The Dragon's Hoard

Edited by Carol Hightshoe

WolfSinger Publications ❨ Brackettville, Texas

Editor's Note

Back in 2011, Maggie Bonham of Sky Warrior Books asked me about being the editor on a Zombie Anthology—Zombified. I went on to edit 3 Zombiefied Anthologies, 2 Vampires Don't Sparkle Anthologies, The Dragon's Hoard and Hoofbeats.

With these anthologies having gone out of print, I wanted to try and see if I could bring them back. I'm starting with The Dragon's Hoard and am looking at Hoofbeats (under its originally planned title of Epona's Children) in 2024. I still have to start contacting the authors to see if they will agree.

I haven't decided on the Zombified or Vampires Don't Sparkle Anthologies yet.

In your hands you now hold the 2nd edition of The Dragon's Hoard. This was a fun anthology to curate and edit. I was looking for stories about the things Dragon's collect and yes…Hoard. After all what kind of Dragon doesn't have a hoard.

Unfortunately, there were three authors who were in the original edition, that I was either unable to contact or who opted to not allow their story to be included in this re-release. But we still have some pretty amazing stories and some pretty amazing dragons—not all of whom are exactly what they seem to be.

Table of Contents

Musings of a Dragon

Joseph P. Macolino

I am a dragon, gathering silver and gold,
Ruby, sapphire, diamond, and gems of old.
I gather them all, holding them in my cave,
No matter the price, I'll make sure to save.
All of the treasure, no matter how large or small,
I swear to persist, until I gather them all.

I am a dragon, full of rage,
No man shall slay me, or put me in a cage.
These treasures are mine, to gather and hoard,
All men shall bow down, and call me lord.
Regardless of size, big or small,
I will obtain, every last one and all.

I am a dragon, lord of the land, sea, and sky,
All bow before me, and praise me up high.
Those who refuse, are left burning in flame,
And those who submit, may be left with some fame.
All treasure belongs to me, me and me alone,
Any who challenge my right, shall be made to atone.

And if you should try to take treasure from me,
You best pray to your gods and prepare for a plea.
I'm not known for mercy but should you show me your fright,
I might even consider letting you live through the night.
But the next morning beware of the price you must pay,
To seek out more treasure and bring it back my way.

To grow my hoard, to make it larger still,
Or I'll burn down your village, just for the thrill.
And watch you suffer, for your indiscretion,
Teaching to you, the full scope of my aggression.
And then I'll return, to my cave full of treasure,
To bask in the glory, and strengthen my pleasure.

For I am a dragon, ruler of these lands,

Bringer of death, and dealer of hands.
My might stays unmatched, my hoard ever-growing,
My breath so hot, it melts men without knowing.
With all my treasure, I'll continue to save,
Never to leave, the comfort of my cave.

~ * ~ * ~

Husband, father, and seeker of truth, **Joseph Macolino** has a passion for nature, philosophy, and all things fantasy. A follower of Christ and dedicated voluntaryist, he dreams of a future human society where people can truly cooperate and voluntarily exchange ideas, goods, and services.

When he's not writing Evorath, he's likely outside gardening, spending time watching a show with his family, or reading a book on philosophy. Considering himself a lifelong student of humanity, Joseph enjoys meeting new people and being exposed to new perspectives. He believes each person's unique gifts can help contribute to stronger communities and hopes his work encourages others to embrace their gifts.

Evorath introduces a rich world full of magic, adventure, and diverse characters trying to find their place in the world.

Dragon Treasure

Irene Radford

"Peel me a watermelon, Jenks," I called to my servant.

"Peel it yourself, Your Monstrousness, Madame Lea," the pixie sneered back at me.

With that attitude, he should have been a gnome. I threw a book at him, the newest in a cozy mystery series I had just finished reading. Jenks flitted up into the cobwebs at the top of the cave. I sent a dribble of flame after him. Any more and I risked the danger of setting fire to one of the stacks of books piled around me.

My aim was off. I sent five spiders scuttling to safety but missed my target.

"Hey, send some more fire this way, Your Volatileness. Helps clean up a bit," Jenks taunted me.

"House cleaning is your job."

"If you'd hire some proper house fairies rather than enslaving an innocent pixie…" He darted into a corner behind the stack of Egyptology tomes.

"You know I can't afford house fairies." Jenks had come to me as part of a trade. I scared a pack of bandits away from a farmer's livestock in return for some books. Jenks had been ensorcelled inside a delectable volume on wheat hybrids (I think the wizard figured no one would ever open the book and discover the bad-tempered brat). I broke the spell in return for services. Someday I'll write a book about that adventure. Someday when I've finished my to-be-read-pile or got bored with re-reading my favorites.

"If you'd get off your fat arse and go hunt up some treasure like a proper dragon…" Jenks ducked as I threw a rotten tomato at him. It was sitting right where I'd left it when I started reading the mystery series—goodness, can that have been two weeks ago? How time flies.

I lumbered off the lounge, displacing the pile of old romances that propped up the broken leg. A fog of dust engulfed me as the books tumbled. I was mad enough to spit fire but had to settle for loosing a stream of ancient curses—gleaned from one of the

Egyptology tomes.

"Where are you, you miserable pixie?" I screamed as I batted my forepaws through the thick air, trying to clear it before I sneezed.

Too late. "Achoooooooooo!" Smoke and fire shot upward as I turned my muzzle away from the precious books.

"Now look what you've done!" Jenks screamed at me as he beat at a flamelet on a hardcover dust jacket with his hands. Unfortunately, his flapping wings only fanned the embers into real fire.

"No great loss." I stomped upon the wildfire, half hoping I'd flatten Jenks in the process. "It's only a duplicate copy of *Astarte, Love Goddess To Unlovable Thieves*, true porn masquerading as romantic erotica, probably the worst book ever written."

"My favorite," Jenks protested as he squeezed between my toes.

Drat! I missed the little gnat.

He examined a bent wing. The fire had singed the tip, and my talons had made a rent down the middle, a least two thirds it's rainbow length.

"I claim the other copy as recompense for damages, Your Addicted-to-Justice-ness," Jenks moaned.

"Fine and clear out some of this other crap while you're at it." I kicked a pig skeleton into the deep recesses of the cave. It bounced back from the pile of refuse and shattered upon impact. I pulled a splinter free of the carcass and picked my teeth.

"You really should do something about the mess, Your Slobbishness," Jenks said, shaking his head.

He rummaged through a pile of rags to unearth a medicine bag from the last wizard who had tried to steal treasure from me. When the spell-caster had discovered nothing but books, I couldn't allow him to leave. After all, my fierce reputation was all that gave me any privacy for reading.

The land was thick with knights and other adventurers; younger sons who couldn't inherit the family homestead and had to make their own way in the world. I guess they hoped to pilfer a few diamonds and such to purchase their own land or make them more attractive to an heiress.

To tell you the truth, if I had a spare diamond or two, I'd sell it and buy more books. That's the only use for treasure, in my not-so-humble opinion. My fractiously feuding family doesn't agree with me on much of anything. Especially the issue of books. Boils and pustules, what can I do with them?

They believe the purpose of a dragon's life is to amass treasure and then defend it against thieving humans. Now if we could just teach more of those humans to read and to treasure books… But that's another matter.

My family, with their hoards of shiny treasures can afford house fairies to keep everything clean and polished and properly accounted for in thick ledgers.

A clean cave is a sign of a sick mind. Or a sign of a dragon with nothing better to do with her time.

I'd rather spend my time reading.

Whenever family obligations require we meet, I always go to their places. I've never invited a single one of them here, nor have I allowed them to "drop by" or escort me to a family gathering. They might discover I'm not just erudite, I'm a total slob.

The doorbell rang. Such a rare phenomenon Jenks and I stared at each other long enough for the visitor to get impatient and ring again.

"Quick, Jenks, get rid of it, whatever it is." I slunk into a dark recess, grabbing my book along the way.

The bell rang again, a long and loud bong that repeated a dozen times, as if someone actually swung from the rope rather than rapping it smartly against the bronze bell. I wasn't curious enough to peek out the window crack to see for sure.

"Keep your greaves on, I'm coming," Jenks groused. He had to walk the ten tail-lengths to the iron-hinged and studded double oak doors. He couldn't lift the latch of course. It was heavy enough to make me think twice about lifting it—so I rarely left the place. Jenks crawled beneath the door, then right back inside.

"Get your scaly chartreuse body over here, Your Immenseness. This is one of yours."

"A knight?" I really didn't want to fight a knight today. They'd left me alone for so long, I'd lost my taste for human flesh. Besides, I was just getting to the good part of the book, the part where the hero says this one special word in ancient Sumerian and the heroine melts into a puddle of oil.

Psst, I should mention I usually recast the characters in the books I read. The ones you might ordinarily call villains are the true heroes. The nice guys are just too…too vanilla.

"A knight of sorts," Jenks choked under his nectar scented breath.

Then I realized the hacking sound coming from his miniature body was laughter. If he'd make a decent mouthful, I just might eat him. But then, if Jenks didn't lure game into the cave, I'd have to find food and cook occasionally. That would disrupt my privacy and my reading.

"Who dares trespass on my property," I bellowed in my fiercest dragon voice. I let a little smoke seep under the door. That usually scared off all but the most desperate and poor of the thieves.

For an answer I heard only a tremendous thud against the stout door.

"What's he got, a battering ram?"

"Better," Jenks chortled. "A trebuchet."

Curses and flames hit the door in equal measure. It caught fire and splintered under the next blow.

Where could I hide? More important, how could I keep the invader away from my books?

Panic made me shrink into a brittle shadow of my robust self.

"Quick, Jenks, sprinkle the place with pixie dust so he thinks all this is treasure and not just garbage. Maybe he'll haul away a pig carcass or three."

"Or six," Jenks muttered. "You know if I dust the books maybe he'll haul away a few stacks, give us some more room."

"Over my dead body!" I puffed myself up and loosed another blast of fire. The knight was attacking the door with a fresh barrage of boulders anyway, maybe if I singed him through the cracks a little, he'd think twice.

"He'll make your body dead if you aren't careful." Jenks threw a handful or two of pixie dust over the remains of my last six meals.

"More, Jenks. That's not enough dust to fool anyone."

"All I can do, Your Gluttonness. Can't fly, thanks to you singeing my wing, so I can't properly dust anything."

"Maybe if you throw it in his face…"

"You willing to hold me high enough, and close enough to reach his face?" The cocky gnat stood, hands on hips, feet spread in an aggressive stance.

"I don't… If I have to." My knees began to tremble and I dropped to all fours rather than fall flat on my face.

Did I mention that besides being an erudite slob I am also a coward?

"That's better," Jenks said. "You're thinking, rather than just reacting and depending upon your size and strength to win this fight."

Yeah, right.

He began climbing my body as he would a mountain. "If you rolled onto your side, I could make better headway on your scales. Not fight gravity."

Whatever. I obeyed his command and he slithered and hitched himself up, scale by scale, shaking loose a few itchy mites along the way.

Meanwhile, the knight made headway on the door with boulders, nearly as large as myself, banging into it every few minutes. Before Jenks reached my muzzle so I could stand up again, the door crashed to the floor.

"Yeep!" I squeaked and scrambled for a more dignified pose.

"All right, Lea, hand them over!" shouted a scrawny man crouching behind a shield made of translucent dragon scales. He brandished a rusty sword that belonged in a museum. His token armor consisted of motorcycle leathers and a helmet—not very stylish or well-fitting leathers at that. They bagged at his shoulders and butt. He'd had to roll up the pant legs and sleeve cuffs to accommodate their bulk and length to his underdeveloped frame.

Jenks swung from one of my neck fronds as if it were a playground toy. "Hey!" he chortled. "It's a girl."

I dipped my head to peer more closely at my invader. The shield was perfectly transparent to my vision. I also hoped to find a way around that shield. Flames were of no use against dragon scales.

If I stalled long enough maybe she'd drop it. It must have weighed a ton and covered the entire length of her body.

"Hand what over?" I boomed, hoping the noise and reverberation would cover the frightened quaver in my voice.

"Your library books. They're one hundred years overdue. The fines alone are worth a king's ransom."

"Yeep!" I gulped. "Library books?"

"You heard me. Hand them over."

"Look around, girlie, you find 'em, you can have 'em," Jenks challenged her.

She poked her pert nose around the edge of her shield. Her eyes went wide, causing a pair of thick spectacles to slide down her miniature snoz, stopping just short of dropping to the ground.

"By Midas, the great god of hoarders!" She tried reaching for a pile of books, discovered both hands occupied by sword and shield.

I could almost see the wheels turning in her head. How to choose between the treasure of books and defense of her body? While she thought, I tried to come up with a strategy to get rid of her. But if she left here alive she'd tell the world not only did I not have a great treasure of diamonds and gold, but she'd broadcast to the world and my family what a lousy housekeeper I was, even with a pixie to help dust occasionally.

The librarian/knight finally opted to sheath her rusty old sword and keep her shield between herself and the smoke dribbling out of my muzzle. Rapidly and precisely she straightened two piles, alphabetizing them as she went.

"My name's Miriam by the way, Miriam de Livres. Some of these books are true rarities. They should be in an atmosphere-controlled room on acid free shelves, not touching each other..." She rambled on about the best way to store and preserve the books. All the while, the square footage behind her shield took on a neatness the likes of which this cave hadn't seen in centuries.

"This cavern is precisely climate controlled. If you'd been less concerned with overdue fines than where you were you'd have noticed how deep you came into this hidey hole. The temperature and humidity do not vary more than ten percent no matter the weather outside," I explained to her. "I bought those books new and they are still in pristine condition."

I puffed out my chest with pride, to disguise the fire building within me. If Miriam of the books lost just a tiny bit of her concentration, I might be able to work a line of flame over or around the shield and she'd be ash. What was one more dead body among the refuse. I just wanted to be done with her and get back to my reading.

"These books are in good condition, despite the dust," she said in a dazed sort of voice. She skootched closer to my chaise lounge, (recliners don't fit my body nearly so well as old fainting couches) leaving order in her wake.

I noticed an old favorite among the rows of books I had

forgotten about. I snatched at it with two delicate talons.

Miriam slapped my paw with the flat of her sword. Where did that come from? "Don't you dare make a mess of these books."

Chastened, I withdrew to sulk on the other side of the chaise. She shifted the shield, still keeping it between us.

Jenks hopped off my muzzle onto my favorite reading chair beneath the crack in the ceiling that allowed a little extra light in. A puff of dust rose around him when he landed.

The librarian stifled a sneeze, still working away in search of "her" books. If possession was nine tenths of the law, then the books should be mine after a century or two had passed.

"Maybe we can work a deal," Jenks said in a stage whisper meant to induce a sense of privacy but loud enough so I could hear.

I'd hear his quiet words anyway; dragon ears and cave acoustics made this a perfect whispering gallery.

"We let you retrieve your books and take a couple of special rarities and you waive the fines. And you keep this cave a secret."

Little Miss Neatness tilted her head to listen. Her free hand kept working.

"No! Not my books. You can't take my books away from me," I wailed, wringing my forepaws. When did I lose control of this battle?

"Hush," Jenks admonished me. "I'm saving your ass. You ever tried to match a librarian for stubbornness, determination, and greed for books?"

"Actually, removing some of these books from this cave might damage them irreparably. But it's a shame scholars don't have access to them. We could learn so much about history, literature, lost sciences…"

"Scholars?" I asked. A plan began to create a pattern in my brain. "Scholars with grant money to pay for access to research material?"

"Scholars with grant money to pay for someone else to do the research?" Jenks looked pointedly at me.

"Scholars with grant money to pay for solid shelves and a card catalogue," the librarian confirmed, eyeing me speculatively. A glimmer shone in her eyes. Those brown orbs grew large with excitement.

"Librarians to help with the dusting?" Jenks asked.

Both the librarian and I stared at him in disgust.

"Okay, I'll dust, you catalogue and shelve." Jenks pointed to

Miriam. "And you do research." He shifted that accusatory finger toward me.

"Agreed." Miriam finally dropped the shield and held out her hand.

Jenks brushed against it, the closest thing to a handshake he could manage.

Then they both turned to stare at me. I extended a talon the size of Miriam's hand. She grasped it and gave it a yank. I guess that sufficed for shaking on the deal.

"Can I get back to my reading now?" I asked plaintively. That was of course my primary objective.

"No!" both Miriam and Jenks screamed.

"If I haul out one armload of garbage, can I read a book?"

"I don't know. How fast do you read?" Miriam looked pointedly at the rotting magician against the far wall.

"Too slow," Jenks said.

"Two piles of garbage per book, and you have to let us put the book back where it belongs when you are done," Miriam insisted, hands on hips.

"Which of course means I don't have to put it back!" I chortled.

"Would you anyway?" Miriam asked. A delightful smudge of dirt graced her pert little nose.

"Well no. I get to pick which book I read next, though."

They both sighed and nodded.

I grabbed a stack of anthropology texts ranging from the Mayan pyramids to Hindu polytheism.

"One book at a time. Your check out limit is cut until we get this place clean, and we have money coming in." Miriam gently removed four of the five books from my hands.

"But..."

"Think about it, Your Laziness Lea," Jenks consoled me. "The sooner we get this place ready for company, the sooner you can indulge in reading anything and everything. Then you can write book reports, you can answer questions about what you just read. You'll be acknowledged as the world's greatest authority. People will actually pay you to read."

I grabbed the nearest pile of skeletons and rotting fabric and practically danced to the cave mouth. "Where do I put it?" I asked.

"Sort it into recyclable categories and dump the non-biodegradable stuff on the plateau above the cliff. That will mislead stupid, uncouth, illiterate adventurers into searching for your treasure further up the mountain," Miriam called through the entrance tunnel.

Good idea. Why hadn't I thought of that? I carefully picked through the stuff to make certain I didn't accidentally discard any books.

Oops! I found a book of alchemy diagrams amongst the dead magician's bones. I peeked over my shoulder to make sure Jenks and Miriam weren't watching, then tucked the book amongst my neck frills for safe keeping. What would it hurt to just look through it to make certain it wasn't damaged?

In loving memory of

My mother
Miriam Bentley Radford
School librarian.
She taught many, including me
That reading is the greatest gift
you can give a child.

~ * ~ * ~

Irene Radford has been writing stories ever since she figured out what a pencil was for. A member of an endangered species—a native Oregonian who lives in Oregon—she and her husband make their home in Welches, Oregon where deer, bears, coyotes, hawks, owls, and woodpeckers feed regularly on their back deck.

A museum trained historian, Irene has spent many hours prowling pioneer cemeteries deepening her connections to the past. Raised in a military family she grew up all over the US and learned early on that books are friends that don't get left behind with a move. Her interests and reading range from ancient history, to spiritual meditations, to space stations, and a whole lot in between.

Mostly Irene writes fantasy and historical fantasy including the best-selling Dragon Nimbus Series. In other lifetimes she writes urban fantasy as P.R. Frost and space opera as C.F. Bentley.

Life with Smokey

John Lance

Doctor Parson leans forward and flashes her penlight in Smokey's eyes. My dragon's filmy pupils slowly constrict, tightening into black slivers on lemon spheres, like cats' eyes.

"Hmmm," the veterinarian says.

"What? What is it? Is that bad?" I ask, peering over her white coated shoulder.

"Mr. Spear, you're hovering, you need to give me room. Please don't make me ask again," Parson says in a polite, but firm, tone.

"Sorry," I mumble, taking two steps back. Despite her white hair, wrinkles, and grandmotherly demeanor, Parson is not above banning 'troublesome' owners from the examination room. Last time it took me six months to get back into her good graces.

Parson gently spreads Smokey's neck frill and runs her thin fingers along the edge. Smokey moans.

"He groans whenever I scratch his frill," I say quickly.

"Of course he does. Everyone loves a good frill rub, don't they boy?" The veterinarian kneads Smokey's frill and he moans louder. The tip of his tail twitches wildly and he nearly topples off the examination table.

Parson continues examining Smokey's scaly, eight-foot length. She extends his wings to check edge wear and peels away some of the dead skin I missed after his midmorning molt.

"He's constantly shedding. And," I drop my voice to a whisper, "his scales are duller than they were at the beginning of the summer."

"I'm sorry, could you speak up?"

I raise my voice a smidgen. "His scales used to be like scarlet rubies and now he looks like, well, a pile of bricks. Do you think he has Scale Mites? Ellen, my wife, looked it up on DragonMD.com…"

"Why are you whispering?" Parson asks.

"I don't want you-know-who, to hear" I casually nod in Smokey's direction. He's trying to slip his snout into Parson's coat pocket, but his ears swivel back and forth like radar dishes. He is obviously listening.

"Ah, I understand, you don't want to upset Smokey. Mr. Spear, I thought we had this conversation. Despite what Hollywood would have you believe; dragons are only as smart as dogs or parrots. And, like dogs and parrots, they cannot have conversations, or solve crimes, or play professional basketball, or do any of the other silly things you see in the movies."

"Yes, I know, but Smokey is exceptionally…"

"When did he break his nail?" Parsons asks, lightly touching a cracked claw. Smokey draws his ivory talon under his belly and gives the vet an accusing look.

"He tumbled down the stairs two days ago. We thought a new one would grow in place like always. Why, is there something wrong?"

"Nope, you're absolutely correct."

"I'm really more concerned about the s-c-a-l-e," I take a breath and continue spelling, "m-i-t-e-s."

"Mr. Spear, how old is Smokey?"

"Let's see, he was a dragonette when my great-great-grand-father received him as a birthday present and he's been in the family ever since. So about," I do some quick math in my head, "one hundred twenty years, give or take a decade."

"Well then, aside from a touch of Frill Fungus, that I'll prescribe some tonic for, what you have here is a reasonably healthy, very, very, old, Flaming Flyer."

"But he hardly flies anymore, and his eyesight is getting worse, and he sleeps all the time."

Parson pats my shoulder. "Despite the myths, dragons are not immortal. We all wear out eventually."

"There must be something I can do," I wave my hands helplessly, like a mime with stage fright.

Taking pity on me, Parson asks, "What's in his hoard these days?"

"Oh, his hoard, well, it's the usual. You know, gold, some silver, a few rubies and emeralds."

"What sort of gold? Eighteen karat? Twenty-four?"

"Mostly fourteen, some ten," I wince at my admission. I don't mention the eight-karat ring I purchased at a garage sale last weekend.

"He goes through gold faster than I remember," I add.

"I'm not surprised. At his age, his scales absorb the gold at an accelerated rate, and the low-quality means there is less gold to absorb. That's why his scales lost their luster. If you want to restore his ruby glow he needs to sleep on pure bullion. If you need a supplier, I can refer you to one. Very reliable."

"No, no, that's okay, I already have a bullion, um, guy." Hopefully the lie sounds more convincing to Parsons than it does to me. A garage sale scavenger has no need for a bullion dealer.

"The silver won't hurt him, will it?" I ask.

"Not as long as you mix in the gold. However, if you continue to use low quality gold you need to keep an eye out for Rubber Scale. You should also consider feeding him some lime."

"Limes?" I raise an eyebrow. Car tires, old sneakers, nasty dead things in the woods, a waffle iron, my dragon will eat anything, except fruit. If a bag of oranges lay beside a bowl of rotting fish, I could count on having fresh juice with my breakfast.

"Not limes, lime, as in limestone. It'll help the sulfuric pee."

Hazy, yellow steam rises from the marble examining table as Smokey's urine rolls down its gutters toward a reinforced drain.

"I'm so sorry. He's been having a tough time with his control…"

"Don't worry," Parson waves a hand speckled with white, tear drop shaped scars. "If you're going to be a dragon doctor, you've got to be prepared for the occasional acid spill. I'll let the front desk know you're all set." She gave Smokey a final frill scratch.

I carry my dragon to the lobby. Fortunately, eighty percent of Smokey's eight feet is tail. Still, seventy pounds is a lot of dragon to tote around. On the plus side, his scales are warm to the touch, like a brisk walk on a spring day, and his spikey mane smells of cinnamon.

"Alright Smokey, I'm putting you down on the linoleum. There is nothing to worry about."

I tell him this every visit in the hope he will believe me.

As usual, I am wrong.

The moment Smokey's toes touch the floor he begins scrabbling his talons as if I've placed him on the icy edge of a yawning crevasse. Finally, he gets his feet set. Legs splayed out, knees locked, one wing half extended for balance, he stands stock still and pants like he's just run a marathon.

I shake my head. "After twenty years you would think he would get used to it," I comment to Muriel, the cheerful, round faced receptionist.

"They're quirky, funny old things. And they get quirkier and funnier the older they get, isn't that right Smokey?"

Halting his panting, Smokey turns his snout toward Muriel's voice, slowly cocks his head, and flicks his forked tongue. I swear, his eyes even grow larger, like a Disney cartoon.

"Oh, you! You know I'm a sucker for *the look*," Muriel says. She reaches into the bowl of meaty, knight-shaped dragon treats she keeps on the counter and tosses one to Smokey. He snaps his jaws shut too soon and the meat knight bounces off the tip of his snout. With a snuffle he locates the treat on the floor and snatches it up.

"His eyes are getting worse, huh? Ah well, what can you do? How was the rest of the check up?" Muriel taps at her keyboard. "Whoops, looks like that stubborn Frill Fungus is back. It happens to everyone when the weather is warm and damp. Let me grab a bottle of Winston's Tonic." She hurries into the back room.

I don't know who Winston is, but he owes me a debt of gratitude. I have purchased enough Frill Tonic to put his children through college.

The bell on the front door jingles and in walks a middle aged, aggressively permed, woman leading a winter wyvern dragonette on a leash. The wyvern's scales are blue with white speckles, and she hops and flaps and twists her head around so much I fear she will literally tie herself into a knot. The spike on the tip of her nose marks her as less than a year old.

"She must be quite a handful," I say to her owner.

"Six feedings a day, three rats each feeding, and she'll only eat albinos. Even my son wasn't so fussy."

Spotting Smokey, the wyvern begins squeaking and chirping like a flock of parakeets. She reminds me of my four-year-old nephew whose favorite phrase is "Play with me!" After ten minutes of incessant nagging, you pick up a Hot Wheels and play with that boy just to shut him up.

Smokey weaves his head back and forth, trying to focus on the bouncing ball of energy skittering her way toward him.

The wyvern squawks and gives him a playful nip on the snout.

I tighten my hold on Smokey's leash and prepare to step in. Fortunately, Smokey just gives a great snort, sending the little dragonette spinning across the floor.

Yelping, the wyvern cowers behind her owner's leg.

"Sorry, he's old," I explain.

"Don't worry, I've been tempted to do that myself on one or two occasions."

"Here we are." Muriel, returns with a liter jug of Winston's. "Four times a day, rub three dabs..."

"Into the creases of the frill. Yes, we've been around the block a few times." Muriel and I exchange smiles. Then she hands me the bill.

I sigh. Another month of eating in. As I turn over my credit card, I wonder how much the visit would've cost if Smokey did have scale mites or something serious. Probably best not to dwell on that question.

I lug Smokey out to my SUV and put him in the rear. The edge of the rubber mat is gnawed and torn and the backs of the rear seats are shredded like a disemboweled deer carcass.

I climb into the driver's seat, hold my breath, and turn the key. The engine roars to life, and I slowly put it into gear. Maybe this time...

Smokey lifts his head and begins to howl. "Crap," I mutter.

Howl is a generous description of my dragon's warbling. While Smokey's stance, with his neck arched and head held high, gives the impression of a wolf baying at the moon, the sound is more like the rumbling "brrr" of an eighty-pound bullfrog followed by the squeak of an equally portly mouse.

The first time, I pulled over to look under the hood. It was only after two more stops I realized Smokey was the source.

Unfortunately, there is only one way to get him to stop.

"The wheels on the bus go round and round..." I sing. Ellen refuses to tell me how she stumbled on the solution or why it works.

It's an open question as to whether the cure is worse than the disease.

Thirty minutes and 622 verses later we arrive home. I am seriously contemplating moving closer to Doctor Parson.

I unload Smokey and he meanders across the lawn toward the front door, stopping every few steps to scratch a random patch of grass or lick the air.

Ellen meets us at the screen door. "Was it s-c-a-l-e...?"

I shake my head. "No, no m-i-t-e-s, but the darn fungus is back. I bought some Winston's. We also we need to feed him limestone."

Smokey wanders to the corner of the living room where his

treasure trove is piled. Three slow spins, a thump and he is snoring.

"What about all the sleeping and the stiffness in his wings?"

"Parson said he's just getting old. She also said he needs more gold and should be sleeping on bullion."

"Bullion? How are we going to afford bullion?"

"I don't know."

I can't ask for a raise. After SiniTar Tec's second quarter results, I'll be lucky to avoid being laid off and Ellen isn't due for a raise for nine months.

The rotten egg, sulfur stink hits us both at the same time.

"Smokey, let's go outside!" I shout, too late.

He made it halfway to the door before his bladder gave out. Hanging his head, Smokey refuses to look at us as the puddle under him burns another hole in a carpet which already looks like radioactive moths have been munching on it.

Ellen sighs. "Your turn."

She slips the leash over Smokey's head and guides him out the front door on the off chance there is still some pee in the tank.

Looking at the size of the puddle, I have my doubts.

I don the my heavy rubber gloves, lead apron, and eye goggles and spray the area with Virturex dragon pee neutralizer. I tell myself it's the fumes causing my eyes to tear.

~ * ~

"Something wrong, Peter?" my boss, Elizabeth Drake asks as she sticks her head in my cube.

"Oh, no, everything is fine," I reply, guiltily closing the web browser showing CheapGold.com.

"You seem distracted," Elizabeth says.

I can't help noticing Elizabeth's gold hoop earrings. My grandmother owned a similar set. I wonder who she left them to when she passed away last year. Might be worth a call to mom.

"Hello, Earth to Peter," Elizabeth waves her hand in front of my face.

"Sorry, you were saying?"

"I was asking if you checked in your code for the final build so we can finish the project?"

"Yes. No. I mean, I'll be done in a few minutes."

"Come on, Pete, be honest, what's bothering you?"

"It's my dragon, Smokey. I took him to the vet yesterday and…" Despite my light tone, my voice quivers.

Elizabeth's expression softens. "I'm so sorry. I lost my Black Scale, Snuffles, three years ago to S.I.S, you know, Spontaneous Ignition Syndrome. Has Smokey been in your family long?"

"Fourth generation."

Elizabeth nods. "Snuffles was second generation. It's so hard. You grow up with them, and they've been part of your family for so long, and then, one day… Well, let me know if there is anything I can do."

"Thanks, he's just really, really, old. I only wish I could afford a better hoard to keep him comfortable." I wonder if Elizabeth will take the hint.

She doesn't.

"Keeping them in gold is always the hardest part. I considered breeding leprechauns, but that's more trouble than it's worth. Although," Elizabeth's eyes glitter mischievously, "my friend, Rose, spotted one nesting in the park. If you caught it, Smokey's hoard would never run dry."

I frown. "Aren't leprechauns protected by the Environmental Protection Agency?"

Elizabeth shrugs. "I suppose. Still, leprechauns are such vile creatures. They spit on couples walking on the trails, give candy to children and tell them it's breakfast cereal, and then there's the public urination. No one would be put out if the one in the park suddenly, migrated, away."

Glancing out the window, she adds, "The rain is stopping. The easiest way to find a leprechaun is to follow a rainbow. Once you finish your work, if you suddenly felt a little sick and needed to take the afternoon off, I would understand."

"Thanks Elizabeth."

She smiles. "We dragon lovers have to stick together."

~ * ~

I splash through the puddles in the park and the verdant scent of wet moss fills the air.

It makes me want to puke.

Hours of searching, and nothing to show for it. I never found the end of the rainbow and my butterfly net is as empty as when I started.

My cell phone buzzes. It's Ellen.

"Some of the folks at the office are going out for dinner and drinks after work, so I was thinking of tagging along."

"Sure, I'm caught up at the office anyway." I fib. Ellen is a rule oriented, law-abiding, woman. She would not be on board with the whole, stalking-leprechauns-and-violating-federal-laws plan.

"What time will you get home?" I ask.

"Not too late. Eightish?"

"Okay, see you then." I hang up.

With the sun starting to set, I resolve to take one last walk around the duck pond.

The pink and purple swirls of the sunset would make an artist salivate.

I am so engrossed I almost miss the leprechaun sitting in a patch of clover with his back to me.

He is a foot tall, with a shock of red hair stuffed under a green, pilgrim hat with a gold buckle. His jacket is green, as are his short pants. A wisp of smoke curls up from his pipe, tinting the evening breeze with a hint of tobacco.

I cast a furtive glance up and down the trail. There is no one else in sight.

Stealthily, I creep forward, net held high over my head. A yard away my foot comes down on a twig with a snap. I hold my breath, expecting him to disappear.

Then I notice the ear buds. He bobs his head back and forth to the music cranked up on his MP3 player. I catch the distinctive thrum of drums, violins, and tapping feet. Riverdance.

I sweep my net down. "Gotcha!"

"Argh, let me go you monstrous buffoon!" the leprechaun shouts, struggling against the net. He only succeeds in entangling himself further.

"I did it! I actually caught you!" I whoop.

The leprechaun stops squirming and starts patting his pockets. "My pipe! My music player! Do you see them laddie?"

"Sure." Bending over, I retrieve his miniature pipe. Straightening up, I take a step back and hear an ominous crunch.

"I see you've also found my music player," The leprechaun glowers at me from within his nylon prison.

"Sorry."

"Not yet you're not," the leprechaun replies, snatching the pipe out of my hand.

"There's no need for this to get ugly. You see, my pet dragon needs more gold for his hoard. If you give me some of yours, I'll turn you loose."

"I don't give a rat's patoot about your stupid dragon. What makes you think I'm even a leprechaun? I might be a pixie."

"You're dressed in green."

"Maybe I'm a fashionable pixie."

"You have an Irish brogue and red hair. Pixies, on the other hand, have wings and sprinkle fairy dust everywhere."

"I can sprinkle too," the leprechaun starts to undo the fly of his pants.

"Do it, and I toss you in the pond," I threaten, wondering if leprechauns can swim.

The leprechaun hesitates. "You wouldn't dare."

"Try me," I growl.

"Fine, fine, there's gold's under the bridge. I'll take you to it, I promise," the leprechaun says.

"I knew you'd see reason."

~ * ~

I peer into the darkness under the stone arch of the bridge. The beams of the rising moon fail to illuminate the darkness beyond the first few gloomy feet.

The bridge is wide, as if the architect expected a marathon's worth of joggers needing to simultaneously cross the shallow stream. Yet, from the weathered rails and moss-covered cobblestones, it's obvious most park visitors don't know the bridge exists. There is a nasty stench as well, like a wet dog rolling in rotten eggs.

"You live under there?" I ask doubtfully.

"Why? Is it not up to your standards, mister fancy britches? Pales in comparison to your elegant mansion, I suppose? I'll have you know this bridge was my father's home, and his father's before him. It has always been good enough for hard working folk such as they."

"I'm sorry," I say. "Where is the entrance?"

"Follow the stream."

"Is there a path?"

"Not one wide enough for your fat feet. What are you, a witch? A little running water will cause you to melt?"

My shoes fill with water as I stride through the shallow brook. Ducking under the bridge, I walk hunched over for ten steps, then stop.

"You've got to go further in," the leprechaun says.

Taking a determined breath, I continue on. Soon we are beyond the reach of the weak moonlight. I take out my phone and turn on the flashlight app.

"Where's the pot?"

"To tell you the truth laddie, I don't have a clue where he keeps it."

"What do you mean you don't…?" My net is empty. "How did you…?"

The leprechaun's voice echoes through the dark, seeming to come from everywhere at once. "Please bucko, if a klutz like you could capture me with a silly little net, why, I'd be broke all the time."

"There's no gold?"

"Oh, there's gold, although it's not mine. Leprechaun gold can only be found at the end of rainbows, I thought everyone knew that. Still, I promised to bring you to the gold under the bridge, and, well, it's here somewhere. You only need to convince its owner to part with it."

"Its owner…"

From out of the dark, the largest, furriest fist ever smashed me in the nose.

"For as much fun as I've had, I must be going. I have to purchase a new music player. Give my regards to your broken-down dragon," the leprechaun cackles.

My witty retort is cut short when a scabby foot kicks me in the jaw and I bite my tongue.

~ * ~

The house is dark when I arrive home. Ellen is still out with her friends, which is for the best since I won't have as much explaining to do.

I am soaked from head to toe and my face and hair are caked with mud. I am missing a sneaker and my dignity.

Needless to say, I don't have a pot of gold. I will also never, ever, return to the park.

I limp into the kitchen, and fill two towels with ice. One I place on my scratched, bruised face. The other, I rest on my groin. Fair play is a foreign concept to trolls and they do so like to work over the tender bits.

There is a groan from the other room. Smokey is asleep on his small hoard, his legs pawing the air. His wings quiver and occasionally give a half flap.

"Chasing hawks again, big guy?" I ask as I slowly, painfully, lower myself down beside him.

"Remember the afternoon you caught two?" I scratch his frill and slowly his twitching stops. A satisfied smile creases his crocodile face.

"I'm sorry old man, I couldn't find any gold. We're just going to have to make due the way we have been. Which reminds me," I reach into my pocket and pull out a molar the troll knocked loose. The gold crown flashes in the light.

"Probably best if you don't let mommy see this," I say, slipping my tooth under his claw.

Smokey half opens his eyes, then curls his leathery tail around me protectively, and places his head in my lap. He emits a deep, satisfied moan, and drifts back into a dreamland where he chases hawks across endless blue skies.

I smile. I don't know how much time we have left, but we'll make the most of it.

~ * ~ * ~

John Lance lives in New England with his beautiful wife and two lovely daughters. His stories have appeared in *Dark Moon Digest*, *Stupefying Stories*, and in the anthologies *Zombified III*, *These Vampires Don't Sparkle*, and others. He has also written a collection of childrens' short stories, *Bobby's Troll and Other Stories* and the picture books *Priscilla Holmes, Ace Detective* and *Priscilla Holmes and the Case of the Glass Slipper*. His blog is at www.johnmlance.com.

Hoard

Deby Fredericks

Strangers were camped at the ford. The dragon Carnisha slithered up to a rock ledge where her tawny scales blended in. Her tail lashed across dead needles under the scrub pines until she stilled it.

"Well, well," she growled to herself.

Two menservants did chores as she watched with cold intensity. One cut firewood while the other swept out a fine, brocaded tent. A well-dressed gentleman stood aside, contemplating the play of morning light on the River Lyre.

"Humans," Carnisha hissed. "They think whatever they see belongs to them."

Long ago, the mighty Cragmaws had been a kingdom of dragons. Until humans invaded the mountains. Other dragons had been killed or forced to retreat, but Carnisha would never give way. At last, the seeds she had been sowing were about to bear fruit.

Carnisha studied the gentleman, with his silken robes and pearly skin. A nobleman, she assumed. However, she had some suspicion about the servants. Though sun-darkened and strong, they worked with little skill. Nor did their rough clothing match their master's finery. They had knives in their boots and sharp eyes glancing about. What nobleman would travel with such ruffians? Perhaps they were bodyguards.

The she-dragon eased back and circled down to the road. Before she left the trees, Carnisha hunched forward. She tucked leathern wings against her back and tail close to her ankles. Concentrating, she coiled slowly, drawing on the powers of sky and land to spin the change. Horny hide and glinting talons reshaped into a dingy dress and ragged hood. Gray hair wisped about a wizened human face.

Disgusting, but needful.

Gone was Carnisha, scourge of the mountains. Instead, an old woman stepped onto the road, bowed by the weight of a peddler's pack. Muddy clogs grated over gravel and dirt. She set off, humming a shrill drone so those ruffians would hear her coming and think themselves clever.

As she neared the ford, a man bellowed, "Hoy! Over here!"

A wide grin split her sagging face as she feigned surprise at seeing the camp.

"Hoy to you, young'un!" Carnisha waved, then tottered as if the pack would drag her to earth.

"Show courtesy to your elders, Robin," the nobleman chided. "Go help the poor woman."

Stone-faced, the man who had been cutting wood strode over the flat rocks that paved the ford. He grabbed her scrawny arm.

"What a kind young man," she beamed, as if he wasn't dragging her along. "Taking care of li'l ol' Nisha."

"Mum," Robin grumbled.

"Are you indeed the famous Nisha?" The nobleman fell in beside them, taking Robin's place. "Fetch us another chair, Nick, and see if there's tea to share."

"Famous, is it?" Carnisha cackled. "How would a grand lord such as yourself know of ol' Nisha?"

"No lord, alas. I am but a humble scholar," the gentleman corrected indulgently. "Edwin Frastian, at your service."

"I be Nisha o'th' Glade." Carnisha bobbed a curtsey. "Well met, good scholar."

"Well met, Nisha o'th' Glade." Frastian continued eagerly, "Recently, a friend of mine acquired a fascinating pendant from an antiques dealer. It was very old. I was truly envious."

"Ah," Carnisha smirked. "Was this an emerald pendant, or pearl?"

"Pearl, dear lady."

"Pearl, you say? That would be Berlack. What a nice young man. So glad he found a home for that trinket of mine."

"Indeed he did," Frastian agreed. "Upon inquiry, Berlack revealed he had acquired the piece from a sweet old peddler woman at the ford of the River Lyre, near Mount Cragmaw. And here I am, ready to buy."

They reached the camp. Robin had built up the fire and Nick unfolded a wooden chair by the fireside. At the mention of emeralds and pearls, they both studied her with hungry eyes.

"Do sit, dear mother." Frastian helped Carnisha into the chair. "Why, isn't this lovely?"

She let him fuss over her, knowing how anticipation would

build. He doted, offering dried dates as well as tea, while the alleged menservants lingered nearby. After Carnisha had eaten and drunk, she bent to unflap the top of her peddler's pack.

"I sell only to a few, like Berlack," she prattled. "Those who have shown I can trust them. An old woman can't be too careful."

Nick coughed a little, and Robin elbowed him.

Frastian frowned, until she twinkled up at him. "Since you've been so kind, I suppose there's no harm."

"You flatter me." A narrow hand touched his chest in modesty.

Carnisha started with a jumble of second-hand wares. Tunics of cotton cloth, only a little stained. A copper pot darkened by use. Wooden sandals with frayed straps. The scholar made interested noises, but kept trying to see into her pack.

At length she unrolled a felt bundle. "Not sure what these are, but I find 'em lying about. They do have a shine, eh?"

Oddly shaped flakes curved from the ground of drab felt. They were tawny brown, no two the same size, and might have been horn, though the glint spoke more of metal.

Frastian leaned forward, knuckles white over his chair arms. "My dear Nisha, these are dragon scales!"

Carnisha knew that quite well, since she had shed them. She bobbed her head. "Dragon scales? You don't say."

Nick stepped closer. "T'would make a fine armor if you had more of 'em." Robin nodded wisely.

"Step back," Frastian snapped. "You're shadowing the wares." Nick gave his master a dark glance but obeyed. Frastian picked up a scale.

"Careful, they're sharp," Carnisha warned.

"So they are." Frastian dropped the scale to suck on a fingertip. He explained, as if Carnisha was a child, "We know there once were dragons in this province, but they were wiped out long ago. The Cragmaws, here, were their last refuge." His other hand gestured to take in the rocky peaks looming beyond the river.

He sounded so pompous, Carnisha could hardly bear it. She brought out her finest baubles.

"Maybe that's why I found these."

The sword hilt was leather, cross-wrapped in a style long out of use. The blade had broken off a few inches down.

"Must've been in a scrum," Robin chuckled.

"'Twould seem." Carnisha shrugged and brought out a silver goblet, now black with tarnish, and a small dog carved of jade. Amber eyes had been picked out, leaving sockets full of dirt.

"These are rare treasures." Frastian breathed. He turned the goblet to see how badly the stem was bent. "This is done in the Beshanthine style, and the sword is from Old Aerde."

The menservants traded lustful glances over his head. Carnisha wondered that Frastian trusted them as much as he appeared to.

"Were these all together?" The scholar's voice shook, words tumbling over each other. "You may have found a dragon's lair. Think what I could learn if I studied the place where a dragon once dwelt!"

"Think of the hoard," Nick murmured to Robin.

Frastian scolded, "Don't be crude. Their value goes far beyond mere gold. Nisha, you must tell me where you found these pieces."

"'Tis my own secret!" She drew back, clutching her pack.

"Nay, dear Nisha," Frastian pleaded. "I am a scholar. I simply must study this location!"

This fervor was exactly what Carnisha needed. She reveled inside, while retorting, "Nay, sir. You could be robbers, after all." She stuffed the sword hilt back into her pack and reached for the jade statuette.

"Please, dear lady! These are not just trinkets, they are priceless relics. Each tells a tale from the distant past. And these are the most precious of all." Frastian gingerly touched a scale. "Allow me to make an offer. I insist!"

"What's your price, then?" She rolled the scales up in the felt, but not too quickly.

"A silver penny for each scale," he ventured, watching her carefully. "There are sixteen, if my count is correct. The other pieces are damaged, but I still may be able to learn from them. Say fifteen pence for the sword, four for the goblet, and..."

Priceless relics, he said? What a cheat. Carnisha's hands didn't falter.

"Berlack pays in gold."

"You overestimate my resources," Frastian protested.

Carnisha cast a canny eye over his silken robes, the black hair pulled into a sleek top-knot, and the shimmering brocade of his private tent. She plucked the goblet from his fingers and tucked it into her pack.

"Wait," the scholar moaned.

Robin put in, "Now then, Mum. Money ent the only thing. How'd it be if we carried a load down for you? Nick and me, we're right strong."

"Less trips for those poor ol' legs," Nick wheedled.

"What are you saying?" Frastian objected.

Carnisha quavered, "You bounders, would you take an old woman's livelihood?"

"Nay, Mum. You've got it wrong," Robin coaxed. "Master Frastian here has enough to pay for all you've got."

"Or he can just buy the whole lair," Nick added.

Edwin Frastian gaped, horrified. Then he closed his mouth and slowly smiled.

"I'd need time to make arrangements, but then I could examine the lair thoroughly and record where the artifacts lie. Brilliant!"

"What a fairy tale." But Carnisha let them see her hesitate.

"Leave the hard work to us young'uns," Nick said. "You can get yourself a little farm or a cottage on the lake."

"Think of it," Rob urged, "living in a warm, dry house 'stead o' these cold mountains."

"Here now." Frastian seized control. "I'll gladly pay a fair price, but I simply must see the location beforehand."

"And if you don't like what you see? You'd still hold my secret," Carnisha whined.

"No need to worry," Frastian said. "If there's nothing to see, there's nothing to tell about."

Carnisha picked at the felt enclosing the scales. The three men watched her with hopeful dread. More than likely, the two servants would follow her anyway. She was tempted to let them do it, but then Frastian might escape with the warning.

"It does sound lovely," she said, tantalizing them.

"Excellent!" Frastian cried, while Robin and Nick playfully shoved each other in celebration.

~ * ~

Some hours later, Carnisha led her dupes up a steep slope, half-way to the summit of Mount Cragmaw. Every so often she pressed a hand to her side.

"Me ol' legs," she would say. Or, "What a hike."

The two servants were hale and hardy, easily keeping pace. However, the scholar struggled. Several hairs had come loose from his topknot and stuck to his pale, sweaty face.

"Surely we'll be there soon?" he puffed with exertion.

Before Carnisha could reply, Nick squinted ahead of them. "What's that?"

Gray-brown rocks loomed, mottled with lichen and moss. A crack angled between them, darkness lurking beyond.

Robin smiled. "Looks like a cave."

"A crag maw, indeed." Frastian chuckled as excitement overcame effort.

They all surged forward, bumping Carnisha. Robin and Nick shouldered each other in the gap.

"You men," Frastian scolded. "Let me see before you trample all over it."

They scowled but let the scholar pass. When Carnisha arrived he was practically crawling over the cavern floor, like a bizarre toad emerging from the spring mud. Holes and heaps of dirt pocked the surface. Only a little light flowed from the entrance. Frastian bent closer to brush at something.

"Another scale. Wonderful," he mused to himself. Nick and Robin edged by.

"Don't see any treasures," Robin muttered.

Nick whispered, "Hoy," and jerked his chin toward a further gap leading off the first chamber. "Think it goes through?"

Frastian was more alert than he seemed. He straightened in time to see the two men slip into the gap. He rushed after them, crying, "Don't touch anything!"

Carnisha sneezed as running feet kicked up dust. Already, exclamations echoed from the rocky passage.

"Worth a hike, I'd say," cried Nick, and Rob gloated, "Nick, lad, the gods must like us." All the while Frastian babbled, "A hoard, a real hoard. I hardly dared hope!"

Carnisha reached the opening. The two ruffians traded back-slaps while Frastian stood rapt. Rays of light from cracks in the ceiling revealed an untidy mound of gold and tarnished silver. Jewels glittered and the occasional shield or urn stuck out. Near the center, several pairs of bright blue eyes flicked open. As soon as they saw Carnisha they winked shut. Tawny scales blended perfectly with the hoard.

Frastian beamed at Carnisha. "Well, will you hear my offer?"

"Gladly, good master," she simpered.

As soon as Frastian's back was turned, Nick knelt beside the hoard. Grinning, he buried both hands above the elbow in clinking coins. Then he winced and jumped back.

"Hoy, something bit me!"

"Where?" Robin wrestled Nick's sleeve up, revealing an arc of four oozing punctures. He glared at the hoard.

Frastian, meanwhile, gave Carnisha a cunning eye. "A thousand should be a fair price."

Playing for time, she folded her arms and stared at him.

"Think of all the work to be done," he reasoned. "Men to hire, bribes to—"

Grimacing, Nick rubbed his arm. "Rob, help me! It burns!"

"Don't touch it." Rob began wrapping his belt around Nick's arm above the bite.

"What are you two getting into?" Frastian demanded.

"Look you," Robin growled. "Nick's been bit."

"He shouldn't have touched anything. Trying to help himself, no doubt," Frastian answered suspiciously.

"What?" Nick stepped forward, still clutching his arm.

The three of them fell to disputing over who needed whose permission for what. While they argued, Carnisha turned around slowly. She straightened her neck and flexed her wings, grateful to regain her superior form.

At this signal, her brood rose from among the hoard. Coins clinked and slithered off horny heads, long necks, low bodies plated with scales. The wings were too small yet for flight, but the talons were sharp enough. Pale blue eyes blazed with glee.

"What are those?" Rob shrieked. He kicked out, but the first of the brood sank its fangs through his trousers. "Get off me, you devil!"

"Gods, no!" Nick tried to run, but the venom had done its work. His knees crumpled. Two of the brood held him down as his body arched in spasms.

"Impossible," Frastian bleated. He turned to flee but skidded to a halt as he saw a dragon blocking the only way out.

Carnisha lowered her horny head to his eye level. "You want to know about dragons, little scholar? We are predators. The hoard is merely bait to attract our prey."

"No," he pleaded, looking around wildly. "You're supposed to be gone."

"I never left. I adapted." Her head snaked forward, fangs piercing skin as she clamped about his middle. Frastian screamed and clawed at her eyes. She shook her head and held him until his struggles ceased.

Shrieks gave way to the rasp of scales as Carnisha's brood gathered. Wings flapped and excited tails lashed the floor.

"We did it," one of the males crowed.

"So sneaky, so sly," a female said.

Another said, "We hid as still as dead bones!"

"Can we eat now?" a different male asked.

"Watch first," she commanded. "These colorful robes will be a fine addition to my peddler's pack."

The brood observed with shining eyes as she demonstrated how to remove clothes from a dead human without ripping them. And then, a good feast for the six dragonets.

"Eat well," she crooned, as her brood tore into still-warm flesh. "With this you will grow strong."

A bloody dragonet raised its head from Frastian's side. "Thank you, mother!"

"Soon we'll be big enough to earn our own names," a female bragged.

Carnisha regarded them without affection, for love meant nothing to her, but rather with fierce satisfaction. One day, she and her brood would drive the human intruders out of the Cragmaws, and they would rule their ancient kingdom once again.

~ * ~ * ~

Deby Fredericks has been a writer all her life but thought of it as just a fun hobby until the late 1990s. She made her first sale, a children's poem, in 2000.

Fredericks has had short work published in *Andromeda Spaceways*, selected anthologies, and small magazines. Most recently, she self-published her fantasy novellas and novelettes, bringing her to 15 books in all. Her latest project is The Minstrels of Skaythe series.

Learn more from her web site: www.debyfredericks.com.

Hosting Happy Hoarders

Sheryl Normandeau

It was a trial by fire, that's for sure. When Bossman Peters came up with the idea, I'll admit I wasn't too crazy about it. Mostly because if I messed this one up, I was out of a job. As I had bills to pay and my mother had told me in her sternest voice she was remodelling my bedroom (in mustard yellow, no less!) and I was not to come begging for a place to live when I failed to make good on my broadcast journalism degree, I desperately needed this particular meal ticket. And there was more on the line than just the paycheck: I had my pride to consider, and that was even more valuable than anything I could take to the bank.

You see, ratings for the television show *Happy Hoarders* had slumped dramatically after inimitable host Dame Diva Diane had tripped over an inappropriately stored cache of garden rakes and shovels during filming, and had left the show without her dignity and use of her right eye. Diane's shtick—a combination of an over-the-top fake Eastern European accent, huge hair, and a domineering personality that bordered on bullying—had made her a superstar among her devoted fans, and we were plummeting without a parachute in her absence. Bossman Peters was determined to halt the inevitable crash, and so devised a foolproof plan: he would pit Jemma-Lee Verity and I against each other over two blockbuster live episodes, and then let the nation hash it out on social media as to who would become the new host of the show. As Jemma-Lee had just come off of hosting the wildly popular *Dogs and Burgs* series for the Food Channel (where she ate her way—just one bite, mind you! —through the best hotdog and burger joints in the country) and I was a nobody straight out of university, it seemed like #Verity was a shoo-in.

I wasn't about to give up and hand it to Jemma-Lee without a fight, however. If there's anything my mother taught me (besides how not to decorate a bedroom), it's to flash the claws and come out swinging. So, on the morning of the shoot, I was primed for battle. I came out roaring by straightaway interviewing the neighbors.

First off: Mrs. Dannick next door, her hair in rollers and her plump arms waving as she described how her neighbor Mr. Fiereno blatantly disregarded the City's notices to mow his lawn and tidy the yard. "Do you see all those garden gnomes?" she sputtered, gesturing wildly. I had to admit, even for a hoarder, there did seem to be an extraordinary amount of bric-a-brac in the front yard, some of it still in shipping crates. Not all of it was ornamental—no less than six washer and dryer sets and at least three refrigerators were planted on the grass, every one of them still on pallets and bound with straps. "It's a disgusting eyesore, and it's driving our property values down!" Mrs. Dannick continued to rage, as we kept filming. This kind of stuff made for great TV, as Bossman Peters was fond of preaching. "And this is nothing compared to the back yard—it looks like a tornado ran through." She lowered her voice conspiratorially. "People in the neighborhood think he's got animals buried back there—why, just the other day, Mrs. Wrightworth from number six-nineteen reported her cat missing. And just a couple of days before that, Lila Lucjek across the street lost her little shih-tzu. Everyone thinks Fiereno is responsible."

I asked Mr. Jackson, the neighbor on the other side, if he had ever seen Mr. Fiereno leave the house. "Well, no," Mr. Jackson acknowledged. He seemed surprised. "I don't think anyone has. He didn't open his door to the Welcome Wagon when he moved in, that's for sure. My wife is on the neighborhood WW—they made three attempts but gave up after that. We figure the guy is some kind of recluse, and a bit off-kilter given the way he keeps his property. I wish he'd move, and soon."

One of the logistical problems with the live show was the fact we sprang ourselves on our unsuspecting guests—which, in Jemma-Lee's case, had meant she met with resistance the second she rang the doorbell of the target in the episode she filmed the week previous. The resident was initially enraged, completely in denial she needed any help from the crew of a reality TV show, and slammed the door in their faces. Unfortunately for me, the viewers lapped that part up—and stayed on in droves to watch Jemma-Lee and Pixie Washington, our De-Clutter Expert, massage the ego of the homeowner and eventually gain entry into an abject pigsty, which they then proceeded, with the help of a slew of minions and four epic hours of airtime, to successfully turn into showpiece of organization. Despite several bouts of tears, screaming hysteria, and threats (mostly, but not strictly, executed by the homeowner), smiles and high fives all abounded in the end, of course.

Bah humbug.

I was positively jangly with nerves as we bashed our way through the piles of car batteries, birdbaths, and RC helicopters that littered the steps to Mr. Fiereno's door, but I kept up a running monologue with the viewers, smiling with my just-whitened teeth and that perfect shade of Revelry Rose lipstick I had picked up at the drugstore the night before. My cameraman, Jonesy, was working the scene beautifully, offering the *Happy Hoarders* fans tantalizing views of the garbage on the walkway and stoop. I paused dramatically to examine the notices stapled by City bylaw officers on the doorframe, the citations giving Mr. Fiereno thirty days to clean up or face severe penalty. Jonesy zoomed in so the nation could see the yellow papers flapping in the slight breeze, the newest one dated four months previous, and Pixie made some vague, but terribly serious pronouncement about the psychological state of people who allow their lives to become dominated by material goods. (Pixie was actually a waitress from New Mexico, so to keep our network's Legal department happy, she tended to not offer much in the way of highly specific counsel).

I could hear our director Barry's voice in my earpiece, offering encouragement from the comfort of the studio. I plunged my finger into the doorbell. The mics picked up the muffled ring within the house. In the subsequent wait for an answer, I chatted with Pixie about what she considered the best ways to tackle a big clean up job, and she rattled off a few pointers she had undoubtedly scooped from someone's Pinterest page the night before.

When Mr. Fiereno did not deign to answer the bell, I knocked, then brazenly tried the doorknob. The actual phrase "break and enter" had not been used at the meeting where the cast and crew had been informed to "make the show happen, at all costs" so I figured I was perfectly in line. To my astonishment (which I was careful not to show), it was unlocked. Barry whooped his approval in my earpiece as Pixie and I ducked inside, followed by Jonesy, who switched on the lamp on the camera and quickly swept our surroundings with his lens.

We only had a paltry few square inches to move around in the entranceway, which made for some tricky camera angles. The place was stacked wall-to-wall with stuff of every description, skids on skids on skids of boxes. I called out for Mr. Fiereno, but the sound of my voice was absorbed by all the cardboard, foam packing materials, and crates marked "TOASTER OVEN", "TOMATO SOUP", "COPPER-BASED SAUCEPAN, 8-INCH", and "ALUMINIUM FOIL".

"Clearly a man who likes to purchase bargains in bulk," Pixie observed. "That's a good idea and can save a lot of money in the long run, but you have to be sure to buy only the things you will use up within a prescribed period of time. Don't just buy things to have them—that's a surefire way to go broke, not to mention end up with a house full of clutter."

I led the way on a tour of the lower floor of the house, plowing through piles of ironing boards, bolts of fabric, pallets containing toothpaste and dishwasher tabs (even though no dishwasher was yet in sight) and totes full of shoes that didn't seem to match. In one room, three billiard tables were racked up in the center, with boxes of tennis balls piled high on top. Below the tables were cartons of refill ink cartridges for a printer I was certain was obsolete. Stuffed in a corner and nearly reaching the ceiling was a rainbow-colored assortment of foam noodles and a skid of algae-skim for a swimming pool Mr. Fiereno didn't own. The kitchen held more surprises: three vintage pinball machines, a rack of wedding dresses (all size 18), five kegs of beer, and a panel of brand-new microwave ovens. We found two bins filled with bark chips in the dining room, sitting next to a display of calendars from 1999 and twenty brand new vacuum cleaners. The dishwasher turned up in the living room, cozied up with more garden gnomes, a fleet of bicycles, and a huge unopened crate that smelled pleasantly like cinnamon.

I had never seen anything like it, and I had been watching *Happy Hoarders* for six seasons now. I was beginning to panic, wondering how the crew would ever accomplish a clean-up on such a colossal scale in the allotted period of time. Barry seemed satisfied with our progress, however; you could tell from the way he contentedly smacked his chewing gum in my ear. But there was still that sticky problem of Mr. Fiereno—the show was nothing without the profile of the man who owned this crazy amount of stuff.

I led the way to the staircase and we plodded up to the second floor, our progress impeded by an array of computer monitors (some still in their original packaging, others which belonged to a recycling heap), cases of soda pop and maple syrup imported from Canada, eight boxes of pine-scented car air fresheners, several tubes of caulking, and a frighteningly teetering collection of variously-sized Mason jars and drinking glasses. I was becoming increasingly anxious; I could feel a line of worry wrinkle the foundation on my forehead. "Mr. Fiereno!" I called again, and this time, there was a reply.

A muffled "Here!" came from the second room on the right, and the three of us barrelled through the debris on the floor of the hallway and barged through the open door.

Mr. Fiereno was sitting atop a huge pile of *Barbecue Monthly* magazines, eating a piece of fried chicken (at least I hope that's what it was) and looking extremely satisfied with himself.

What followed was the most uncomfortable moment of silence the television industry had ever recorded—or, at least that's how it felt to me. I was so terrified I could hardly breathe, and I could hear Pixie gulping audibly beside me. I didn't dare look at Jonesy but I didn't hear the camera drop, so I figured he still had some sort of grip on it. Barry was freaking out in my earpiece, hollering "Say something! We're LIVE, Meredith, or have you forgotten?"

Hardly. My mind was racing, fast-forwarding to the point where this episode would be wrapped and I would be watching this meeting on a viral YouTube video, thanks to Jonesy's stellar work behind the camera and my perky, attentive hosting skills. Well, and obviously the dragon, of course.

For that's what Mr. Fiereno was—a living, breathing, certifiable dragon. In the fairy tales of my youth, dragons had been as large as mountains, holing themselves up in ancient volcanic caves, sucking on lava and steam for sustenance. Any wayward idiot—knight or knave—who wandered by the dragon's abode was instantly turned to ash by virtue of the dragon's great exhalations, and every once in awhile, the gargantuan lizards would take to the skies on mighty wings and incinerate random villages or something equally nasty.

Mr. Fiereno was no larger than a house cat, but he had the requisite wings and tail, and he was covered in scaly armor that sparkled prismatically in the light of Jonesy's camera. His eyes were intelligent, containing just the right ratio of beadiness to humor, and they were fixed directly on me.

I gathered myself and stepped toward the creature, offering both him and the nation my winningest smile. I hoped Jonesy was focused on my upper body; my knees were knocking something fierce. Thankfully, the dragon seemed more amused than angry, astonishing what with these crazy humans barging in on him in his lair at breakfast-time. But then again, what did I know about dragon facial expressions? "Good morning, Mr. Fiereno," I said breathily. My voice sounded less like 'Fifties Beauty Queen than Asphyxiation by Fear. "You're on *Happy Hoarders*, the show that transforms your place into space! I'm Meredith Sun, and we're here to help you overcome and organize your clutter in a special four-hour live episode!"

Mr. Fiereno looked unfazed, which I optimistically took to mean he wasn't going to make crème brulee out of us as the whole country watched. I was directly in the line of fire, after all, and my vinyl skirt was particularly flammable. "Well, now, Miss Sun," he said, flashing a toothy grin, "if I had known you and your delightful viewers were going to show up at my house today, I would have put the kettle on for tea." His voice was gravelly, like he was storing up a few small fireballs in his gullet, but his tone was exceedingly polite. He eyeballed the camera lens directly, yellow irises gleaming. "Or kettles—I have three dozen or so of them somewhere." He returned his gaze to me and plucked a piece of sinew out of his teeth with an exquisitely pointed talon. "Bought 'em online at a restaurant supply store at a deep discount."

I could imagine Bossman Peters now, sitting in the control room with a cronut dangling from his dropped jaw, dollar signs strobing neon-bright in his eyes. We had just hit ratings gold.

Eat your heart out, Jemma-Lee Verity.

~ * ~ * ~

Sheryl Normandeau is a Calgary-based writer who spends an inordinate amount of time at the library (mostly because she works there). Her stories have appeared in several North American publications.

Meltdown

Chris Barili

Wink gazed out the window of the reactor's control building into the cold winter night. Outside, snowflakes mingled with the ever-falling ash, a sign the era of murderous dragons waxed, while the age of men waned like a guttering candle. The lights of New Manhattan flickered, making the squat, filthy expanse of shacks and hovels dug in around the power plant look like a cloudy night sky, stars appearing and disappearing as clouds passed.

A straw-thin engineer named Mayfield stood beside Wink, tapping his foot on the hard concrete floor. The pasty, sweat-drenched man had insisted Wink remove his Kevlar and weapons before donning a loose-fitting, paper-thin coverall, ridiculous booties, and uncomfortable rubber gloves. Mayfield wore the same gear, and while it looked natural on the engineer, Wink felt more like a clown than a hardened dragon slayer.

The power plant had three reactor buildings: two with tall domes and a squat, flattened one between them. They stood inside an annex to one of the taller ones—the only operating reactor—in a cavernous room with steel girders in the ceiling, pipes and wires running everywhere, and a collapsed ceiling crane nearby. Behind them stood a rolling steel door, thick and gray, labeled, "Material Removal."

"Let me get this straight," Wink said to Mayfield. "You want me to *help* a dragon?"

Mayfield nodded, fidgeting with the black rubber of his gloves. "We—the city of New Manhattan—will pay you to help him, yes."

The thought of helping one of the foul beasts turned Wink's stomach.

"I'm a dragon killer, not a dragon helper."

"You can't kill him," Mayfield said, his voice reedy and weak. "He keeps the reactor operating. He's why our hospitals operate, and our homes have heat."

"You sold your souls for convenience."

"We sold them to survive."

Wink gave the door a dubious look. "I want my weapons."

Mayfield placed the baggy, white hood over his head and Wink's breath fogged the face shield.

"Radon doesn't allow weapons inside," Mayfield said.

"You named it?"

"All dragons have names," Mayfield said, "but we never ask."

Communicating with a dragon, much less helping it, gnawed on the center of Wink's being.

"They're monsters," Wink said. "Killers to be eradicated like disease."

Mayfield sighed. "Do you know Radon's primary weapon? Some dragons breathe fire. Others ice. Some molten metal or scalding gases or poisonous venom. Not Radon. He breathes radiation, anything from a microwave oven to a small mushroom cloud. He's already threatened to cause a meltdown—do you really want to make him angrier?"

"He'll probably nuke me as soon as I walk in."

Mayfield shook his head. "He needs you. You're quite safe. I hope."

Wink rolled his eyes and slipped his hood over his head. In front of him, the ponderous steel door rolled left. A pulsing blue light leaked around its edges, fraying Wink's already raw nerves.

"The reactor vessel is sealed," Mayfield said. "The dome is just a containment shell in case the vessel is breached. The suit is just a precaution."

Something streaked past the opening in the door, moving so fast Wink only made out a long, spiked tail. The door stopped wide enough for him to slip through. After one last glance at Mayfield, Wink stepped inside.

An automated female voice, calm and emotionless, said over the loudspeakers, "Cooling system at minimum efficiency."

Heat buffeted him. Sweat ran down his scalp and dripped on his face shield. The containment chamber's domed ceiling stood at least fifty feet overhead, its concrete surface reflecting blue light, steel beams shining. Before him, a metal railing surrounded a hole in the floor, thirty feet across, from which the pulsing blue light originated.

"That's where the reactor vessel sits."

Wink jumped and snapped his gaze up, instinctively reaching

for the forty-four magnum that no longer rode at his hip. Hanging from a low beam, Radon stretched his long, scaled neck downward until his face hung no more than a foot over Wink's. Steam rose from his nostrils.

Smaller than Wink had expected, his body looked about the size of a lion or a bear, his wings folded against the glittering green scales on his back. Wink couldn't tell if his glowing blue eyes pulsed in time with the reactor, or if the reactor pulsed in time with them. Either way, he longed to extinguish that blue, to snuff out the life in those cold, reptilian eyes.

"See why I don't allow weapons?" the dragon asked. The corners of his mouth turned up, forming an almost human smile. "Your first instinct was to kill me."

All around them sat piles and piles of books. Hard cover, paperback, magazines and notebooks. Picture books, novels, even comic books stood in stacks nearly ceiling high.

Radon's hoard.

Wink unconsciously took a step back.

The dragon seemed to sense his concern, his forked tongue flicking out, sniffing at Wink's suit. "You needn't fear radiation poisoning. This ugly outfit is quite functional, and the little bit of radiation I emit on a regular basis is harmless. Of course, I *could* cook you from the inside out. But I don't want to…*yet.*"

He chuckled again, but Wink found it less than amusing. "What do you want from me?"

"What else would I want of someone in your barbaric profession? I need you to kill a dragon. After all, you are the great Rudolf Winkelried, son of Heinrich and Margaret Antioch Winkelried. You carry the blood of both dragon-slaying families in your veins. Quite the assassin's pedigree."

"So you know I hate you," Wink said through gritted teeth.

Radon puffed steam out of his nostrils. "I know your parents were both killed by dragons. I know you've been avenging them ever since. With prejudice."

Wink's fists clenched. One titanium round to the creature's pulsing blue eye would do the trick.

"Why would one dragon want another dead?" he asked.

"Because he stole my book."

Wink looked around; eyebrows raised. "Seems like you have

enough."

The dragon dropped from the ceiling, gliding lithe and serpentine to the floor. His stubby arms seemed almost human, perfect for holding books under his snout. As he rose to look Wink in the eye, his body glowed, an iridescent blue that emanated from between his jade-colored scales.

"We dragons are protective of our hoards," Radon said, "and this is a special book. One I need badly enough to hire a murderer. Badly enough to melt down this reactor if I don't get it back."

"Aren't you worried I'll turn on you?"

"You could no more kill me than you could the innocent people of this city. The people we both serve, in our own ways."

"You say you serve this city," Wink spat out the words like spoiled meat. "So why destroy it over a book?"

"It's not just any book," Radon moved whip-quick, popping up behind Wink like a snake poising to strike. Wink faced him, unarmed. "It is crucial to running this reactor. The uranium used in this core is no longer suitable, so my job is to keep the fuel rods radiated so the reactor can run. I also dispose of waste and keep the whole thing from melting down."

"You're a real philanthropist."

"We all have our talents. Yours is killing dragons, not nuclear physics, so let me be simple. I keep the reactor on a precipice, ready to melt down if I let it. You kill the thief, return my book, and I return the cooling system to full power. Fail and I allow a meltdown, killing everyone within a ten-mile radius."

"What's in it for me?"

"If saving all those people isn't enough, you can keep the other dragon's hoard."

"Wow, a ton of books. I *so* love to read."

"Save your sarcasm. The other dragon—his name is Ferron, by the way—is a metal dragon. You know, scales of titanium and tungsten, breathes molten metal? Brain the size of your thumb."

Wink turned to go. "Find someone else."

"Metal dragons hoard metals," Radon said. "Steel. Copper. Silver and gold. Especially gold."

Wink stopped.

"So why does this one want your book? And how did he get it?"

"Ferron took it while I was inside the reactor vessel, refueling.

He killed three people to get it. I tried to stop him, but was too late. This book is rare, and until it's back here, it's in grave jeopardy."

"What is it called?"

Radon's melancholy smile surprised Wink. He'd never seen a dragon smile, hadn't known they could. "It is called 'Help.' It should be easy to pick out from the tons of metal in his hoard, and I suspect it will identify itself to you."

"A talking book?"

"You might say that, yes," Radon answered.

"Tell me where to find it. You and I will settle our differences when I get back."

Radon's lips peeled back, revealing gleaming, sharp teeth. It almost looked like a grin.

Almost.

~ * ~

Wink trudged across the frozen lake, flinching every time the ice popped or snapped. He'd crossed ice like this dozens of times as a child, never thinking twice, but with age comes fear, and Wink was getting older every day.

Snow flurried around him, and a light wind kicked the flakes into whorls and eddies that ticked on his thick jacket, sticking in the fur lining his hood. He wiggled his fingers inside his gloves.

The lake had a name once, before the wars and the dragons. Before his parents had died. No one remembered that name now, but the lake stood between Wink and Ferron's lair, an obstacle he could cross in an hour or go around in a day.

He'd already been gone three days. He couldn't spare another.

So Wink summoned his childhood courage, fixed his gaze on the far shore, and trudged on.

Helping one of the beasts still disgusted him. It flew in the face of all he believed in. But then, so did seeing another city laid waste by a dragon's brutality, its citizens dying on the whim of a giant reptile. Once the reactor was stabilized, he would deal with Radon personally.

Past the far shore, the mountains loomed behind a curtain of snow, peeking through as if lying in wait. He had a half-mile of ice left to cross.

He hoped to sneak up on Ferron, maybe catch him napping.

Metal dragons were notoriously deep sleepers, but also notoriously huge. The last one he'd killed was thirty feet long and stood over three stories high. It melted the armor of two other slayers right onto their bodies while Wink slipped in for the kill. This time he didn't have two more slayers for distractions.

Most metal dragons had soft spots underneath, where the heat from their kiln-like lungs softened their metallic scales. The trick was hitting that spot before they encased you in molten iron.

Wink checked his weapons. His titanium sword rode high on his back, pommel jutting up over his left shoulder. An alloy shield as big around as his chest hung on his left hip, while a loaded forty-four magnum clung to his right thigh, armor piercing rounds loaded. And in his left hand he carried an old Mossberg shotgun, loaded with depleted uranium rounds for penetrating Ferron's tough alloy scales. Radon had fashioned the rounds himself, and while Wink didn't trust the dragon, the rounds looked…well, amazing.

Wink paused. A sound came to him, soft at first but growing louder, skating light on the wind. The sound of wings beating in the winter air.

He cussed and swung the shotgun up. So much for sneaking up on the monster.

A pillar of fire ripped through the snow over the far shore, and Ferron emerged from the clouds like a wraith. He was massive, with wings twenty feet across and a head bigger than Wink's torso. His reptilian eyes glowed orange and his long, barbed tail whipped behind him. He circled Wink's position once, then dropped to the ice feet from the dragon slayer.

The metal dragon extended its long, silver neck until its head towered over Wink, then let out a horrifying roar. The ice cracked again, louder.

"Radon's puny human?"

Wink aimed the shotgun at the beast's eye. "You want to die slowly or quick?"

Ferron laughed, a coughing, hissing sound that slithered over Wink's skin and down his spine.

"You funny. Go now. I no kill you."

The dragon didn't want to fight him here, in the cold, where a giant reptile would be slower, weaker.

"I have a better deal for you," Wink proposed. "Give me the

book and I will return it to Radon without killing you."

Ferron lowered his gigantic snout to Wink's face and sniffed, the smell of sulfur tickling Wink's nose. The dragon snapped back its head.

"Dragon blood!"

Wink shrugged. "It's sort of the family business."

He hefted the shotgun again for emphasis.

Without warning Ferron leapt into the air. Wink fired twice to no effect before the dragon disappeared into the clouds. He listened for a full minute. No flapping. No beating of wings. An instant later, Ferron swooped from above, gliding over the lake in deadly silence.

Wink ran as the dragon fired a column of molten metal over his head, destroying the ice before him. Wink leapt the hole of now-steaming water, his feet slipping out from under him on the other side. He slid on his back as another ball of fire struck to his left, showering him with water and ice, making the water hiss with steam. He jumped to his feet and ran again.

The ice fractured, cracks streaking in juts and angles ahead of him.

Fifty yards to go.

A ball of liquid steel whooshed over his shoulder, the heat searing his right ear, and slammed into the ice. Water shot up, cloaked in steam. The water boiled where the molten metal had hit.

Thirty yards. He could feel the ice giving way beneath him, melting as the water under it boiled. Maybe Ferron wasn't so dumb after all.

Ten yards. His boot plunged into the water, splashing it up to his face.

Then he reached the shore, streaking for the concealment of the pines. He hunkered down, shivering under a towering spruce, thankful he'd worn waterproof boots. Ferron streaked overhead twice, searching, but when he didn't find his prey, he torched a strip of forest a few meters south of Wink. He circled back and burned a spot to the east.

Wink knew the tactic—he was trying to smoke out his prey, hoping Wink would run from the fires like a sheep.

Wink wasn't a sheep.

As the dragon descended for a closer pass, Wink aimed the shotgun and fired. Sparks flew off the dragon's snout and he jerked wildly up and right. Ferron circled high above for a moment, clearly considering another pass. Then he flapped off to the north and the safety of his lair. Wink slung his shotgun over his shoulder and followed.

~ * ~

With an inch or so of soft, fluffy snow on the ground, moving quietly came easier than normal for Wink, and within an hour, he found the cave entrance. It gaped dark through the snow and looked tall enough for him to walk through upright. Dragons could squeeze themselves into tight spaces, but this was obviously not Ferron's way into his lair, which meant it was either a trap, or a secret. Wink leaned toward trap.

He edged up to the trunk of a birch tree, its papery bark frozen stiff, and peered at the cave. No movement, no light.

Sucking in as much frigid air as he could, he sprinted into the opening. Just ten yards inside, he knew he'd found the lair. The rotten-egg stench of sulfur assailed his nose, and the temperature rose steadily as he walked. The tunnel led downward, and as he descended, Wink kept his shotgun pointed ahead.

The tunnel shrank as he went, its ceiling dropping so far he had to sling the shotgun across his back and crawl on hands and knees until it opened up to full height again.

A few minutes later, as sweat beaded on his forehead, Wink reached the opening to the main cavern. He stopped a few feet back from the opening, and looked out at the cave. The opening seemed at least twenty feet up. He needed to know more, so he inched forward a step at a time, testing the ground with every step. He'd almost reached the opening when the floor beneath him gave way and he slid on his back, rocks and scree pelting him as he went. He lost the shotgun, scrabbled with his fingers, trying to slow down. Then he was falling. His butt landed on a sandy floor, the shotgun cracking him across the back of his head.

White light exploded around him, then all went dark.

~ * ~

Wink jolted upright, the remnants of sleep fleeing like bats from a cave as his eyes adjusted to the orange glow around him.

He sat in the sand where he'd landed, inside a rudimentary cage built of steel girders of varying thickness slammed into the floor. His weapons lay in a neat pile on the sand just out of reach beyond the girders.

The cave towered a hundred feet overhead, its ceiling vaulting upward, with frightening stalactites biting down like fangs. On the floor, piled high along every wall, sat piles of metal. Steel. Iron. Copper. Alloys Wink didn't recognize. The closest group consisted of random piles of scrap metal—parts from cars, buildings, trains, and so on. Past that, a more organized ring of coiled wires, cut girders, and other harvested metals formed a low wall. Finally, against the farthest wall stood a ten-foot-high pile of silver, and a slightly smaller one of gold. Coins, jewelry, and other artifacts glittered in the dancing orange light, beckoning for Wink to grab an armful and run. Even an armful would buy him new weapons and food for a year.

Sprawled on the floor between Wink and the hoard, however, lay Ferron, his gargantuan chest rising and falling, tendrils of smoke wafting from his nostrils. Beyond the dragon, the main opening to the cave stood, gaping and dark. The tunnel he'd entered through opened behind him, too high to reach.

He'd fallen right into the trap.

Wink climbed to his feet, groaning as pain stabbed through his lower back.

"Quiet or you'll wake him."

He spun, fists coming up, and found himself face-to-face with a woman. She peeked in through the girders, expressionless and calm. Straight midnight hair fell to her shoulders, while bright green eyes stared out from under falling bangs. Her cloud-white skin reflected the cave's orange light. She wore a simple gray t-shirt that hung loose on her slender frame, and baggy jeans that looked like they'd been snug some years before. Just above her left ear, a handful of hair had fallen out, revealing an angry sore—her only imperfection.

"He knows you're here," she whispered, her finger to her lips. "He fell asleep waiting."

"I need my weapons," he whispered back. "And I need to get out of here."

"Ferron put me inside the cage." Her voice sounded familiar. "He made me take your things."

Wink studied his prison. The girders were placed at irregular intervals and angles, forming a mesh of steel, welded with gobs of metal. The top was open, but barbs and spikes marred the steel walls and made climbing impossible.

Wink searched the mesh, mentally measuring each gap, but finding nothing big enough.

"What's your name?" he asked the girl, his voice soft, his back to her as he checked out a hole about waist high. When she didn't answer, he knew it meant trouble.

He turned an inch at a time, hands up, and found Ferron's enormous head looking at him through the top of the cage.

"You awake. Die now," the dragon said, steam puffing from his mouth. "Much pain!"

Wink needed an exit, and there was only one way to make one. He moved all the way to his left, against the wall of the cage.

"Boy, you really are as stupid as Radon said."

Ferron's giant head darted toward him, and a forked tongue flicked out.

"He didn't tell me you were ugly, too," Wink went on. "You have the most hideous face I've ever seen."

"No talking!" Ferron roared, his mighty head pitching up.

"Did you seriously think this woman would ever love something as ugly as you?"

"No talking!"

"I guess you were wrong. She wants to go back to Radon. Now *there's* a real dragon! Powerful. Handsome. And—"

Ferron struck, firing a column of molten metal at him. But Wink moved fast, diving out of the way. The cage rocked as molten metal pounded it, blowing a hole in the front. The metal pooled under the hole, forming a puddle. He dove through the hole, heat baking his face and chest as he held his breath against the noxious fumes. He rolled to his feet right under the dragon's snout. Radon drew back his head to strike, fangs gleaming.

Then the woman sprang between them.

"Don't hurt him!" she shouted.

Wink tackled her just as Ferron fired again. The pillar of flaming metal arced over them. Wink jumped to his feet, shotgun in-hand.

"My turn!" he bellowed.

Wink fired. The heavy bullet tore scales away from the side of Ferron's neck. The dragon screamed, his tail whipping around at his attacker, but Wink dropped to the ground and the steel-spiked tail whistled overhead.

Jumping up, Wink grabbed the girl, shoved her ahead of him, and ran for the main tunnel. A blast of liquid metal vaulted over them striking the wall and raining down rocks to block the entrance. It left a space just big enough to crawl through while lava-like metal steamed and hissed on the ground.

"Get in the tunnel!" Wink yelled.

She nodded and sprinted past him, awkward and gangly. Wink followed on her heels.

Ferron took flight, trying to get between them and the obstructed exit. Wink spun to a stop and fired again. This one took Ferron in the chest, the bullet going molten as it hit, penetrating the soft spot in the armored scales. The dragon dropped to the cave floor, towering over Wink, and chuckled: a low, violent sound, like an earthquake or a distant roll of thunder.

"That didn't work like I'd hoped," Wink muttered to himself.

He dashed for the tunnel, but he knew he couldn't make it. He jumped behind the charred shell of an old school bus as liquid metal blasted the spot where he'd stood an instant earlier. The bus rocked with the force of the impact.

He sprinted to the far end of the bus, far clear of the toxic gases rising from the pool of liquid metal. He peered around the hood and fired again. He hit Ferron's right arm, blasting it from his shoulder. As the dragon roared in agony, Wink fired again, this time hitting the same spot on the chest he had before. The round exploded out Ferron's back in a shower of blood, liquid metal, and fragments.

Ferron wheezed, fire spitting through the holes both front and back, his tiny left talon scrabbling at his chest. The light in his eyes went wild, erupting through the cavern.

Wink ran for the tunnel, dodging the still smoldering gobs of Ferron's fire, and squeezing through the hole to find the girl huddled against the wall inside. He wrapped his arms around her as Ferron roared one last time and crashed to the floor. Dust and pebbles fell on Wink and the girl, and the heat of a blast furnace buffeted them, but when it ended, they both lived.

She shoved away from him and threw up in the dark, retching and spitting. When she was done, she started down the tunnel, her footsteps echoing in the dark.

"I need to get what I came for," Wink said. "I need Radon's book."

She looked at him, the green in her eyes flashing.

"You have it. I'm Help."

~ * ~

"I'm dying," she told him as they walked along an old road with buckling pavement and faded signs. They'd found warm clothing for her in a burned-out shop, so now she wore thick boots and a warm wool coat with the collar turned up. "When Ferron took me, Radon tried to fight him. It exposed me to radiation."

Wink's stomach tightened. Help tugged out a fistful of her hair and tossed it to the ground. It did little to dim her beauty.

"Now I know why he wants you back," he told her.

She kicked at the ground with her toe. "I look like hell now, but I was pretty when he found me."

Her green eyes sparkled, extra bright against the pallor of her skin.

"You're still pretty."

She blushed again. "It's flattering to have a dragon fall in love with you. They're very particular."

The snow on the trail before them glittered in the light of the full moon. The flakes had stopped falling, but bits of the ever-present ash still fluttered down, the calling cards of dragons.

"Particular how?"

"They accept only purity. Only…"

She let the sentence trail off, and it took Wink a moment to realize she meant virgins.

"You're awfully calm for someone who's dying."

"Radon can help me," she explained. "He's done it before. It's one of the things a reactor dragon can do. But…"

"But what?"

She turned her face away, trudging through a snow drift on purpose.

"But there are limits. If the sickness progresses too far, he won't be able to save me."

Wink's breath caught in his throat. "How long do you have?"

She shook her head, raven hair flying through the falling ash. "I don't know."

Wink frowned. They were still a day from the Hudson River, and crossing could take a lot of time, depending on the condition of the ice.

"Two days," he told her.

She nodded, her expression stoic. Her voice remained monotone. "It will have to do."

"And if it doesn't?"

"Then you will have to kill Radon, too."

Tears froze on her cheeks, causing Wink an instant of doubt. "You're crying for a dragon?"

"He'll die without me. Without love."

Wink changed the subject. "Why does he call you a book?"

She took a deep breath and let it out in a rush of steam.

"He needed instructions to run the reactor," she said. "Mayfield was the only technician left alive, and he'd been little more than a repairman. He found an automated help program, though, and played it for Radon. My name was listed in the program credits as the 'Voice of Help.' He sent dozens of people looking for me, scouring Old Manhattan and New, promising them he'd get the reactor going for their families. Eventually, someone got lucky and found me."

"He fell in love with your voice?"

She nodded. "He said my voice is pure, chaste like a virgin. He provided for me, made sure my family had power, water, and food. So I stayed with him."

Wink grimaced. "It's the lack of emotion in your voice. That's what he meant by pure. Your voice relays pure knowledge, no emotion. Dragons hate human emotions."

"Except for love," she said. "They fall in love. Especially with virgins."

Wink snapped his jaw closed, hoping she hadn't seen. She laughed, the first emotion he'd seen from her.

"I was fifteen when he took me. He protected me from danger, so here I am thirteen years later, still pure thanks to Radon. I suppose, in a way, I grew to love him, too."

Wink's head spun.

"What was your original name?"

She shrugged. "It's not important. He's not a terrible monster, you know?"

Wink met her gaze.

"They all are to me."

But his words rang hollow.

~ * ~

Help lay prone on a shining steel table in the outer containment shell of the reactor. Vomit clung to her hair and stained her gray t-shirt. Splotches of bare scalp showed through her thinning, black hair.

In the background, her voice still droned over the intercom, warning about the cooling system.

Radon's wedge-shaped head swung around on his long neck, and his nostrils flared as he took in her scent. The blue in his eyes flared brighter.

"We don't have much time," he told Wink. "Leave."

His voice dripped with worry, his scaled brow drawing down as he looked at his love.

"Fix the cooling system," Wink told him through the clear face mask of his radiation suit. "I upheld my end of the bargain, now you do the same."

"There is time for that later!" Radon lunged at Wink. "I need to save her now. You have my word I will stop it. Now go."

Wink recalled Ferron's betrayal and opened his mouth to argue. Help's hand on his arm stopped him.

She looked up into her dragon's eyes, a sad smile touching her lips. Wink's mouth hung open at the affection passing between them. "You must start," she told him. "Reactor systems are critical. The core is overheating. You need to reactivate the tertiary cooling system, then work on me."

Something about her expression must have convinced the dragon, for he rushed away, snapping orders at Mayfield as he went.

Help squeezed Wink's hand. "It is too late for me," she said. "You must evacuate the city. Promise me."

He nodded as Radon flew back into the chamber; the steel door sliding closed behind him.

A humming sound began in the reactor pit.

"It is started," Radon told her. "Now let me save you."

As Wink turned away, a tremor shook the building. Bits of dust and cement fell from above.

"Did you kill Ferron?" the reactor dragon asked. "Put out his fire?"

"I kind of skipped that part," Wink replied. "I was busy getting her back to you. But the tunnel was sealed."

Radon shook his head. "Well, you did enough to anger him. He's back for revenge. Now go finish your job."

Wink sprinted from the room, the door sliding open as he neared. As it rolled closed behind him, Mayfield followed him out.

"I'll handle Ferron," Wink told him. "Start evacuating the city. This may not end well."

The engineer blanched, then ran from the room.

Wink ripped off the radiation suit and buckled on his Kevlar and weapons. The building rocked again.

"Hurry, Slayer!" Radon's voice called from inside the dome.

~ * ~

Wink burst out the front door of the reactor building as Ferron swooped in from the north, low and fast over the river. Security guards opened fire on him, but he obliterated their position with a pillar of molten metal. The dragon took aim at the working reactor's dome, so Wink raised his shotgun and fired, the heavy metal round ripping into the dragon's left shoulder. The column of fire missed the dome and smashed into a brick building beside it, blasting a hole in the wall. Ferron swerved, his left wing folding into his side, then disappeared behind the reactor.

Wink chambered another round just as Ferron reappeared, eyes fixed on his new enemy. Wink fired again. Ferron dodged and let out a tree-sized beam of liquid steel. Wink dove to his left, and the fire slammed into a generator shed behind him. Pain arced up his left leg, and he reached back to find a long piece of metal jutting from his calf.

Ferron passed overhead and turned south along the Hudson. Wink managed to climb to his knees. He'd lost the shotgun, so he drew his forty-four, hoping the armor piercing rounds would be enough to slow the dragon so a sword could finish the job.

Popping up from the river, Ferron spit fire again, this time a short, thin burst that quickly solidified. Wink hit the deck as the iron ball shot over him.

He raised his pistol, but Ferron had already shot a column of hot iron at the reactor. Even as Wink blasted away, the fiery shaft struck the dome, exploding it in a shower of concrete and steel.

Wink kept shooting as the dragon passed over him again, and his last round found home, hitting the already weakened spot in Ferron's underbelly. The dragon veered violently right, then crashed into the tall dome of the vacant reactor building.

For a galvanized instant, all went silent. Wink counted his heartbeats as he waited to see if the dragon would emerge. He holstered the empty pistol and drew his sword, the titanium gleaming in the moonlight as he marched toward the downed dragon, still fifty yards away.

Then Ferron's mighty head peeked above the shattered wall of the dome, eyes dimmed, but not dark. When he saw Wink, the fire in his eyes flared to life. He let out an enraged howl that shook buildings and sent a shockwave through Wink's body. Then he turned his head toward Radon's reactor building and drew in his breath.

Wink's heart stalled. He'd failed. He couldn't reach Ferron in time to stop him.

With a roar, Radon—wrapped in glowing blue—burst from the hole in the working reactor's dome. Perched between his wings sat Help. Her head, now bald, shone in the light of her dragon's skin, and her eyes flashed as bright blue as Radon's.

Ferron hesitated.

"Wink, run!" Help cried.

He limped for the remaining dome, the squat one with its roof intact. His leg burning in pain. Both dragons roared. Help screamed. And as Wink ducked through the door, the night sky flashed red, then blue, then brilliant white as the door clanged shut behind him. He ran for the iron door, jumped inside the containment dome, and hit the red button to slide the door closed.

~ * ~

Mayfield found him the next day and sent a radiation suit in through a delivery passage. Wink had already bandaged his injured leg, and he met the engineer as the iron door slid open.

Wink's questions must have shown on his face, for the engineer babbled.

"Ferron is dead, vaporized really. And the reactor is operating. Radon fixed it before he came out to fight. Well, Radon and Help."

"Are they…"

"Radon did not have time to cure Help's radiation sickness before he had to defend the reactor. She is dying."

Wink's heart dropped into his stomach.

"And the beast?"

Mayfield shook his head. "Ferron blasted him in the chest. He's asking for you."

Wink found them both in the rubble of the dome, the dragon curled in a ball, his tail wrapped around Help as she rested against him. She looked even worse than before, eyes sunken, skin pocked with sores. Still, her green eyes lit up when she saw Wink.

"We stopped the meltdown."

"So I heard."

Radon's head rose. His blue eyes had gone almost dark. The scales on his chest had been burned away, leaving seared flesh exposed.

"Looks like you don't get to kill me after all, Slayer." His voice barely hissed from his lips.

"You saved the city."

"I couldn't let all those people die," Radon whispered.

"I didn't know you cared," Wink said.

"Neither did I."

"What will they do without power?"

"I re-energized the fuel rods before the fight," the dragon hissed. "If they follow Help's recordings, they will have power for years."

Wink noted a kind of wild beauty in the dragon's gleaming scales, with their mother-of-pearl iridescence. For once, he didn't find a dragon repulsive.

"And then?"

"Then they will adapt," Help said, coughing up blood and spittle.

"Why didn't you tell me Help was a woman?" Wink asked the dragon.

"You'd have tried to kill me," Radon said, eyelids slipping lower. "And you'd have died without saving her."

"Or I might have killed you and saved her."

The dragon's laugh rumbled through the ground.

"It is time," Help said to the dragon. Radon nodded and lowered his head to the ground. Help looked at Wink again. "Take what payment you require. Both hoards are yours."

"But I failed," Wink said. "I didn't kill Ferron."

"You brought Help back to me, Slayer," Radon said. A thin, weak tendril of steam wafted up from one nostril. "I can ask no more. Go home, as you wish."

Wink thought about it, then shrugged. "The city needs another reactor dragon, and I seem to be able to reason with them."

"You won't have Help to lure the next dragon."

"No, but I have two hoards for bribery."

Radon laughed, a belching sound deep in his chest, then fell silent, the steam from his nostril stopping.

"Goodbye, Slayer," Help said.

Her smile brushed away her illness for a moment, lighting up her face the way he'd first seen it. Then she, too fell silent.

Wink stood for a long time, fighting his own inner dragons. When he had control of his emotions, he started hunting again.

~ * ~ * ~

When not oppressed by his day job, **Chris Barili** writes all kinds of stories, and has published fantasy, science fiction, horror, western, paranormal romance, and most recently crime, with a noir story in the inaugural print edition of *Toe Six Magazine*. He is the author of the self-published, weird western *Hell's Butcher* series, and also writes under the pen names B.T. Clearwater (Supernatural romance) and T.C. Barlow (western). He sold his first novel, a supernatural romance called *Smothered*, to Permuted Press in 2016, and in 2019, his fantasy novel *Shadow Blade* debuted from WordFire Press. Chris lives in Colorado.

When the
Next Wind Blows

H. Holt

On a morning of wispy magic in an ivory tower overlooking the sea, Constance (who possessed no surname) was singing to her only companion in the Known Boundaries. Ramouille, as was the dragon's one and only name, sat at the base of the tower and watched her sing, his neck stretching until he was face to face with her.

When he could find no peace in the evening, she sang to him until he was lulled to sleep. Since he was burdened by forever remembering the robberies he committed in his past life (a curse by the Wizards of Yesteryear, as was his current bestial form), she sang him to sleep every night. Her voice would make him forget all the gold in the world; for it was she, with her little hands and lilting voice, that he treasured above all else.

This morning, Constance of no surname and Ramouille of no other name found sadness in each other's presence, for the time had come for her to leave him.

Every princess in the Known Boundaries was placed in an ivory tower guarded by a dragon when they reached the age of thirteen, only to be released when they came of age. In all honesty, it was a precaution to protect their sanctity, and Constance was no different. Since she was almost eighteen, she knew such a time had come, though she dreaded leaving her beloved friend.

As her voice trailed off, reaching the highest he'd ever heard it, Ramouille found himself gazing at her, wishing she didn't have to depart. Even though he knew her leaving would break the curse, he couldn't resist wanting her to stay with him.

Watching the crystalline tears flow down her face, he found himself longing to wipe them away. He wanted to touch her hair, which shone like silk beneath the sunlight; he wanted to touch her anywhere…and everywhere, but such was not to be. He loved her more than he'd ever loved anyone or anything. He hated to see her go.

Her sapphire eyes danced upon his brown and she smiled, but it wasn't genuine because sadness lingered at the corners of her trembling mouth. "I will miss you, Ramouille. Five long years we've known each other, but it feels like I've never lived a day without you."

"There, there, princess. All will be well, you'll see," he said, though each syllable pained him. "I will be the wind; you'll forget me in time, when the next wind blows from the west."

"I shall not."

He said nothing further, then lowered his head, ducked under the stairs and headed for the large doors. He heard her calling after him, but he didn't stop until he came outside and stretched his wings to their full extent. When he first came to guard the castle, his wings were as dark as night. Now they, and the rest of his scales, were gray. The time had come…

"Ramouille!" she exclaimed.

He turned to her for an instant, then looked towards the other side of the plateau to see her father and servants arriving. He smiled. The curse was almost broken, if only he could tear himself away. If only he didn't look back…

"Farewell, maiden," Ramouille said as he dived off. Before he hit the water, he surged up into the sky, seeming like a gray cloud filled with rain. He didn't look back as she called his name, but his heart beat hard in his chest so much so he could hardly breathe. He wondered briefly if her rubied vital organ was hammering like his, threatening to break free of its ivory-boned prison.

~ * ~

As the caravan moved away from the tower, Constance looked back for the last time and sang quietly, tears streaming down her face, "When the night is lonely, on me you can rely…"

A man watching her departure with much sorrow completed the verse. "To be there if I can, until we say goodbye."

As the caravan proceeded, a warm wind blew from the west. Constance sighed deeply and the wind proceeded, stealing the memory of her adored friend from her mind and bosom. Ramouille watched quietly, tears slipping from his eyes. Her love had been his treasure; now, with his new-found freedom, he was worse off than a penniless vagrant.

~ * ~ * ~

H. Holt has been published by various magazines and blogs, including: The Blue Mountain Review, Burning House Press, Philosophical Idiot, Eunoia Review, Yellow Chair Review, Hobo Camp Review, and Ishaan Literary Review. She has been published in "Stone, River, Sky: An Anthology of Georgia Poems," alongside former president Jimmy Carter.

She holds a Bachelor's Degree in Creative Writing & English from Southern New Hampshire University, and graduated summa cum laude July 2020.

The Problem with Princesses

Sarina Dorie

Chained to the wall of Prince Bruno's dungeon, one tended to ask important questions like, "What did I do to deserve this?" or "How long will I be here?" and "I know I said I like whips, chains and dungeon masters who are into bondage, but couldn't I get chained up next to someone with flesh on their bones?" The decaying corpse looked like it had been there for ages. And he sure didn't look like he died of ecstasy. Maybe this situation would have been kinky to some dragons, but I wasn't into necro-bestiality.

My beautiful, scale-covered body might have been the hottest thing this side of the Mountains of No Return, but that didn't mean just anyone would get some tail. Of course, part of the problem was I didn't have a tail at the moment. I was stuck in human form after a witch's spell.

Mayhap I should back up. The true problem that started this misunderstanding was when Merlot the Wizard came to me in my underground cavern. I was still in my dragon form then. As usual, I sat on top of my hoard of gold, reading an ancient tome about bondage gear by the glow of sconces.

Merlot staggered in, reeking of wine. The gray hem of his robe was stained purple and the "L.I.G." crest on his robe was speckled with purple as well. Probably a sign he'd been chasing maidens around the vineyard again. He was the newest addition to the League of Impossible Gentleman, though I suspected he was only a junior member since he didn't wear white.

He gazed up at rows of gold-plated sex toys hanging from the wall, restraints, gags, and diamond studded collars. His wrinkled lips puckered into a frown. He didn't voice his contempt for my fetish, but he didn't need to with the way he wore his disgust on his visage. He eyed the two tons of my curvy dragon body and rapped his staff on the stone floor–as if his stench hadn't already drawn my attention.

"Dragonacia the Wicked," he was speaking with a slur and not exactly stable on his feet. "I come to you on a matter of great importance. The kingdom is in ssserious danger. The League of Imposssssssible Gentleman wishes for you to bring aid to this land in its greatest hour of need. And by the way, do you have anything to drink? I'm a bit parched."

I set a jeweled bookmark between the pages I was reading. "When you say drink, if you mean water, yes, I have plenty of that. There's that magic wishing well in the adjoining cavern." Too bad the wishes didn't work for dragons, otherwise I would have wished for a big, handsome dragon to fulfill my wildest fantasies. But alas, all the males had been hunted to extinction, so here I was, wasting my best years away alone. "And if you mean the League of Impossibly Stupid Gentleman, I don't qualify for membership. I'm neither a knave, nor male." I cleared my throat. I remembered the slight from when I'd applied a century back. They didn't want females of any breed. Only recently I'd decided they were simpletons when they had changed the residence of their secret lair to a volcano—which had incidentally blown up their hideout. I had no idea where they were these days.

"This issss your chance to show your worth." He plopped himself on a chest of jewels and hiccupped. How he had managed the trek into the mountain I had no idea. Maybe he'd hitched a ride with a witch. "And what about ssssome pipeweed? Have you got any of that lying around?"

"All out. But I do have some roasted dwarves over yon if you're hungry." I nodded to the far end of the mountain of gold. "You're welcome to an arm or leg if you wish." The place was crawling with dwarves, knights and would-be heroes pining for my treasure. I usually didn't mind if they were cute—I mean, not that I'm into humans. But there's no harm in looking, right?

A whole band of dwarf gangbangers was a dragoness's wet dream come true. Only, those particular dwarves had insulted me and called me a freak all because I'd wanted them to tie me up and ravish me.

Merlot's face turned as gray as his robes. "I'm fine, thank you. I had better get to the point then. The kingdom hasss become overrun by princessssssses needing to be rescued. They lock themselves up in towers, eat enchanted apples, magick themselves into deep sssslumbers and do all ssssundry of insipid things as a means of catching a prince."

I shifted on my piles of gold, causing jewels and coins to roll toward him. "So where do I fit into all this?"

He scrambled to stay afloat of the rolling riches. "It wouldn't be sssssuch a problem if there wasn't a shortage of princes, which may have ssssomething to do with ssssomeone's enormous appetite and her cavern of gold."

"Wait a minute! You think it's my fault humans, elves and dwarves keep coming to my cave to steal my treasure? It's not like I *want* to eat them." Much. Although, when I thought about crunching into more of their fragile bones, it was kind of…kinky. No, I would not think about the polished metal of their armor. I would not fantasize about being tied up and spanked. I did not find knights one bit sexy or hot. My nostrils flared with smoke at the thought.

"Easy now. No need to upset yourself." Merlot stumbled back, probably thinking he'd sparked my temper. "The League of Impossible Gentleman issss willing to offer you a reward if you can eat at least a hundred princesses."

I perked up at that. "What kind of reward?"

"Ten pounds of gold per head."

One thousand pounds of gold? That in itself was an incentive. I doubted there actually was a princess surplus, but it could be advantageous if there was less competition for knights in shining armor around. This would be like killing two birds with one stone. I stood, my body looming larger than a peasant's hut. "Out of the kindness of my heart, I will go on a quest to fix the princess problem."

His mouth curled into an impish smile.

"Wait a minute. What about the rest of the princess?" I asked. "What are you doing with the bodies?"

He scratched at his wiry beard. "Whatever do you mean?"

"Well, you get the heads? I can eat the bodies, right?"

"Of course. Mwa-ha-ha-ha-ha!" He rubbed his hands together and laughed maniacally in the way the League of Impossible Gentleman were wont to do upon the closure of a business deal.

~ * ~

I wasn't about to leave my current treasure unguarded just so I could acquire another. I did the sensible thing any dragon would do and hired myself a regiment of goblins to haunt the entrances of the mountain. I was leery when I saw what the temp agency sent to me. One of the nasty little creatures rocked back and forth, staring at me with glazed-over eyes as he muttered, "Precious, my precious."

What a creepo! I was definitely complaining to the agency when I got back.

My next task was finding, not one, but one hundred princesses. I wasn't about to go after each one locked up in a tower or feigning sleep. That would take way too long, and there was no way I would leave my treasure with that batch of goblins for more than a few days. I flew to the cottage of the nearest wicked witch in Forget-Me-Not Forest. The edges of her gingerbread siding looked as though it had been nibbled on since the last time I'd been there.

"Well, hello, Dragonacia. It's been ages since I've seen you," Mysteria said, blowing air kisses at my cheeks as I crouched down to her level. "Is this a social call, dearie? Why don't I set a cauldron to boil us some tea and pop a child in the oven for dinner?"

I shook my head. "Excuse me, but I'm here on a business matter. I wondered if you could tell me if there are any large social engagements happening any time soon. Something with a high number of princesses in attendance."

"Oh? Looking for a princess for your hoard? I hear they're excellent for luring princes to dark, dangerous places. My cousin Brunhilda caught her prince that way after she lured him into her tower and trapped him there." Her deep, gravelly voice turned creaky as she spoke.

My words came out a little too quickly. "Why would I want a princess when I already have too many princes trying to break in?" And what dashing princes they were! Not that I was into that sort of thing.

She leaned against a lollipop tree. "Then what do you want a princess for?"

"I don't need one princess. I need as many as I can find. It's a paid job. I need to off them to get more gold."

"This doesn't have anything to do with that group of unpossible men, does it? Nothing to do with a certain task they've decided to give you to prove your salt? If you ask me, I haven't heard anything about the kingdom being overrun by princesses."

Likely she was right. I scratched my chin, regarding Mysteria. I hoped she didn't suspect my true reasons for wanting to get rid of princesses. "You've been consulting your magic mirror? Your cards?"

She waved me off. "No, I gave a ride to that drunk old fool, Merlot, on my broom yesterday. You should have heard the way he rambled on. Anywho, let me consult my magic ball to see what kind of social gatherings might be coming up."

She opened the cottage door. Two pathetic voices cried out from within. "Please save us! Help us! The witch is going to eat us for dinner if we don't do a good enough job cleaning her house."

Mysteria came out carrying her crystal ball. She slammed the door behind her. "I hate food that talks back, don't you?"

I shrugged. I didn't mind the tall, dark and stubbornly sassy knights who came to my cave. They were such an improvement over the whiney ones. The problem with witty humans who had a good face—and a good personality—was that I just didn't know what to do with them. Sometimes I wanted to curl up and cuddle with them and sometimes they were just so darned cute I wanted to bite their heads off. The rumble of hunger in my stomach wasn't so far from the flutter in my heart. It was rather embarrassing to be unable to tell the difference. Had there been other dragons around to consult, I'm not even sure I could have admitted this weakness in my character to ask advice.

Mysteria placed a pair of spectacles on her wart-covered nose and waved her hand over a crystal ball. Red mist fogged up the sphere. "I see invitations going out to every princess in the land. I see carriages pulling up to a beautiful castle. Oh, it's the Riverdor castle where Prince Bruno resides. There will be princesses in fluffy, pink gowns arriving at a ball. Banquet tables will be set out with so much food it could feed a village for weeks. I see royalty on the throne, servants, and plump, juicy children. Oh, yes, it's a ball! There will be so many tender, delicious children." She licked her lips.

"When is this ball?" I asked.

"In about an hour. Just enough time to be fashionably late."

I stroked my chin. This sounded too easy. Did the princesses know I was coming? Had the League of Impossible Gentleman set me up for something? I would need to be careful as I went forward with my plan.

Mysteria continued to drool into her crystal ball. "You don't mind if I come along, do you? I'm a bit peckish."

"Is there a trap? Is the League of Impossible Idiots going to sit in wait at the castle to play a trick on me?"

She shook her head, making her gray wisps of hair fly about in all directions. "No, I see no wizards, ogres, evil genies or invisible men at the party."

"Well, that's the thing about invisible men. You can't see them."

She lifted her chin. "The Great Mysteria sees all and knows all, dearie."

Wouldn't you know it, at that moment a blond boy in lederhosen climbed out the window of the gingerbread cottage behind her and helped a girl in pigtails climb out after him.

"Really? The Great Mysteria sees all?" I asked. "What does your magic ball say about the most recent children you caught nibbling on your gingerbread house?"

"It says they will make—" She squinted into her bifocals, removed and polished them, and put them back on before gazing again into the mirror. "Oh, drat! Not again. Well, it looks like I'm definitely coming to the ball with you then."

~ * ~

Mysteria flew on her broom at my side as we travelled. It was nearly dusk when we arrived in the forest outside the castle. Mysteria-the-not-so-teenage-witch waved a magic wand over her shabby black dress and transformed herself into a young, blonde woman in a fluffy pink gown. Her head was even topped with a tiara.

"What are you doing?" I asked.

"I need to blend in. You don't think the guards at the castle are going to actually permit a witch looking to snatch up children within their gates, do you?" Her voice remained rough and gravelly, incongruous with the soft, delicate form she now occupied.

I eyed her demure façade. "That's very well and all, but you've got to think up another disguise. I'm going to mistake you for a princess and accidentally eat you."

She tsked. "Princesses are too giddy and silly to be good for a dragon's constitution. They'll give you indigestion. You should try children."

I rolled my eyes.

"Besides, I'm not a princess, I'm a countess. You can clearly see from the single row of ruffles my gown is meant to blend in and not outdo the royal families in the room. Notice my tiara only has ten gemstones, not two dozen. And these puff sleeves are truly nothing. What we need is a good disguise for you. How about a viscountess?"

"I don't want to be a viscountess."

"A marquise? A duchess?"

Smoke fumed out my nose. "I'm going to go up to the castle, tear the roof off and pull out anyone wearing pink. I don't need a disguise for that."

"But the night is still young! Imagine how many more princesses you can have if you wait until they're all here. Or you could even take them off one by one as they arrive if you look inconspicuous. Hmm?"

I hesitated, considering her point. I did need a hundred princesses in order to make this worth my while. "Ugh! Fine, you can do your bippity boppity magic. But if you're going to make me into a human, it should be a prince. That way I can lure away all the—" It was too late to complete my sentence.

She raised her wand, a sparkly trail of magic flying out of it. Pink glitter spiraled around my large figure, making my scales tingle. My tail receded and neck shrank. My contracting flesh burned like cold fire.

"—a princesses," I finished. The harm had already been done. I wore a pink, fluffy gown with four tiers of ruffles. My shoulders felt burdened by puff sleeves and my head was weighed down under at least fifty gemstones. I took off the gold crown, pulling a few blonde hairs out with it. The diamonds caught the light of the setting sun, shimmering with an unearthly beauty only a dragon could truly enjoy.

"Wow! This would be a nice piece to add to my treasure."

"Alas, it's only twenty-four-hour gold. It will expire at that time or when you click your heels together and repeat three times, 'There's no place like my big, beautiful dragon body.' Whichever occurs first."

She nodded to my slippers. "But you can keep the heels."

I had a feeling the glittering rubies on the shoes were phony. Oh well, they would be a good keepsake. Mysteria linked her arm through mine and we walked out of the forest, across the drawbridge and into the castle. The guards didn't even bat an eyelash. Not that I can say I did the same. I couldn't help staring at the knight's polished armor. There's something about a man in uniform.

I called out, "Hey handsome, you ever consider going out into the mountains to seduce—ahem, I mean, slay a dragon? There are great rewards in doing such deeds."

"Stop that! Now isn't the time." Mysteria elbowed me in the ribs. "You're going to give us away."

"How can I give us a way? I'm acting like a princess."

She hissed. "Princesses do not flirt with inferiors. Only dragons with carnal appetites for handsome young men do that."

I stopped in a huff. Smoke fumed out my nose. "What are you implying?"

She shook her head. "Your knight fetish isn't exactly a secret, dearie."

"I don't know what you're talking about."

She let out a cackle that looked out of place on her blonde, royal aspect. "Do you really think after all these years I wouldn't notice? I don't judge you for your lifestyle. And you've never judged me for mine. That's what friends are for, right?"

Maybe. Only, I did think her craving for children could be a bit much at times. So what did that say about me as a friend?

When the servant at the door to the ballroom took our names, Mysteria told him, "Countess Cordelia and her cousin, Princess Geraldine." As we entered the hall, they announced us. The room was spotlessly white and as immense as my cavern. Candlelight sparkled off chandeliers. An orchestra played music on one side of the room. A young couple whom I took to be the king and queen sat on the thrones overlooking the guests. The queen wore a blue gown with an excessive amount of bows and even more ruffles than mine. She propped her chin up with a hand, looking absolutely bored. Yeah, the life of royalty must be tough.

There were quite a few noble-looking men but fewer royal ladies.

I nudged Mysteria. "Where are all the princesses?"

She shrugged. "I suppose they might be fashionably late." I had a feeling I'd been duped by the league but to what purpose if it wasn't some kind of trap?

Her gaze followed a servant boy placing glasses of wine on a banquet table. "You don't mind if I slip off for a little snack, do you? You can handle yourself, yes?" She licked her pink, pouty lips.

No sooner had she taken her leave of me than a gentleman

bowed before me. "May I request this dance?" He was young, but he wasn't wearing nearly enough polished metal to tempt me.

"No, thank you. I'm not much of a dancer. I would prefer to watch."

"Surely, you're being modest." He hooked an arm through mine.

Initially I tried to resist and was pleased to find my dragon strength had actually diminished! I'd never experienced the sensation of being small and feminine. It was quite novel. My enthusiasm for my new condition brightened my mood. There was something adorably stubborn and bullheaded about the young noble and I couldn't help finding him attractive—even if he wasn't wearing any armor. He did wear an impressive gold necklace with a giant sapphire attached. I wouldn't mind having a rich prince for a suitor who might gift me with shiny accessories on occasion. Or better yet, a lover who would tie me up with gold chains.

If I couldn't have a hundred princesses for a few more hours, I might as well enjoy myself in the meantime. It might even be possible to do things in this human body I couldn't do as a dragon —namely, bed a hot, handsome prince or knight. I shivered with delight at the thought.

Unfortunately the prince soon realized I couldn't dance. After stepping on his feet a number of times, he bowed to me and limped off. If he thought his feet were aching now, he had no idea how lucky he was I hadn't retained my dragon strength and weight.

The second dance with another noble went no better. I bumped into a circle of dignitaries and a man spilled his sherry on another. I blame the heels, really. I didn't know how human women did it. They were so uncomfortable to dance in. I may also have drawn an excessive amount of attention when I went to the punch table and downed the entire punch bowl.

The dragon-sized belch didn't help. Apparently, I had retained a few dragon qualities.

I glanced around for Mysteria. She was on the far side of the room, crouched down as she spoke to two servant children. She held candy out to them but they backed away. She lifted her skirts and chased after them. Apparently, her plan to catch children for dinner fared no better.

The room had filled, though there were only about twenty princesses at present. Still not enough to convince me it was time to return to dragon form.

My true form might have gone undetected, but then Prince Bruno—the man I had assumed to be a king previously—introduced himself to me. His entire ensemble was made of silver and gold. He wore rings on nearly every finger, several necklaces and a heavy crown. Now he knew how to tempt a dragoness!

The young woman on the throne sat up straight and tall, watching us closely. She shook her head at me, eyes wide. Ah, she was jealous.

He eyed my temporary human figure with a gleam in his eyes. "I've never had the pleasure of making your acquaintance. Where exactly are you from?"

I tried to think of something plausible. It's not like I could say a cave. "Um…Far away."

"Ah, a woman of mystery. How delightful. And what lovely shoes you have."

"Yes, the better to step on your feet with, my dear."

He laughed like he thought it was a joke. "I would be honored if you would allow me a dance." He tugged me to the floor, but I planted my feet firmly on the ground. It would have been thrilling for a master to dominate me and humiliate me—only not in public on the dance floor.

"No, really, the dancing isn't working out so well," I said. "I'd rather sit out and watch all the other princesses. Where are all the other princesses, by the way? You did invite more than the ones here, right?"

He raised an eyebrow. "You would refuse your host? A prince?"

"It's not you. It's me. Well, the shoes, actually. They are killing my feet."

"Oh, your shoes!" He laughed. Of all the audacious things, he reached under my dress and pulled off one of the ruby slippers. It was so unexpected; I didn't stop him. I was pretty sure stealing lady's shoes was a faux pas. Then again, rulers of small kingdoms pretty much had the right to do as they pleased. If he had a foot fetish, who was going to object?

It didn't mean it vexed me any less that he should steal my pretty high heel.

"Exquisite," he said, eying the jewels encrusted on the shoe.

I grabbed at it, but I couldn't pull it from his hands. I was weak and less powerful than him. I might have savored the novelty of it, but if I didn't have my heel, I wouldn't be able to return to my dragon body when I needed to.

Smoke fumed out of my nose as anger flared in me.

Prince Bruno glanced around. "Where's that smoke coming from? Is something on fire?"

"Not yet," I said. A few sparks may have shot out of my mouth. The cloth on the punch table evidently was not fire retardant from the way it went up in flames. People leapt back. A plump woman I was pretty sure I recognized as a former sea witch, but now with legs, screamed.

"She is an enchanted princess!" one man said.

The prince circled me, eyeing me like I was prey. "Is she? Or is she a witch!" He pointed at me like that was a bad thing.

The young woman who sat on the throne came forward. She placed a hand on his arm. "Let's not jump to conclusions. Perhaps we should speak to our guest privately on this matter and see if a curse ails her. I have read that—"

I wondered if I misheard her. I didn't think princesses did much reading. I thought they spent their days doing embroidery, spending their kingdom's money, and giving their husbands heirs— not that I had anything against sexual appetites and making babies, it's just that the rest of it sounded pretty boring.

"We will take her to the dungeons and interrogate her. I have a way of persuading." He cracked his knuckles. I couldn't help feeling tickled by the way he tried to act intimidating. It was quite endearing he should take such an interest in me. My face flushed with heat at the idea of being tied up and doing unspeakable things with a prince wearing gold.

"This method of persuasion wouldn't happen to have any whips and chains involved, would it?" I asked.

His eyes glinted and his grin broadened. "I see my reputation precedes me. We'll see what you have to say after a few minutes on the rack."

"Actually, I prefer paddles and bondage gear," I said in an attempt at being helpful.

The princess beside the man covered her mouth and stifled a giggle. I hated it when my sexual fantasies had that effect on people. I wasn't even in dragon form and someone was scoffing at my true passion.

The prince glared at me and stomped his foot. "You mock me? You'll pay for this insolence." His face turned red, and a vein bulged in his temple. I had no idea humans could be so hot when they were angry like this.

I licked my lips, imagining I was licking his. "I hope that's a promise," I said.

"Guards, seize this witch!" he roared.

"Dear, I do believe the young lady misunderstands you," the princess said. Interestingly, she lacked the vacant eyes of an empty-headed princess. I had a feeling she knew what I was talking about. "And more importantly, I am sure she isn't a witch."

"Silence! I didn't ask for your opinion."

The guards were pretty puny for humans. I hoped that wouldn't keep them from fully man-handling me. "That's right," I encouraged. "I like it rough. Put more back into it as you drag me off."

~ * ~

As a dragon, I was used to dark, dank caves and underground lairs. I liked the perfume of underground springs, sulfur and mildew. Other turn-ons: swords raking over my scales; leather gloves sliding over my long neck, and strong, dominant men who knew how to make me feel weak and feminine—a hard thing to do to a plus-sized dragon. And gold. Lots and lots of gold.

This particular dungeon where I was chained was a little less glamorous than I'd hoped for. It smelled more like sewage and rotting bodies than the earthy aroma of minerals, there were rats, and I didn't have a private room like I'd hoped. Bodies in various states of decay lined the walls. It wasn't that I minded voyeurism; I just wanted my voyeurs to be alive.

The guards chained me to a wall. I was quite disappointed neither of them tried to grope me. The prince didn't even come down with them. They just left me there.

So there I was, stuck in a less-than-erotic dungeon wondering what I was going to do. I tried clicking my heels together. Naturally it didn't work since I had lost one of them. I struggled against the bonds. They held.

"Maybe the anticipation is supposed to arouse me," I said to the skeleton chained to the wall next to me. I did my best to imagine all the kinky things Prince Bruno and I were going to do together.

Nearly a half hour later, I heard footsteps approach. A female voice echoed down the hallway. "I insist you have a trial before resorting to such measures. I'm sure the poor young lady is innocent."

"Hold your insolent tongue, Katherine!" Prince Bruno said. "I say she is a witch, and I am the prince, therefore I'm right."

"No, I will not remain silent as you kill one more innocent. Leave her be."

Ah, the princess was jealous. I couldn't blame her. I was pretty far from innocent, and she knew it. They rounded a corner and came into view.

The young lady stepped in front of the prince, but he pushed her aside.

"She's no innocent," he said. "I bet she's the one behind all the magical events that have been interfering with my kingdom. First it was the bread falling from the sky that fed the peasants when I was trying to teach them a lesson by taking all their grain after they refused to pay my taxes."

I listened intently to the argument. Pompous and arrogant were sexy, but stingy not so much. I tried to overlook this fault.

He went on. "Then there was the magical rainstorm that put out all the fires at my annual book burning."

What? This was the reason I hadn't been able to find books of late? Literature about bondage had been especially scarce.

His voice grew annoyingly whiney. "I bet she was the one who cast a spell on me to make me sprain my ankle two weeks ago."

"Of all the knavish things! You sprained your ankle because you're a clumsy oaf, not because of magic. And the other things had nothing to do with that young lady. I did them." She lifted her chin.

Well, this little spat had taken quite the turn. If anything, I was quite diverted.

"Ha! You are a princess, and princesses do not do magic. Furthermore, as my betrothed, I should find it…" His voice trailed off into a gasp.

The princess lifted her hand and drew a symbol in the air. She chanted words to a spell. An aura around her body radiated with light. Her feet lifted from the ground, and she floated a few inches into the air. Electricity crackled around her body and tiny surges of lightning flashed around her. One of them zipped in the air and zapped her hand.

"Ouch! Blast it!" She dropped to the gritty dungeon floor and stumbled into Prince Bruno.

The prince screamed and leapt back. "Guards! Save me! Another witch! She's trying to assassinate me."

She began to chant again, but he covered her mouth with a hand to stifle her spell. I was quite dismayed when they gagged her with a handkerchief and chained her to the wall next to me. Even a dragon like myself could see she hadn't been trying to kill him, but to show off her magical skills to prove she was the witch. It was a far nobler deed than I expected to see from most royalty, and a princess at that.

Seeing her chained up, he said, "I'll be back with the executioner for both of you upon the morrow. But I won't let this get in the way of my party." He stomped off.

"Hey, what about me? Will you gag me?" I asked. "You promised me some S and M. Where are you going?"

The princess next to me said something, but her reply was muffled and I couldn't understand her.

"How long is he going to make me wait? I'm not a patient girl. He is coming back for me, isn't he?" I asked her.

She gave another muffled answer I couldn't understand.

"Oh, bother," I said. This wasn't fun at all. "That execution business he mentioned wasn't for me too, was it?"

She nodded.

This would not do. I struggled against my restraints. I had neither dragon strength, nor dragon weight. What did I have? I'd managed to drink quite a bit of punch, so I still had some dragon abilities. I could still breathe fire.

I studied the chains attached to the manacles. I tipped my head upward and blew a small stream of fire at the place where the chains were pinned into the wall. The metal glowed orange and then white. The manacles around my wrists grew hot against my human skin. I yanked myself forward, pulling the chains free of the wall and falling onto the gritty floor. I worked at the chains on my manacled feet next until I'd freed them.

The princess stared with wide eyes. She said something and nodded at the wall across from us. Keys hung from a ring and I fetched them to unlock my manacles. My delicate human skin was chaffed from where the metal had rubbed.

I was tired of being in this human body.

I reached behind the princess and untied the handkerchief. "There. Now, is he coming back for me?"

"How'd you do that?" she asked. "Was that a spell?"

"The fire? No. It was simply a natural talent. Pray tell me, what does a girl have to do to get a rich, handsome man to tie her up and spank her?"

"Oh, that really isn't Prince Bruno's thing. He's more of a foot fetish kind of guy."

"I knew it!" I said disappointed. My shoulders sagged.

"I beg your pardon, where are my manners? I'm Princess Katherine. Pleased to make your acquaintance."

"I am Dragonacia the Wicked, but you can just call me Dragonacia." I extended a hand, forgetting she was chained to the wall. I shook her fingers instead.

"Oh? I've heard of you! You're a dragon known for your bountiful treasure, great library, and...appetite for knights. How delightful to make your acquaintance."

My face flushed with heat. I toed the gritty floor with a ruby heel. "I have no idea what you're implying. I don't have an appetite *like that* for knights. I simply like to eat them like every other dragon. I'm sorry that—"

She shook her head. "Stop! A woman shouldn't feel ashamed of having desires." The more she spoke, the more I liked this Katherine. She was most unusual for a princess. Or perhaps I hadn't met enough princesses to know what they were like.

"I just don't understand how you ended up looking like..." She made a face that summed up the contempt I also felt. "A princess?"

"A fairy god-witch. Long story."

"You don't mind unlocking my manacles, do you?" she asked.

I stroked my chin, eyeing her blue gown. She was rather sweet and endearing and she was growing on me. "You did say you're a princess, didn't you? It's sort of hard to tell. You aren't wearing pink."

"It happens I don't like the color pink. I'm not into fashion trends that everyone does simply for the sake of doing it. Will you free me so I can escape before he comes back to execute me?"

I sighed, my heart feeling especially heavy. "Well, the thing is, there really would be no point in that. I'm going to have to eat you."

She raised an eyebrow. "Why would you do that?"

"Oh, it has to do with the kingdom being overrun by princesses who cause so many problems since there aren't enough princes to go around these days. I've been hired by the League of Impossible Gentleman to solve this by eating the princess surplus."

She shook her head. "Surely you jest? You saw how many princesses were at the ball, didn't you? We haven't more than twenty in all eight kingdoms."

"No, more like a hundred."

"Oh, and where are all the princesses? It's nearly midnight. This is the prime time single princesses leave in haste in order to appear mysterious. Why are you *really* here to eat princesses?"

I swallowed. "Well, I am being paid, and the bodies will make an excellent meal." But that hadn't been my true reason for accepting the mission. I toed the ground with a ruby slipper. "I guess I wanted them out of the way so I could have all the knights and princes to myself." Surely they wouldn't refuse me then.

"That's your reason. What about the League of Impossible Gentleman? What do they have against princesses?"

As far as I knew, they had no qualms. What could their true motivation be? A jest? To be rid of me...for at least a while. I thought about my treasure. Smoke fumed out my nose. They wouldn't dare!

I unlocked Princess Katherine's manacles.

"Shall I show you how to escape to the servant halls?" she asked.

I knew I should probably find Mysteria before departing. It should have come as no surprise that I found her in the servant passages, chasing after children.

"I'm ready to go home," I said. "This princess quest has been a big sham. Are you ready?"

Mysteria wiped the drool from her chin. "I didn't catch one child. But it's after midnight, and I'm beat."

I bowed to the princess. "Thank you for your assistance. I am in your debt. If there's anything I can do to repay—"

"Take me with you! I'm tired of insipid princes and pink dresses. I would like to put some space between myself and here."

Mysteria and I exchanged glances. Ugh, a princess. I needed one of those cluttering up my cave like I needed another hole in my scales of armor. On the other hand, she wasn't as annoying as the ones I'd eaten—er—met in the past. We both liked to read, though I suspected the books I devoured were slightly steamier than what she read.

"I could be useful to you. Dragons need a princess for their hoard. If knights hear you have a princess, they'll try to rescue me."

Mysteria nudged me. "This will bring in more knights." She waved a wand around herself, exchanging her blonde hair for gray wisps and her pink dress for a tattered black one.

I didn't deny the appeal of a cave filled with hot, handsome armor-clad men for once. "It does seem like a win-win situation." I nodded, coming to a decision. "I'm willing to give it a try." I lifted up the hem of my dress to show Mysteria my missing shoe. "The only problem is I lost my ruby slipper."

Mysteria pursed her lips. "What is it about princesses losing shoes at balls? You're lucky I brought an extra." She tapped her hand with her wand and an identical slipper appeared in her palm. She placed it on my foot.

I clicked my heels together and chanted three times, "There's no place like my big, beautiful dragon body."

Immediately I began to change.

Princess Katherine stepped back. "Oh my! You are big and beautiful."

I was pleased I'd captured her already.

~ * ~

I was immediately suspicious when I returned to my cave and no goblins greeted me. I hastened toward my treasure room. The gold was gone. Not a trace of it remained. I felt as though I'd been punched in the gut by a mountain.

On an empty treasure chest was a note that read:
Mwa-ha-ha-ha-ha!
Yours,
The League of Impossible Gentleman

"Uh oh." Mysteria shook her head in dismay. "I suppose we now know why the League of Impossible Gentlemen wanted to get you out of the way."

I roared, flames licking the walls and illuminating cobwebs on stalagmites I hadn't known were there. I might have burned Mysteria and Princess Katherine to a crisp, but Mysteria waved her wand over the two of them and muttered a spell. An invisible shield protected them from flames.

"That is a splendid spell!" the princess said. "And very practical."

Mysteria waved her off. "Oh, that's nothing. A simple heat shield spell, really. I could teach it to you sometime."

I blew a geyser of fire at the ceiling. I was so angry I could probably have gone on for hours but where would that get me? It wouldn't bring my gold back.

I turned to Mysteria. "Can you use a locating spell to find the league's current hideout?"

"Certainly."

"And are you still hungry?"

She rubbed at a wart on her chin. "Well, I never did catch any children."

"Have you ever considered trying wizards and invisible men?"

"For eating or practicing depraved acts with?"

I might not have gained gold, a hundred princesses to eat, or even some sweet bondage action with a prince, but I did have two friends who were encouraging and nonjudgmental of my sexual appetites. And I was going to have a tasty supper in my belly after I kicked some wizard ass.

~ * ~ * ~

Sarina Dorie has sold over 200 short stories to markets like *Analog, Daily Science Fiction, Fantasy Magazine,* and *F & SF.* She has over a hundred books up on Amazon, including her bestselling series, *Womby's School for Wayward Witches.* She is the first-place winner of: Golden Rose RWA Award, Golden Claddagh RWA Award, Allasso Humor Award, and Penn Cove Literary Award. Sarina teaches workshops and classes on writing craft, writing business, cover design and art, and belly dance.

A few of her favorite things include: gluten-free brownies (not necessarily glutton-free), Star Trek, steampunk, fairies, Severus Snape, and Mr. Darcy. She lives with twenty-three hypoallergenic fur babies, by which she means tribbles. By the time you finish reading this bio, there will be twenty-seven.

You can find info about her short stories and novels on her website: www.sarinadorie.com.

Ugly Girl

Lyn McConchie

In the village of Hadiaa there lived an ugly girl; at least that was how the inhabitants of Hadiaa thought of and referred to her. In truth Verisi wasn't ugly, not if you thought of "ugly" as distorted or damaged in some way. But on a world where the population emigrating from earth had been selected for their looks as well as other qualities, she was—well—not pretty, which made her ugly as everyone else saw her.

"Ugly girl, ugly girl, Verisi's come out to play. Ugly girl, ugly girl, why don't you hide yourself away?"

And that was the least of the comments chanted by the village children. None of them threw stones, that would have been culturally inappropriate, but for a six-year-old the comments were painful enough. The whole thing was disruptive, and irritating for the village occupants and it became more so as Verisi's first year at school wore on. Eventually the Mayor of the settled area of Hadishaa continent spoke to her father.

"James, I know it isn't your fault, there may have been a throwback gene they failed to sift out before we took ship, but the child distresses her age-group. Home schooling would be a viable alternative and the school board will grant it if you petition."

James grunted. "If you agree that I can give up my ordinary job and I'm paid seven hours a day tutoring fees. And we should have a larger home, I want two more rooms added, one as a specific schoolroom, and another for supplies."

"Agreed."

Not that Verisi received more than the basic teaching. The village provided an electronic on-line tutor and the screen-embedded desk for that which was placed in the so-called supplies room. James took over the larger schoolroom, finding the shelving and space a useful resource. And with his house and goat field the furthest from the village he took more time away from home, scouring the slopes of the mountains a day's long-striding walk away where he found interesting specimens. A man who found something new or unique to sell in the spaceport could make real money. And with Verisi at home, and with his having all the time with no one over-looking him, and the fees the village paid for her, he could safely vanish all day—or longer.

"Cover for me, Veri, I want to get down into that ravine, so I'll be gone all night."

"Yes, father." And when the vid signal buzzed late morning the next day. "Hello, Verisi Taylor here. May I be of assistance?"

"Mayor Morson here. May I talk with your father, child?"

"I'm sorry, Mayor, he's milking the goat, and he won't be back for a while."

"That'll do. Just ask him to vid me once he returns."

"Yes, Mayor Morson."

After that Verisi scampered out in the rain to the far side of the goat field with the relay vid in hand. She extended the antenna, clicked in direction to prevent the whole village hearing her and called. "Father, Mayor Morson wants you to vid him back. I said you were out milking Pretty and you'd call back."

"Stay where you are then and I'll call him in another forty minutes."

James called and had a useful exchange as his outcome. Verisi had a bad cold as hers.

It was useful to have her home-schooled, James thought as he tended his snuffling daughter. Deep in the ravine he'd found a large crystal that broke down into smaller ones. The smaller sections glittered entrancingly and he was certain he could sell them to some spacer. A small independent trading ship only touched down once every four or five years, but that was what the shelves in the school-room were for. He added the crystals to a shelf and hoped. He wanted to be rich and once he was he'd think up some way of rid-ding himself of his ugly girl also.

In Verisi's tenth year there was excitement amongst local scien-tists. James returned from a village meeting and explained. He should have taken Verisi to the meeting but since everyone including Verisi preferred she not attend, she'd remained at home.

"They took a hopper over to the other continent and they found dragon bones!" James announced portentously. Verisi's eyes widened. "Yes, dragon bones. The brutes seem to have been wiped out in a volcanic eruption on the other continent as much as a thousand years ago. However the scientists are claiming the creatures may have been intelligent." James snorted. "Imagine, intelligent?"

"Were they real dragons, father?"

James snorted again. "They flew, they were large, and they have the approximate shape. Really they're big flying lizards, and as for their intelligence, I suspect the homes the scientists claim to have scanned under the lava, were merely rock formations. No doubt the brutes roosted on the mountain slopes for warmth."

Verisi dreamed after that. Of great soaring beasts that didn't know she was ugly and might like her for herself.

She hit puberty in her fourteenth year, and if life had been difficult before, puberty made it far harder. Whatever gene had prevented her from being pretty (as were other settlers on Hadishaa) may have had other attributes. Or perhaps it was a different gene, also left un-sifted, because Verisi began to empathize with those in the village if she was anywhere near them. She felt such things as Granny Jackson's dislike of her daughter-in-law and her suspicion the woman was cheating on Granny's son, Mayor Morson's desire for the daughter of his partner, and his partner's angry suspicion of that.

She only slipped a few times when speaking to a villager, but that was enough.

"Sneaking little spy!"

"Nosy troublemaker."

And this time, here and there, surreptitiously, a stone *was* thrown. That was the year a trade ship landed too, and the captain bought almost all of the contents of James' shelves.

"Some good stuff here, I'll ask for you next time we land."

"When's that likely to be?"

The captain shrugged. "Not for quite a while. Traders aren't coming to planets like yours much anymore. Not enough profit. Erissa in sector three hasn't had a landing in a generation. And I've heard to steer clear of Chanto, they say the last time a ship landed there they found the population had reverted to primitive."

"Primitive?"

"Yes, primitive," the Captain said irritably. "You know, sacrifice and stuff."

James informed the next meeting about Chanto so everyone could be properly horrified. He didn't see the thoughtful look in several pairs of eyes. In a primitive society a person could do what they wanted. It didn't occur to those thinking that way that it might apply to others thinking about what could be done to the parties of the first part.

~ * ~

And on the other continent the scientists finished their excavations and went away again. A find like the dragon town happened once in a lifetime, but the creatures had been dead for a very long time, and off-planet no one was that interested apart from two or three universities back on earth and the Space-Peacekeepers who checked before filing their report.

"Dead, you say? All of them? And no sign of any living beings?"

"No, commander. We estimate the last of the dragons must have died in the eruption. From excavations it appears they were never numerous. A few hundred of all ages, no more."

"And no evidence of separate dwellings?"

"No, so far as we could ascertain they lived close together. It may have been cultural imperative or biological necessity. However I assure you that while it appears from the artifacts they do seem to have had intelligence, they died out around one thousand years ago and we've certainly seen none in the almost two hundred years we've been here. A pity, the inderi on that continent are over-breeding."

"And you believe these inderi were originally prey for the creatures you call dragons?"

"We found middens full of cooked inderi bones, so yes, we do."

~ * ~

Verisi was twenty-seven when there was a drought and the goats dried up, fields lay parched in the savage sun, and grumbling escalated. The woman studied herself in the mirror; that stone had actually grazed the side of her forehead. It was uncivilized, uncultured —but not entirely unexpected. The people of Hadishaa were beginning to panic knowing a world sank or swam on its own once it had been listed in the database of settled planets for a hundred years. Even if they were starving there'd be no aid unless they had something to report, a valuable find, a scientific breakthrough, and of these there were none.

~ * ~

What no one on Hadishaa knew was that on the other continent something had made a breakthrough of its own. In the last days before the eruption one of the inhabitants of the small town had taken to the skies to hunt, caught by unexpected spasms it had landed to lay the latest egg in a deep crevice near the opposite side of the volcano. The egg had rolled into a lower section, and the inhabitant had left it there. The creatures' eggs could be left for centuries and still be viable. It was why they had a building that held a few eggs from each of the last fifty generations. Hatching one of the older ones now and again kept the bloodlines from narrowing and they saved only those eggs laid by the talented who would contribute to later society.

The inhabitant would recover the egg when it had time, and take it to the hatching bed.

It never did have time. Eleven days later the volcano erupted with vigor and drowned the town in lava. The building that held hundreds of eggs and the lone egg in the crevice were both lightly covered, but the town and its inhabitants died. The egg vault had been dug into the ground, it was strong and the roof held. The crevice egg was rolled deeper still in the ground's convulsions, into the furthest part of the crevice to where the side met in a roof, and the lava that poured over the crevice never touched the egg.

It had been a new and fortunately minor eruption that brought the scientists. That eruption had opened the crevice again, and the warmth had begun the fertile egg's development. It hatched a month after the scientists departed. The inhabitant, who knew his name to be Hnli as soon as he hatched, had no initial problems. Prey were numerous, there was ample water in rock pools nearby and in streams that laced the other continent, his kind had racial memory from the egg-layer, which took Hnli up to the time when the egg had been deposited, and all was well so far as Hnli was concerned for around twelve years. By which time Hnli was into adolescence and realizing two things. He had the usual insatiable curiosity of his age and genus, and he was lonely.

~ * ~

Mayor Morson rocketed down the main street of Hadiaa, eyes popping, legs moving faster than they'd moved since he was a teenager, and as he ran he yelled incoherently.

"Ahhh, help…awful…ahhh."

James Taylor was shopping, with the drought it was dangerous for Verisi to show her face in the village and he preferred not to have his groceries with added dirt from being dropped as she dodged stones. He caught the Mayor and asked questions. Those of the village that joined him asked more until the story emerged. After which the people of Hadiaa looked at each other, the Mayor, the sky and retired, firmly of the opinion their leader had gone off his hypothetical trolley.

James went home to his daughter and recounted the tale. "He says he was looking along the village boundary. Granny asked him to approve an extension of land for her family. It's just a formality but you know Morson."

Verisi did, the man was a pompous ineffectual windbag who adored to be asked in his official capacity for anything that made him look good and didn't cost money.

"So the Mayor says he was checking GPS figures to mark on the main map when a dragon flew over. When he yelled it dropped lower and looked at him. He claims it tried to catch him but he cleverly evaded it, then he ran all the way back to tell us about it." James guffawed. "I don't know what he's been drinking, but I'd like some of it."

"Did he say what it looked like, how big it was?"

"It was gray and black, and he swore it was a hundred and fifty feet long if it was an inch. I'd doubt that myself, I talked to one of the scientists and he told me the dragon bones they excavated suggested that full-grown the brutes weren't much over half that. No, Morson's finally lost it, we'll have to vote for someone else next year."

That calumny went around all the villages and towns of Hadishaa in a week. The Mayor was semi-vindicated two months later when the owner of the Hadiaa fresh fruit and vegetable shop saw the dragon too. By the time the exceptionally dry summer was done, almost everyone across Hadishaa was hysterical and Verisi's village, having been the scene of the only two visitations was in turmoil. The rain put a stop to the outdoor indignation meetings, but not the indoor ones. Feelings boiled over winter and when in spring Hnli made a final foray before he hibernated to shed his skin, things moved closer to boil-over.

James had a bad cold, and Verisi did the shopping that week. "Ugly girl, yah, yah, ugly girl. Go home so we don't have to look at you." A stone whizzed past.

Verisi ducked and scowled. "Better an ugly face than an ugly nature, Mertin Andrews, shouldn't you be helping your wife instead of running after Josey Giles?"

The wife in question was pregnant, six friends made sure she heard about the accusation Ugly Girl had made, and her husband paid the price. It didn't make him love the one who'd made the accusation—which was true, and how had she known?

Verisi went home and stared into her mirror. She was, she decided again, not *that* ugly. She was plain, but her hair was thick even if it was an average brown, her nose was straight, and while her eyes were an indeterminate gray-green, they did good service. She didn't have the well-rounded figure of the other women, but she was healthy, energetic, and fit. What more was expected? Next time she shopped in the village *that* was made plain to her.

Mertin Andrews cornered her and snarled softly. "Look, you nosy, tattling cow, I don't know where you get your information but you better shut up about anything you think you know. I'm not the only one who thinks that, keep tattling and find trouble. Understand?"

Verisi lost her temper for once. "Make trouble and I could tell a lot more about you." She turned on her heel and marched home, not seeing the look Mertin shot at her retreating back. He had secrets he'd rather not have told, and so did some of his friends. It looked like it would be another dry summer, and there'd been a recent rumor the dragon had been seen again, and...Mertin's thin lips curved in an unpleasant smile.

~ * ~

On the other continent Hnli came out of hibernation and stretched. He was forty feet from nose to hindquarters and his tail added another twenty feet. His wings and claws-fingers had grown well with his hibernation and skin-casting and he could pick up and kill a full-grown inderi. He'd found a suitable cave that went deep into the fire mountain, but he was considering moving. He'd come to realize the danger and the thought of his dead kin bothered him. It was likely he would be alone for all of what was usually a long life for his species, and with no one to *farn* with, egg production was impossible.

He ate well, drank deeply, rested a day to let his dinner go down and decided to look at the odd little creatures on the other continent. It was easy to fly there, Hnli stood twelve feet at the shoulder and in the shallow sea between continents there were a number of semi-submerged reefs. He rested on those, pausing to eat some of the larger reef fish for variety. With his appetite assuaged he flew on to land by the mountains that backed Verisi's home.

Mertin was out that way hunting, saw the dragon land and that was all it took. Mertin was an efficient and effective rabble-rouser and he did his best.

"I'm a what?" Verisi squirmed against their grip.

"A sacrifice. The dragon's come for you and we're giving it what it wants."

The outcome was a foregone conclusion. It must be admitted James protested; but not too loudly. Verisi ended up tied to a post sunk into the rocky ground in the mountain foothills near where Mertin had seen the dragon. Then everyone went home, convinced the rain would now fall, the crops grow, no one would tell secrets that were meant to remain secret, and all would be for the best in the best of all possible worlds.

Hnli saw some of the events from a ledge high on the mountain and blinked. These small creatures had some odd habits but with this one anchored Hnli could at least look it over at close range without it running for cover. Hnli stepped off the ledge and glided down. Verisi saw the dragon coming and was abruptly struck by the creature's beauty, the mayor had said it was gray and black, and it was—mostly. But where the sunlight caught the underside of the great wings they flashed shades of purple, crimson, and even gold.

She waited quietly, knowing screaming and thrashing provoked any animal, and would do nothing to free her anyhow. In many ways she was resigned. She was Ugly Girl who knew too much. Now she was a sacrifice. What was the use of fighting? She watched as Hnli landed, reached out his nose and touched her. Then she spoke quietly.

"I don't want to die, and I *really* don't want to be eaten. But if it happens then at least you're beautiful, and please do it quickly."

Hnli opened iridescent eyes wide in horror as her emotions and mental pictures sank in. He took two steps forward allowing the front half of his body to curve around the creature, it was bound and he dealt with the problem. Carefully, very carefully, he curved his claw-fingers around the small body and his wings hurled him skywards. They arrived on the other continent a day later. Verisi had eaten raw fish, been shown a rock pool with fresh rainwater, and now she slept exhausted but reassured in the bed of dry grasses Hnli provided.

And that was almost the end of the story. Almost, I said. The rains came to the village of Hadiaa and they smiled, assuming they'd done the right thing with that ugly girl. The crops did well, Mayor Morson was elected for another five years, and Mertin the blacksmith persuaded Josey Giles to lie down with him a time or two without his wife finding out. James took over the whole house and, since some were feeling slightly guilty about his daughter, he managed to convince them his salary for home-schooling the girl should continue. After all, she could return.

~ * ~

On the other continent.

"Hnli, your colors have become so bright."

"I know," Hnli smiled at his friend, savoring the warmth of her in his mind.

"You're more beautiful than ever."

"Those who give life are always beautiful." Hnli agreed. He'd had to teach her to open her mind further than she'd managed on her own, but it had been easy enough. And being able to touch minds, he'd also taught her to *farn*. How had her own kind ever so misunderstood her? The human was all beauty when minds touched, power, and warmth, love, and loveliness. And she could *farn* with a strength that engendered startling results beyond those that had prevailed in the last generations of his kind before the eruption.

"When will the eggs hatch?"

"In another month, my *esfarner*. Five at one hatch, it is wonderful." Hnli's chuckle vibrated in Verisi's mind.

"I know," she said aloud. "If you lay that well again this year you'll have no fear of being alone."

His tail curled around her warmly. "Nor you, *esfarner*. If it wasn't for your ability to touch my mind I'd not have fertile eggs, let alone so many."

Verisi giggled. Just the bones of a people didn't tell you about their sex lives. The scientists hadn't been able to tell the Draco were hermaphrodite, that egg fertility depended on their having a friend who would touch mind to mind and generate what was required in the portion of the brain that started egg formation, determined numbers, and created egg fertility. She was Hnli's friend and *esfarner*, she could *farn* and there would be fertile eggs, many of them, and Hnli's race would be reborn.

Verisi and Hnli excavated the egg nursery and hatched dozens of those as well. That had been their hoard, the precious eggs saved as the very best of them from the very best and most talented of their people. In twenty years there were many Draco, more than one bore some version of her name and would for thousands of years into the future, even though her father and the villagers had long forgotten her until the next event. That occurred when a flight of adolescent dragons went to look over the creatures on the other continent. One dragon may be disregarded if it does little damage. A flight of twenty isn't so easily ignored.

The village of Hadiaa screamed its head off severally and in chorus. Peacekeepers arrived on Hadishaa at speed, certified the dragons as intelligent, the original race on Hadishaa, and hence the world was theirs. The dragons announced that if this was so they'd like it to themselves—and got their wish, for all but Verisi whose existence wasn't known to the peacekeepers. Two million people, removed from a world no longer theirs, wept, protested, and raged, none of them knowing the seed of the event or what their cruelty had returned.

Verisi died at nine days over a hundred years old, loved and honored. In her last years she had come to be known as *Esfarnerle*, which could be loosely translated as Draco Creator. With adult Draco now numbering more than seventeen hundred her funeral was spectacular. Her body was laid in the crevice in which Hnli's egg had lain, and the crevice filled in and covered with a reclining slab of the black lava. Hnli's grandchild Esali carved the slab, which had been inlaid with Draco colors. In the ancient language it said *Verisi. Draco Esfarnerle*. The line below that title would have amused the woman who lay beneath. In elegant script it made the final pronouncement. *She was very beautiful.*

~ * ~ * ~

Lyn McConchie began writing professionally in 1990, since when she has seen 50 books published and over 300 short stories. Her work appears in nine countries and four languages. She owns a small farm in New Zealand and shares her 19th century farmhouse with a feral named Sooty and 7469 books by other authors.

Over the years she has received awards both from New Zealand and America, and her pastiche collection, SHERLOCK HOLMES: REPEAT BUSINESS (Wildside 2014) was shortlisted for The Silver Falchion Award.

The Young Dragon's Hoard

V. Hartman DiSanto

"Will you be part of my horde?"

Three large heads turned to look at the smaller creature.

Puff pulled back slightly but then steeled his nerve and lifted his head high. No, it was nowhere near as big as the heads of the larger beings, but why let them intimidate him? "Will you be part of my horde?"

Again there was a pause as they regarded him, though only a slight one.

The first breaking of the silence was a snort from Nidhug, followed by a louder sound and a burst of flame that barely missed Puff's tail as it scorched past him. This was followed by more sound from the others, different in tone, but again accompanied by flame.

Laughter.

Puff recognized that. He knew the sound of laughter, and he joined them, his own giggle accompanied by short hiccups of smoke, no flame. He had no idea why they were laughing, no idea what the older dragons considered to be so funny, but if they were laughing so boisterously it must be hysterical.

The laughter died down then erupted once more, finally stuttering to a close. By that time the dragons were surrounded by the sulfuric scent and the cloud of smoke that always accompanied dragon laughter. Except, of course, for Puff, who had not yet mastered flame at all.

As the laughter faded the older dragons regarded him with as much solemnity as they could muster.

Chua's massive head snaked closer to the young dragon. "Why did you ask that?"

Puff backed away. "Ask what?"

"Why did you ask if we'd be part of your hoard?"

Through all of that laughter, Puff had forgotten the reason for the guffaws. "I...I just wanted your help."

"How would that help you?" Adelinda regarded him from her full height. The others might lean down to watch Puff and to speak to him, but not Adelinda. She was truly the queen of this community of dragons and her very stance exhibited that to anyone who might see her.

"Because of what Longwei said."

Adelinda and the others turned to regard the elderly green dragon, but Longwei was not paying attention. His eyes were closed, his head raised to catch a ray of sun, oblivious to the conversation surrounding him.

Chua turned back to Puff. "What did Longwei say?"

Puff stretched his neck upward, striving for more height, yet still needing to look up to the older dragon. "He said that every true dragon has a horde."

Three pairs of eyes regarded him Chua, Nidhug, and Adelinda. Not Longwei, who had lowered his head and now chomped slowly and noisily, something he seemed to do more often nowadays. But the three watched him, silent, their expressions unreadable.

Confused, Puff stared back at them.

Finally Nidhug spoke. "That is true, but why would you ask us to be your hoard?"

The young dragon felt a wave of relief at this question, something he could answer. "Because a horde must be more than one, and all I have is Jackie."

"More than one?" Chua's head lowered toward Puff's.

"Jackie?" Nidhug's massive snout pointed to the young dragon.

"What in the name of gold do you mean?" Adelinda joined the others, surrounding Puff.

Again Puff found himself the center of uncomfortable attention, any of the three sets of jaws around him capable of crushing his own smaller skull. *I am a dragon,* he reminded himself. *I show no fear.*

"Of course more than one" was his reply. "It takes more than one to make a horde. And Jackie" —he tried to turn toward Nidhug but was too hemmed in to do more than to shift his gaze— "is the boy I met last week. As to what I mean, I've been trying to explain that to you."

As uncomfortable as he had felt with those older and larger dragon heads surrounding him, it was even worse as they all sat upright, looking from one to another, the three of them in silent conversation far above his head. He backed away slowly, looking upward to watch them and to try to discern what they might be conveying to each other.

Finally, all three moved in unison to look down at him, though it was Adelinda who spoke. "Exactly what do you think a hoard is?"

"A large group or crowd." He gave a quick nod of his head. "I memorized that. I didn't know what it meant, so I asked Jackie, and he looked it up in his dir…dis…dictionary."

Chua let out a short burst of flame. "That makes no sense."

"Horde. H-o-r-d-e. He is correct. 'A large group or crowd.'" Apparently Longwei had not drifted to sleep. His eyes were half-lidded as he pronounced the letters, but he had clearly been listening to the conversation.

Nidhug addressed Longwei with deference, as was proper to the eldest of the dragons of these mountains. "That's what you told Puff he needed?"

"No." Longwei sat up, stopping to stretch his wings and refold them before continuing. "I told him that every true dragon has a hoard, h-o-a-r-d."

They processed that silently, Puff and the three larger dragons, considering the two words Longwei had mentioned, though the letters meant little to them.

Finally, Puff responded. "I don't know what that means."

Adelinda, Chua, and Nidhug were silent. If they knew, they weren't saying. If they didn't, they had elected to allow Puff to be the ignorant one.

"Hoard, h-o-a-r-d. 'A supply or store of something held or hidden for future use' or 'to accumulate as much of something as one can.'" With that wisdom imparted, Longwei apparently felt his instruction was ended for the day. He turned from the others to lie upon the rocks, his body drawn into a circle, his head pillowed upon his tail, his eyes closing once more.

"Oh." Puff barely noticed the other dragons leaving his side, nodding their heads as if they had known this all along. He was busy considering how he could accumulate enough of something, anything, to be a true dragon.

~*~

"I've started my hoard."

The others turned to him, heads whipping about quickly.

"It's Puff's hoard." Longwei faced away from the rest of them as he spoke, his words a reminder.

"Of course it's Puff's hoard," Nidhug snapped. "We'd never take it."

"We'd never even try," Chua agreed.

Adelinda poked her nose closer to the young dragon. "Where do you keep it?"

"It's right here, near the mouth of my cave." Puff entered the cleft in the rock and turned, pushing something into the light so that the others could see.

"That's…" Nidhug leaned closer to regard the pile of items in front of her. "That's… what is that?"

"String!" Puff's eyes shone brightly in the sunlight as he looked up at them.

"String?" Chua glanced at the others but found no answer there. He lowered his head to study the item more closely. "Was it wrapped around your treasure?"

"It is my treasure." The youngster hooked a claw and lifted the once-white item, a small clump of sealing wax clinging to it. "See it's tied in a loop. Jackie plays some game with it. He tried to teach me, but my claws aren't shaped the right way."

"Cat's Cradle," Longwei murmured—as well as a dragon of his size could murmur.

"That's it," Puff agreed. "Cat's Cradle."

"It's string." Adelinda glared at the item still dangling in front of her.

"It's very nice string." Puff dropped it on the ground and covered it with his talons, drawing it closer to his body.

"String is string," the larger dragon insisted. "It's not treasure."

"It's the young one's treasure." Longwei swung his head toward the others. "Let him enjoy it."

At the eldest dragon's words, the others returned to basking in the last rays of afternoon sun, leaving Puff to contemplate the string and how to unstick it from the softening wax.

~*~

"What's that?" Chua leaned closer to Puff to inspect the ball that bounced in front of the young dragon.

"It's made of gum bands."

"Gum bands?"

"Kevin gave it to me." Puff picked it up, held it above the flat rock, and dropped it. It bounced and bounced again, each upward movement slightly lower than the last, until it lay still on the rock.

"Foolishness!" Chua turned away to lift his wings and catch the sunlight.

Puff picked up the ball and dropped it to watch it bounce once more.

~*~

"Playing with your hoard again?" Adelinda glanced back at Puff, her red wings extended to either side, glittering in the sun.

"It's not a hoard." The young dragon flicked his foreleg, sending the assortment of items scattering across the flat rock on which he perched. "It's just a collection of junk."

Adelinda folded back her wings and turned to him, as did the other dragons. Even Longwei opened his eyes and stared.

Puff looked from one to the other as the silence stretched between them. Finally he could stand it no longer. "It is. Junk, that is." Even so, he now reached for the items, one by one, drawing them closer with his talons. String spotted with blue wax, a ball of yellowing rubber bands, a shiny white piece of gravel, a folded paper airplane splitting at one of the creases. "Junk."

"This one has left you as well?" There was something unfamiliar in Chua's voice. His words lacked the mocking tone Puff's hoard usually evoked.

"Brian." The youngster provided the name. "He didn't come yesterday or the day before that or any day for over a week." The green dragon lifted the slingshot, the latest boy's contribution to the pile of treasures. "I saw him yesterday. He was walking with a girl, talking to her. I stood by the path but he acted as if he didn't even see me."

"He didn't," Nidhug murmured. "He didn't see you."

"He's growing up," Adelinda added. "As they get older, we fade to them."

"But they never fade to us." Longwei reached forward to the rock where Puff stood.

Instinctively, the younger dragon grabbed his treasures, pulling them closer.

"They're yours, little one." Longwei withdrew his paw, revealing a box beneath it.

Puff had never seen a thing so beautiful. Gold, but encrusted with jewels. Red, green, blue, purple, brown sparkled in the sun, but the gemstone that dominated was a dark yellow, glinting black as the elder dragon tipped the box.

Dark yellow, the color of Longwei's scales. Flashing black as the edges of his wings.

With a deftness betraying his size, the old dragon tapped the box with the tip of a talon. The lid sprung open. "Look inside," Longwei instructed.

The other dragons drew back to give the younger one space.

Within the box Puff expected to see treasure beyond any he had encountered before this day. After all, what else would a dragon keep in such a beautiful container?

No. The contents were much simpler than expected.

A smooth river rock.

A piece of stone sharpened to a point.

A crude chain, its metal showing hammer marks.

A brass coin unreadable for the scratches upon it.

Puff stared at them, confused at first, but slowly realizing…

He glanced up at Longwei, whose attention was fixed upon the contents of the box.

"Yes, young one," the eldest dragon whispered. "I had my children as well, the ones who saw me, who shared with me, and then left, unable to recognize me as they grew to adulthood. I remember each of them, though they forgot me." A claw tapped on the sharpened stone. "Sheng." Then the chain. "Qian." Abruptly, the massive hand swept forward, closing the box. "I remember them all."

"Cleo, Markos, Sofia, Lucas." Adelinda nodded. "I remember."

Nidhug took up the litany. "Alvis, Magda, Fiske, Rika."

"I remember," continued Chua. "Rangi, Hau, Malu, Wiki."

Puff looked from one to the other, sadness emanating from the older dragons, sadness to match his own. "Why didn't you tell me?"

"It hurts," Adelinda told him.

"Hurts," Nidhug repeated.

Chua said nothing.

Longwei cleared his throat, resulting in the expulsion of wisps of dark gray smoke and sulfuric odor. "You deserved your happiness. If we had told you they would leave you, you'd have spent your time worrying over that." He tucked the box out of sight, but another appeared in the grip of his talons.

This box was plain, gold in color but lacking the sparkling gems of the one Longwei had first shared. "This one is for you."

Puff stared at it for a long time as the other dragons watched him. Finally he reached for it, the tip of one claw drawing slowly over the long side surface as he had seen his elder do. The point caught in a small opening, and the lid creaked open.

A plain gold box.

Empty.

Puff looked at his treasures, the small pile of items the children, his children, had shared. His claw hooked the string with its melted mass of wax. "Jackie," he announced as he placed it in the box. Next the folded paper plane. "Hannah." One after another, his hoard was placed within the box, each accompanied by the name of the child who had entrusted him with the object. "Brian," he pronounced as an interesting piece of bark joined the others.

The young dragon closed the box.

Longwei reached out and swiped the gold coffer to himself, his movement swift and completed before Puff could react. Leaning over the box, the eldest dragon spoke softly. "We remember." He blinked, and a tear eased from the corner of his eye, elongating, then falling, to splash slightly and land in a drop upon the lid of the box.

No. Not a drop.

Where the tear had hit was now embedded a gem, deep yellow with black highlights, the color of Longwei's hide.

He passed the box to Adelinda.

"We remember," she intoned as she added her own tear to the box. Red, deep red, glinting as the sun hit its facets.

Nidhug was next. "We remember." As his tear fell, he shook his head and the droplet split in two, both remnants landing upon the box. The resultant jewels were smaller but sparkled in shades of blue.

Finally, Chua. "Remember," he choked and left behind a crystal of deepest purple.

And then the box was once again in front of Puff.

The youngster stared down at it, beautiful in its decoration and even more beautiful in its contents. "I remember." His own tears spattered, dotting the box with emeralds to match his own scales.

"You have grown." Longwei waited for Puff to look up before speaking further. "No longer will you use your child name, but the true name to which you were born. Apophis."

"Apophis," the others reiterated.

"Apophis."

The young dragon nodded, accepting his new name and his adulthood.

He drew the adorned box to himself, the first piece in his grown-up hoard.

~ * ~ * ~

By day **V. Hartman DiSanto** is an advocate for appropriate early education and by night she is a procrastinating writer. She is the author of several speculative fiction novels that have stagnated at various stages of editing. Someday, these may be completed, but in the meantime, her publication credits include short stories in several anthologies.

While most people keep a bucket list of places to visit and things to do, she has found that with disasters seeming to follow her wherever she goes, her list is more achievable: finding destructive events to add to surviving tornados, floods, a nuclear meltdown, and other minor inconveniences.

Feed the Dragons

CHM Singerie

My husband started feeding them even though we'd been warned. The feeder was a gift from his sister. It was a trough of stainless steel about four feet long that hung from a large branch on a large oak tree in our backyard. The trough had to be secured at both ends because sometimes, the dragons got a little feisty.

Once a day, sometimes twice, my husband would stock the feeder with a few pounds of ground beef, chicken or pork chops depending on what was on sale. After he manhandled the meat into the trough, the dragons would wait for him to come inside, then congregate at the feeder; the larger ones chasing the smaller ones away until they had their fill, the little ones skittering into the fray if they thought they had a chance.

He'd always watch them from the table, through the sliding glass door, in our dining room. There were books piled up that he used for reference, a pair of binoculars (I don't know why, those beasts were huge), and a diary he used to record the sightings and sketch the dragons, complete with a full complement of colored pencils.

"Look at that one," he exclaimed. "It's a yellow crested Cuelebre. They're from Spain originally. Aren't the colors on it amazing? The yellow and the blue. Wow. They really won the genetic lottery! And the little red ones, they are Niohoggr from the Arctic circle. Red in the Arctic, interesting, isn't it? Wonder how they used it there. They are cute. The blue ones, the Wyvern, are assholes. They're so bossy. Look at that one chasing all the others away. What a jerk."

He delighted in categorizing the dragons from his perch. Me? Not so much.

"Dad," our daughter, Lili, said, "those dragons have chewed the swings."

"And pooped all over them," our son, Steve added. "POOP. Poop. Poopy-poo-poo." he giggled.

I could hear my mother's voice echo in my head, "He's a free spirit! Free spirits don't feed your children." Yea, but apparently, they feed dragons.

Within a few weeks, we had three feeders and George continued to stock them two, then sometimes three times a day. We started to get Yilbegans and Nagas. They nested in our oak tree with what turned out to be the missing screens from our windows. The neighbors complained it was an eyesore and an odor menace. Gladys, who lived next door, started giving me the stink eye, which turned out to be less potent than the sour smell our yard had developed. The people who passed by our house on their walks started crossing to the other side of the street. I thought that was the worst of it until the cat came into the house, the fur on her back singed from dragon fire.

"Cats shouldn't be outside anyway," my husband said, "It's too dangerous." "And what about our kids? Should they be outside? You're so into these dragons, you're sacrificing our lives, our kid's lives. You're gonna have to get rid of them. Besides, we can't afford them. Our grocery bill has doubled."

"Look! A Drake! We have a Drake. Ha, that Wyvern's gonna get it now! It's about the size of a Lab, don't ya think?"

He didn't hear a word I said. What I heard was my Mother in my head, "Love is fine, but don't forget the mortgage." Ugh.

Late that night, I heard a crash and a boom and then scratching. "George," I shook him awake, "what was that?"

"Hmm? What? Maybe you're dreaming. I didn't hear anything."

I stayed awake for a long time after that. Listening to his soft restful snore, I cringed at every inhale, wishing I could smack the breath right out of him.

The next morning we found out the Drake had made a nest in the top of our chimney. The uppermost bricks were laying on the ground in front of our house and the top of the chimney seemed to be filled with straw and copper (there was a building site not far away) and screens (which weren't from our house—ours were still in the oak tree.)

Lili looked up and asked, "How will Santa ever get in?"

"Don't be stupid," Steve said, "Santa's magic, he'll be fine! But I think we're gonna have to call the satellite company. The dragon's using the dish as a bed."

"This is too much," I spat. "This has gone too far! Now we'll have to call someone to repair the chimney AND the cable. Those dragons are eating our savings!"

My husband turned away and went back outside, a garbage bag in his hand.

I love my husband, I really do, but this made me think my Mom had pegged him. "He's a flightless bird, tittering away at this and that." "He'll never be a good provider." "He's got no ambition except for games." Certainly he had obsessions before: playing games on X-Box, golf, LARPing—all of them slightly expensive and even a bit questionable, but nothing that involved our family like this. Didn't he see how hard he was making it on the rest of us? I wanted him to be happy, but not at the expense of the family. I take it back; I wasn't even sure I wanted him to be happy. While he might enjoy the dragons, they were ruinous to our family. Couldn't he see that?

I couldn't finish the tirade in my head because there was a knock on the door. I opened it to see a man with a badge, and a clipboard in his hand. He tilted his hat to me.

"Morning, ma'am. I'm Constable Miller and I'm here to serve you papers for a small claims suit. Your neighbor, Danny Sherry, is suing you for the cost of his outbuilding that your dragons have destroyed."

"They're not my dragons!" I said.

"Well, intent is three fourths of the law, and it seems you've been feeding them. So…"

"They're dragons! You can't own dragons."

"Ma'am, they live in your yard. Therefore, they're your dragons. I don't know how you people live. It's disgusting. The smell alone…but your lack of consideration? You people deserve what you get."

"Ugh. Fine." I was fuming and embarrassed. I reached for the clipboard and signed the space with our name on it.

I noticed the Drake at the left of my vision, on the driveway side of our house. He was keeping his distance, but hissing. I stuck my tongue out at the little monster, made the angriest face I could, and handed the constable his clipboard. The constable gave me the envelope, a scowl, and turned to walk away.

The Drake matched his exit down the path, getting closer to the constable, crossing the grass, and hissing the whole way. The constable tried to play it cool, but you could see the tension in his walk, the veins popping on his neck, and eventual sprint to his car, parked at the front of the house. The drake spit a fireball at the passenger window once the constable was inside and then jumped on the trunk of the car and bounced on it like a trampoline. I couldn't help but laugh. I was delighted. Fear replaced all that stupid scowly judgment on that stupid constable's face. The tires squealed and the car drove away. Serves him right, serving me papers! The drake hovered over the street in front of our house and whooped a screechy victory cry.

I went to the back door. The Drake flew into the yard in a tree branch above my family. He was a giant reptilian watchdog. I think that was the first time I'd laughed in weeks. My shoulders relaxed a little. I watched my husband outside as he finished the chore of bagging all the poop, and then at the feeder. Our son and daughter, waiting patiently, packages of burger meat in their hands. They unwrapped the plastic as he scooped it in the feeder. He pointed up to what was left of the swing set where the iridescent red, blue and purple Drake waited, spitting sparks. Steve grabbed a stick and mocked a sword fight with the beast who flapped his wings lazily. George and Lili laughed, and George grabbed the leftover beef wrappers and motioned them all inside, hugging them as he walked.

All three stood at the window to watch as the Drake got first dibs on the meat, cooking it a little with his fire as he ate. The Wyvern chased away the others until the Drake hawked a ball of fire at him. The Wyvern flew to the top of the oak tree, continuing to squawk at the smaller dragons from a safe distance. George let out a happy cheer, "Look who's all talk now! HA!"

All the smaller dragons flew in to feast. Our daughter sat next to my husband, both of them at the dining table, sketching the scene outside the picture window. Our son played with knight figures at battle on the floor at their feet. As I watched them, I realized he was taking care of, caring for, the kids as well as the dragons. Even when he was off on his own, he always made us part of his interests. We all played X-box; dressed up and ran around; used clubs to hit balls. The kids were fine, he was fine, the adjustment that needed tweaking was me. Maybe I wouldn't get those new shoes and I would have to ignore the scowls of the neighbors and the smell and inconvenience, not to mention the money it would cost. But the kids weren't in front of a video screen, and they were happy. My husband was happy. I needed to tell the cop-neighbor-Mom-in-my-head to shut up. I needed to be happy. And these were my people.

Just then, there was a crash in the living room. I had deluded myself. What was I thinking? Being happy? Get real! I need to turn up the Mom in my head. What if they tore our whole house down? Shit!

We all raced to the front of the house.

Coins and jewels of all kinds were spilling out of the fireplace onto the living room floor. They shimmered and glittered as they piled onto the carpet. I watched the golden flow in awe as my family came to stand beside me.

"Drakes are well known for their hoards. Aren't they Daddy?" Lili took my hand and her dad's hand.

"See, Santa knows!" Steve turned and dove into the treasure to explore.

~ * ~ * ~

CHM Singerie is a wife, mother and web developer who has been hoarding treasure for a very long time.

You can find her at xtinamorris.com.

Time of the Month

Carol Hightshoe

All those men running around with swords, I knew someone was going to get hurt. What I didn't know was that it was going to be me.

Krystall paused as she approached the doors to Duke Jucaysa's hall. All she had done was ask what was causing the near panic when she entered the town gates and the next thing she knew, a group of guardsmen were telling her the Duke wanted to see her. Apparently someone had pointed her out as being the warrior who had slain the dragon Gramudyus; and since everyone was concerned about the appearance of another dragon, the Duke believed she was the one to handle it.

As far as Krystall was concerned, they needed to find someone else. It had been fifteen years since she fought Gramudyus. She was feeling her age as well as all the leagues she had traveled. What she wanted right now was a hot bath, a hot meal and a relaxing drink. Then to hole up for about a week.

"Ah, Krystall, Sword Maiden of Malytta. I welcome you to my hall." The Duke stood and extended his arms.

Krystall frowned. She hated that title. Some other Duke had given it to her. Then he'd promptly commissioned a bard to write the tale his daughter's rescue from a dark mage. Still the tale usually earned her a free meal and several drinks in taverns when someone realized she was the one being sung about. Having a reputation did have a few perks. Of course, the downside was everyone wanted you to solve their problems for them, regardless of whether you wanted to or not.

Besides, she definitely wasn't a maiden.

She smiled and bowed her head slightly as she studied the Duke. He was an older man, maybe a year or two younger than she was. However, while her hair was still full and black, his was thin and gray. His brown eyes were dull and his face was weathered and lined. Based on the threadbare cloak he was wearing, and the lack of adornments in the hall, this was one of the poorer areas of the realm.

"My Lord." She paused, choosing her next words with care. "May I know the reason I was brought here?"

"My apologies for the abruptness in summoning you here." He gestured to a nearby bench. "As you saw when you arrived, things are a bit confused. The dragon Freynia has been holding our town hostage for many years and has demanded we pay her a steep tribute each year. Recently, a traveling seer told us Freynia would be vulnerable during the two days before the moon is at its fullest." He paused and took a breath. "Many of the men in this town think to be the ones to dispatch the dragon. However, none of them have the training or skills to do so."

"And…" She waited.

"And, with your reputation…" He swallowed hard then looked down at the floor. "I was hoping to hire you to slay Freynia for us."

"Sorry, but this is not a good time." Was it ever not a good time—but men never understood these things. "I doubt I'm up to handling dragons anymore. I would be willing to give some training and advice to the person who goes after her. She turned toward the door. "It won't be me."

"Please."

Krystall hesitated. She heard the Duke's desperation. *Why do I always have to be a sucker for hopeless causes.* She turned back to face the Duke.

"I know it doesn't look like we can offer much, but I will grant you half of the dragon's hoard, which should be considerable, considering the number of years it has been demanding tribute from us," he said. "As well as anything else you want that is within my power to give you." His right hand was wrapped around in his left.

Krystall looked at the Duke. She almost expected him to drop to his knees and beg the way his hands were now rubbing each other.

"If the hoard is as big as you say it is, I only lay claim to one quarter of it. From the looks of this place, your people need it more than I do."

"Thank…"

She held up her hand. "I'm not finished."

"If it is within my power."

"I want a place to retire. Where I can be left *alone*."

"I will grant you a landholding within my domain. And, a title befit…"

"No!" Her hand went to her sword. "No more titles...please. Just a small place—not too far from here, but as isolated as possible."

"I will review the maps and will find you several locations to choose from."

She let a heartbeat pass before she spoke. "Where do I find this Freynia?"

"She makes her lair to the east, near one of the older emerald mines. It is about two days ride."

"Two days." *Might be enough time.* "And this traveling seer told you Freynia would be most vulnerable during the two days before the moon is full."

"He did."

"That gives me a day to get ready before leaving," she said. "Do you have an herb-witch in this town?"

"Herb-witch? I am not familiar with the term."

"I will introduce you to the one I consult with," a soft voice said from behind the Duke.

"My Lady." Krystall inclined her head slightly as an older woman stepped from the shadows and stood next to the Duke. Like her husband, the Lady wore a threadbare cloak and her face, though it still reflected the beauty of her youth, was lined. Her green eyes sparkled as she smiled.

The Duchess stepped forward and held out her hand. "Come with me. I will show you your chamber so you can rest."

Krystall nodded and followed her hostess out of the room.

~ * ~

Krystall grimaced. The morning sun cut through the clouds, creating shimmering mirages in the distance. Her abdomen was in knots from the stronger than normal mixture the herb-witch had given her. The witch had explained the timing was too close. The normal mixture wouldn't work properly.

However, she hadn't been sure this would work either. Now after two days of travel, her insides were protesting and she *still* had a dragon to deal with.

"Why did I agree to this?" she growled.

She patted her horse's neck and surveyed the area. Even though everyone only talked about her defeat of Gramudyus, she had fought an even dozen dragons in her life, and probably understood them better than anyone else.

This Freynia had made her lair in the remains of an emerald mine. Krystall had no doubt the dragon would have made use of the tunnels to create numerous exits. The question was, which one did she favor as her main route into and out of the lair, and which ones might she have forgotten about?

As her gaze moved over the area, she spotted a large open tunnel entrance and nodded. That was the one the dragon wanted others to think was the main one.

She continued to scan the area. There, behind a group of boulders, was another entrance. The edges of the boulders were worn and there was a greenish-metallic sheen to them that showed where the dragon had rubbed against them as she came and went.

She continued to study the area, but found no other signs of other possible tunnels. Now that was odd. The last dragon she had fought, Leystav, had been young, but he still had over twenty maze like tunnels into his lair. Gramudyus had almost a hundred. It had taken her three months to find all the entrances and study them before she had been willing to tackle the ancient dragon.

Kyrstall guided her horse to a sheltered area behind some weathered boulders. She tethered the animal there. Perhaps she wouldn't need to worry about the other entrances if the dragon was supposed to be vulnerable, like the seer had said. A wolf howled in the distance. She felt a chill wrap itself around her heart at the painful sound. Making sure her horse could free herself if necessary, Kyrstall headed for the dragon's lair.

~ * ~

Part of her secret in fighting dragons was a charm she wore. It helped her eyes adjust to the darkness of the tunnel and lair. So she didn't need to risk announcing her presence by carrying a torch or lantern.

Another howl stopped her. The sound echoed in the tunnel. Similar to the wolf she had heard outside, but with a deepness that reminded her of a dragon's roar. She frowned. There was something else in the sound. She listened. It choked off into a painful whimper.

What, by all the Lords of Chaos, is going on here?

She drew her sword, cringing at the soft scraping as it came out of the scabbard. There were no other sounds from the tunnel and she continued on her way.

The tunnel widened and she stopped. Her breath caught as she stared at the creature. Lying in the large black walled chamber was the dragon. Only it wasn't a dragon—not anymore.

Her stomach twisted.

The dragon was caught in the midst of a shape change into what appeared to be a wolf. Freynia was curled up as tightly as her dragon body would allow. Her scales had patchy fur and her legs looked like a dog's but shiny. She looked up at Krystall, then dropped her head back on the stone floor. A barking hiss escaped her mouth.

Krystall shook her head. She lifted her sword and cautiously approached the dragon. This was *not* the way one of these great reptiles should be killed.

She raised her sword and glanced down at Freynia's golden eyes. The dragon blinked once, then nodded her head. Not taking her luck for granted, she drove the sword hard into the dragon's chest, then twisted the blade as she pulled it out.

The dragon's lips curled as her eyes closed. The transformation stopped. The dragon returned to her own form.

"May the great mother of dragons spread her wings over you," Krystall whispered.

"Nicely done."

Krystall spun around; her sword held ready. An older man with long gray hair and matching beard, dressed in silver robes stood there. His blue eyes twinkled as his gaze moved past her to where the dragon's hoard was piled against a far rock wall.

"Peace," he said. "I am only here to recover something that belongs to me. Nothing more." He stepped past her, not looking down at the dragon as his robes rustled against her scales.

Krystall waited as the man reached into the pile of coins, gems and other trinkets and removed a staff. Topping the carved wood was the figure of a wolf's head—nose raised and mouth opened in a howl.

"Taken from me a few weeks ago, shortly after the last full moon. A very foolish bit of thievery on her part." He glanced at the dragon's body and shook his head.

Now she knew who the seer was. "You're the one who told Duke Jucaysa she would be vulnerable at this time?"

"I am." He bowed his head slightly. "I am known as the Wolf Seer and this creature came to me with a question. She didn't like my answer and stole my staff because of it."

"If I may ask, what was the question?"

The old man smiled. "She wanted to know how to gain true immortality. It is the one thing all dragons seek." His fingers tightened on the staff. "They know they can never have it."

She glanced back at the still body and nodded. Despite their long lives, dragons were not truly immortal. Some had been known, or so she had heard, to offer their entire hoard to any mage who could grant them true immortality. None had ever achieved it.

"Why did she seek you out?"

"I am the Wolf Seer. I asked the pack and the other creatures of this area to spread the story that I knew the secret to dragon immortality."

"Why?"

"Because I had an answer for her." He straightened his back and raised his chin, as if daring her to challenge what he said.

"What did you tell her?"

"That to gain the only form of true immortality, she would have to die in battle, at the hand of a true warrior."

"What nonsense is that?" Krystall stared at the seer and shook her head. "To gain immortality she had to die? Where is the immortality in that?"

"It is the same immortality you share with Leystav and Gramudyus. The only true immortality there is," he paused, "to live forever in story and song." His staff glowed.

Krystall raised her head as a low howl echoed in the room.

"Even though I can call the wolves, there is no danger to you," he reassured her. "I am the Wolf Seer and I run with the pack."

The glow faded and the old man vanished. Standing in front of her was a large dark gray wolf. The staff shimmered then flowed around the wolf creating a twig collar around his neck.

She held out the back of her hand and the wolf touched his wet nose lightly to it before he trotted out of the chamber.

Krystall sheathed her sword and looked at the dragon's treasure. She only had one horse and it was a two-day ride back to Duke Jucaysa, then another two days back here, if she wanted more. She filled a sack with various gems and headed out of the cave.

Her stomach twisted into a knot and she almost doubled over from the pain. *I hate this time of the month,* she thought as she mounted her horse and headed back.

Originally published in "Different Dragons" - WolfSinger Publications, 2013

~ * ~ * ~

A native Texan, **Carol Hightshoe** found her way back to Texas after of a five-year detour in The Nederlands and over thirty years in Colorado. Both detours were courtesy of her husband Tim and the US Air Force.

An avid reader at a young age, her strong desire to write came from her love of (her husband calls it her obsession with) Star Trek. It was this early love of Star Trek that led her to the Science Fiction and Fantasy genres.

In addition to her writing she has worked as a receptionist/office manager for two veterinary clinics, a deputy sheriff in El Paso County Colorado, and Assistant Fan Club Manager for the Professional Bull Riders. Her last day job was as a Rodeo Keyer for the Professional Rodeo Cowboys Association. She is now retired in Brackettville, Texas where she spends most of her time writing and publishing other authors as the editor and publisher of WolfSinger Publications and the online magazine The Lorelei Signal.

She has been published in various anthologies and magazines including "Creature Fantastic", PanGaia Magazine, "Stories of Strength", Baen's Universe, Tales of the Talisman and "Kepler's Dozen". Her books include: Call of Chaos, Chaos Embraced, The Road into Chaos, and Chaos Challenged.

Dragon's Tooth

Alexis Glynn Latner

The ticket said FLIGHT #19.

If only, Neil Weiler thought.

He found a place at the front window of the tram car. Other passengers filed in behind him in pairs and small groups. Neil was by himself. Starting college at the University of New Mexico in a few days, he didn't yet know anyone here.

Big rotors in the wheelhouse started the cables in motion. The tram car glided up the face of the Sandia Mountains above a steep slope of huge boulders and gray-green plants. Standing at the front window seemed so much like flying that Neil grinned. The tramway guide in his uniform vest warned everyone passing the first tower up ahead would make the car sway. It did. "Oooh," a woman tourist said uneasily. But Neil loved it. When the car swayed it *felt* like flying.

The mountainside under the tram car changed into deeply seamed blocks of rock and deep rough folds. The tramway guide announced, "If you look in the canyon below us, you may see pieces of metal from a plane crash years ago."

"That pilot sure flew into a tight spot," the uneasy woman said.

Looking down into the narrow canyon, Neil glimpsed a piece of metal with the letters *TWA. Wow. It wasn't just a pilot in a small plane. It was an airliner.* By some trick of the sunlight, the wrecked aluminum shone like silver. The letters TWA gleamed ruby-red. Neil blinked and then saw nothing but gray-green plants in the canyon.

Two couples stood beside Neil. He heard one of the women ask her friends, "Are there any ghosts from that crash?"

"Ghosts have been seen on the tram," one of the men answered. "They never knew what hit them. That's how you get ghosts."

Past the second tower, where the car swayed again, Neil looked back through the tram car to the west. In the valley below lay the sun washed city of Albuquerque. On the far horizon stood the blue silhouettes of distant mountains. Neil wondered what it would be like at this altitude in a small airplane, actually *flying.*

Flight #19 ended too soon. First on, last off, Neil watched the other passengers file out. No one looked hazy or sad and Neil didn't feel any drafts colder than the outside high-altitude air. No ghosts on the tram this time. But there was interesting activity on the platform. Several of the passengers were taking long bundles from the top of the tram car. Neil asked one of them, a man with smooth gray hair, "What's that?"

"Hang glider."

Neil stared at the man. "You hang-glide from *here*?"

"All the time, kid." The man's weathered face seamed as he grinned. "Want to come watch?"

~ * ~

Neil watched the hang-glider flyers assemble their V-winged rigs. He helped a couple of them by holding on by a strut until they were ready to launch. It was a good day for hang-gliding, with thermals of warm air lifting up from the valley floor a mile below and rising even higher than the ten-thousand-foot mountain crest. The hang-gliders rode the thermals under a clear blue sky. Neil had never seen anything so wonderful in his life.

He got a ride back down the mountain with a pilot who wasn't flying today. James Johnson—known to the hang-gliding crowd as JJ—was a grad student at UNM. Having been in the physics lab all night, JJ was too tired to fly but didn't want to stay off the mountain. After loading a great deal of spare gear into JJ's Toyota Corolla, there was just enough room for Neil in the passenger seat with his feet among duffle bags and a bulky aluminum hang glider part in his lap. "Good thing you're a compact kind of guy," JJ observed.

The western face of the Sandias was dramatically steep, but to the east the mountains tumbled down through foothills. That was where the roadway to the Crest ran. As the road zig-zagged down through rugged, pine-forested slopes, Neil told JJ his last name, Weiler, and that his family pronounced it "Way-ler."

"Ever have a nickname?" JJ asked.

"Not really." His mother called him Neily. He wasn't going to mention that.

"We've already got a guy called Rusty with redder hair than yours." Neil's hair was a dark, coppery red. "Why don't you go by Way?"

"Sure!"

JJ drove to the landing zone in the valley below the Crest where the hang-glider pilots gathered to drink beer and swap flying stories. The keeper of the cooler handed Neil a beer, saying solemnly, "Dunno how old you are but you look over twenty-one. "

Neil privately thanked Grandmother Weiler for insisting he go to college with a grownup haircut. The beer slid down his throat cold and tasty and made his head swim, or else what made his head swim was the unexpected acceptance into a fellowship of flying.

A late pilot angled out of the sky, tilted up, landed on his feet on the field of desert grass, and stumbled. His friends helped him get out of the harness and roll up the hang glider. He announced he needed a beer and downed most of it in one gulp.

"Hard flight, Rusty?" somebody asked.

"Downdraft near the Tooth. Almost crashed." Rusty swore.

"Today is August nineteenth," the pilot who went by the nickname Salt said. As in *old salt*. He was the gray-haired man Neil had approached on the tram platform. "Maybe that's too close. It was the nineteenth of February at seven-thirteen a.m."

There was a sudden silence.

"What was?" Neil asked.

"When Flight two-six-zero crashed into the back side of that." JJ pointed at a blunt pinnacle on the Sandia Crest. "Dragon's Tooth."

"The wreckage in the canyon?"

"Yeah. It was a winter morning with clouds and snow obscuring the north end of the valley and the Sandias. The flight was en route from Albuquerque to Santa Fe on instruments, but an instrument lied. The airliner flew into a canyon and hit a rock wall. When the tram was built above the wreckage, they hired helicopters to remove the pieces that said TWA, which wasn't going to be good for TWA's image."

But I saw one of those pieces this morning. Neil found the ticket in his jacket pocket. It said what he remembered. FLIGHT #19. Was a tram ride called Flight #19 *too close?* An unpleasant chill crawled up Neil's back. He tore the ticket up and threw the pieces on the grass.

Salt spoke harshly. "Rusty and the rest of you, and you if you take up this sport," he pointed a stubby finger at Neil, "and I think you will, because I recognize the shine in your eyes, stay away from Dragon's Tooth. It's got something bad inside. I'm not saying there's mountains that are bad. *Mountain* is just a human word for the floor of an ancient sea buckled by the collision of continental plates. But there's ridges, cliffs, scarps in the world that have *something* inside that hates hang-gliders. Geologically, maybe it's a pluton—igneous rock intruded into an overlying formation. I know about a cliff like that in Australia and a rock face in the French Alps. That one nearly killed me. Don't fly near Dragon's Tooth."

~ * ~

Just before he transferred to Embry-Riddle Aeronautical University in Prescott, Arizona, Neil hiked into TWA Canyon. He was about to commit his future to flying, but he needed to make his peace with the reality of tragic aviation accidents. This seemed like a way to do that.

He reached the canyon through a field of big boulders, the work of wind and water and time carving the mountain across eons. The mountain twisted the wind and trammeled the water. Water and wind wore away at the mountain. It was an ancient enmity, a kind of long slow elemental war.

TWA Canyon was narrow, vegetated with thorny plants, and quiet. Dragon's Tooth loomed overhead. Neil had never been this close to the pinnacle in a hang-glider.

The pilot and copilot of TWA Flight 260 had believed they were ten miles west of the Sandias. But the fluxgate compass had lied. It misled them into a cloud-obscured canyon under Dragon's Tooth. A rift in the clouds must have given them the shocking sight of a wall of rock off the right wingtip. Thinking they were near the west face of the Sandias, they made a climbing turn to the left. The airliner slammed into the canyon's other wall. The flight crew and thirteen passengers perished instantly.

What remained of the wreckage lay off the main trail but was reachable with good directions, which Neil had in JJ's precise handwriting. He worked his way up through thorny bushes beside a stream. Loose rocks slid out from under his boots. He started seeing nuts and bolts underfoot. Then larger chunks of rusted metal lay beside the trail.

He found the marker with the names of the crash victims and their hometowns.

This was New Mexico. Ruins, whether centuries or decades old, got respect. Last year there had been a memorial service with families of the crash victims and other mourners hiking up here and placing the marker. JJ's fiancée Karen, who was a native of Albuquerque, thought there would be no more ghosts from Flight 260. They finally knew what had hit them and could find their way to the next world.

Neil crouched beside a large scrap of bent aluminum. It had red numbers on it. *416.* That might have been part of the airliner's serial number, scratched and dull from long exposure to the harsh climate. How it was he'd looked down from the tram that day and clearly seen the red letters *TWA*, he still didn't understand.

The weathered numbers blurred. He frowned. The air over the numbers turned hazy. The metal shifted in a sudden breeze. The breeze felt cold. Inexplicably, he had a strong metallic taste in his mouth.

The bent aluminum rattled urgently. Startled, he crabbed away from it.

With no warning but the rattling metal, a boulder tipped out of the steep canyon wall and crashed down where he'd been until a moment earlier.

He skidded back to the main trail. He didn't stop running until he got to JJ's car and drove away with his chest heaving, hands sweating, and arms bleeding from oak-thorn scratches. When he got home to his dorm room, he finished packing that same sleepless night. By morning, he still wasn't at peace with the reality of aviation accidents. In fact, he now felt sure there could be mysterious and inimical reasons for them.

That didn't make him give up on a flying career. It had the opposite effect. Now that he knew unexplainable accidents could happen, he'd never be unwary.

He started classes at Embry-Riddle two days later.

~ * ~

To the dismay of his family, instead of getting a degree in engineering from UNM followed by a good job in the mining industry, Neil graduated from Embry-Riddle with a degree in aeronautical science, with good grades but not the best, and started the low-pay, long-irregular-hours, rootless life of a would-be airline pilot. He gave flight instruction to build up hours of flying time. He flew cargo in Arizona. Then he got a job flying checks at night from Houston Hobby airport.

Houston occupied a coastal plain where hang-gliding, at least as Neil knew and loved it, didn't happen. Instead he got involved in a B-25 restoration project at Hobby. The project needed volunteers and one with an aviation degree and a compact build was welcomed with open arms. Like the young men who had originally crewed the old warbird, Neil fit into the bomber's tight spaces.

Working in the tail of the bomber one hot, humid, summer morning, he began to feel cold. Soon he felt chilled all over. Even the roots of his hair felt cold. Then he tasted metal. He wormed his way back to the bomb bay. By the time he got there he was shivering uncontrollably. He crawled down the ladder and tripped over a toolbox.

It was a weekday with no other volunteers around. The chief of the restoration project, Mannie Alvarez, was in the project office. When Neil overturned the box of tools Mannie ran out. "You okay?"

"Cold." Neil could barely talk through chattering teeth. "C-can't see. Maybe breakbone fever." Hadn't he heard about that tropical disease turning up in Houston?

Mannie took off Neil's safety goggles. They were frosted over. "Nah. You found the ghost."

"G-g-ghost?"

Mannie shoved Neil into a folding chair under the bomber's broad wing. Then he stepped into the project office and came out with a mug of coffee.

The first swallow slid down Neil's cold, tight throat as warm as life. He looked up at the looming hulk of the bomber. "Somebody died?"

"Two. Last mission she got shot up. It was about nine o' clock in the morning. I see it's nine-ten now. Huh. The rest of the crew barely managed to get back to the Allied airbase. But it's not a human ghost. It's a memory of death and fear soaked into the metal. Call it a spirit, maybe."

With humid air infiltrating his cold-soaked clothes, Neil felt unpleasantly clammy. "Maybe it needs exorcising," he muttered.

"It's not an evil spirit," Mannie answered. "It just needs to find its way. When the old gal is restored and she flies at altitude, the spirit will see how to move on."

Neil took another swallow of the coffee. Being Mannie's private brew, it was strong enough to cut the taste of metal in his mouth.

"How do you know?"

"*Curanderas* on the family tree back in Mexico, including a Tia, my aunt Alma. I asked her about this stuff the last time I went down there. You're the second guy to feel the spirit in the bomber. Tia Alma says not many people can feel ghosts and other spirits, but if they do, the ghosts can feel *them*, and will come to them for help, or if they need *curanderismo*. That means healing. I guess you got druids in your ancestry?"

Neil shook his head. "My ancestors came from Germany. They were miners, some of them mine engineers."

"Huh. Where'd you get your first name?"

"After Neil Armstrong because I was born the day of the Moon landing."

"Ever see spirits anyway?"

Neil hesitated. "Maybe." He told Mannie about seeing *TWA* from the tram, what Salt had said about Dragon's Tooth, the cold and haze in TWA Canyon, and the falling boulder.

"Huh. Next time I go home I'll ask my Tia if any of that matters," Mannie said.

Six months later, on a cold rainy Houston winter afternoon, Mannie beckoned Neil into the office and shut the office door for privacy. "I went home to Mexico over Christmas, talked to the aunt I told you about. She says with miners and engineers in your blood, and born on Moon Landing Day, yeah, you can maybe see the spirits of machines."

"The world is full of machines," Neil objected. "They can't all have spirits."

"Nah, just machines that are hope or fear or dream incarnate. Ships, trains, rockets, warbirds." Mannie jerked his thumb toward the B-25. "War creates spirits for sure. Or a crash like that TWA airliner. Seems my family has some German blood from way back, news to me. Tia Alma says that has something to do with seeing machine spirits."

Neil let this highly unusual information sink in. "Who else saw the B-25 spirit?"

Mannie grinned, white teeth a contrast to his tawny face. "Me. So you're off the hook for this one. The first time we take the bomber on a long flight at altitude, I'll have a bundle of herbs and ashes Tia Alma makes for the occasion. She thinks that'll set the ghost right.

"By the way, the dragon under the tooth is maybe a rock spirit. She's heard of them, knows one or two small ones personally. They hate mining—they resent it when miners take copper or silver or salt, and if they get a chance to claw back metal or minerals, they will. They're hoarders with a vengeance. What you said about the wreckage and the boulder in the canyon, Tia says something like that happened a century ago a few valleys away from her village. Train wreck in a gorge. After the wreck some people who tried to salvage or steal the wreckage died. There was a rock spirit hoarding the wreckage and killing anybody who tried to take anything. It held the spirits of the dead too. The place was haunted but good. Finally a new padre decided to do something about that situation. He led a procession with a crucifix and holy water and Bible and deacon reading prayers and acolyte with incense, the whole works, into the gorge. Every man in the procession heard a loud crack—like a stone wall splitting in an earthquake. At that moment the captive spirits were set free and they followed the padre and his procession out. The padre was smart enough to lead the way out at a run. The wall of the gorge came down in an avalanche behind them.

"Tia Alma told me to tell you to remember, if you can tell a ghost spirit is there, they know you're there. If they need help they'll approach you for *curanderismo*. If you've got the gift, you're going to get asked for it, that's how it works in Mexico, and New Mexico is still Mexico, Tia Alma says. She's old school that way."

~ * ~

Neil landed a job flying for a commuter airline out of Tulsa. He stayed in touch with Mannie. Three years later he got a laconic e-mail that said, *Took the bomber to West Texas and it was vaya con Dios to the spirit.*

In the aftermath of September 11, 2001, Neil lost his job. Two lean years later, he got another commuter job and moved to Boise. Along the way he had several girlfriends, none of whom became a wife because he was too rootless, too moneyless, and too obsessed with flying, which was too dangerous for their liking. His girlfriends had a point. He finally counted up five hang-glider friends who had died from accidents. Some of them had been careless. But he heard about a few hang-glider and airplane crashes in mountainous terrain that were damn near impossible to explain rationally.

At last he got an opportunity to fly for a major air carrier: American Airlines out of Albuquerque. He thought long and hard before he took it. For the next seven years he was exactingly careful on every approach and departure into and out of Albuquerque Sunport. Nothing ever went wrong.

His personal life could have been better—with a marriage followed by a moderately unpleasant divorce—but flying made up for that. By then, his knees had aged out of hang-gliding. He'd had too many hard landings with his legs being the landing gear. He took up soaring out of Moriarty in the high-desert Estancia Valley east of Albuquerque. He bought an old fiberglass glider, a Libelle, that had once been owned by his namesake. Neil Armstrong's Libelle had no engine, long wings, slick white skin, and a high glide ratio. A first-rate hang-glider in calm air could glide twenty miles for every mile of altitude it started with. The Libelle had double that glide ratio, and in a thermal it climbed the sky like a nimble angel.

Then he bought a newer and higher-performing sailplane—a Ventus. It made him feel like hang-gliding once had: like a creature of the sky. In honor of his old hang-gliding nickname, he registered a unique identifier with the Soaring Society of America and proudly marked the T-tail and the long white wings of the Ventus with the bold black letters WAY.

A week before his forty-fifth birthday, conditions looked excellent for soaring cross-country. Neil took an aerotow in the early afternoon. He followed the tow plane into the sky at the end of the long tow rope, pulled the tow release at 2000' above the ground in a thermal, and circled up to 15,000' in air as clear as glass with the mountains of New Mexico rimming the horizon. From there on he didn't even have to circle in the plentiful thermals. He simply dolphined south past the white sheen of the Salinas salt flats, then westward over the pass at the south end of the Manzano Mountains. From there he worked his way northward along a ragged line of cloud-marked lift above spine of the Manzanos.

Further north, above the lesser mountains named Manzanitas, the thermals were strong but sparse and narrow. Turning a few circles at a forty-five-degree bank in the thermals regained the altitude he lost between them. He easily stayed above 14,000'. There was strong sink between the thermals. What goes up must come down and that included air. He wasn't worried. If he got below 12,000' he'd turn east to glide back into the Estancia Valley. If the day turned into hellacious sink and all else failing, there was Albuquerque Sunport—not that he really wanted to declare an emergency landing in their midst on a busy day. And it wouldn't come to that. This was a flight-of-a-lifetime kind of day.

The oxygen system seconded his every breath with a soft click and a puff of oxygen. His forearm rested on his thigh. He moved the control stick with his wrist and the Ventus responded instantly. The variometer chirped when he gained altitude. That was the only electric instrument he was using. The flight computer was off, a blank screen. He didn't need its lurid electron show. The clear canopy of the Ventus gave him a view to every horizon. Life was very good.

The Sandia Crest was an immense fold of rock, deeply contoured with canyons and granite spires. The blunt pinnacle of Dragon's Tooth stood on this end of the Crest. He checked his altitude: just over 14,000'. Almost a mile higher than Dragon's Tooth. Staying at least a half mile away had worked in his hang-glider days. He was faintly aware of his mind discarding several other relevant considerations because this day was giving him a dream flight. He intended to fly the length of the Sandias and then turn northeast to the Sangre de Cristo Mountains and finally south to Moriarty. Such a flight was everything his younger self had yearned for but hadn't even been able to imagine that long-ago summer morning when he took the nineteenth tram ride and discovered hang-gliding.

Over Tijeras Canyon, he hit a wide swath of strongly sinking air. To minimize his sink rate he flew faster. Over the slopes of South Peak, he found a thermal, pulled up and circled. The variometer chirped approvingly. After several turns he glanced at the altimeter, and frowned. The instrument read 13,000'. Despite what the vario thought, he'd lost a good thousand feet of altitude. He needed more. He worked the thermal, which didn't cooperate. The altimeter barely budged while the vario falsely reported an excellent rate of climb. In irritation, he turned the vario off.

The thermal tilted toward the Sandia Crest. He found himself looking over the down wing at Dragon's Tooth. He didn't have much thought to spare for it. He was too busy. The thermal was weak, narrow, turbulent, and elusive. He turned steeper to milk the thermal better.

Between one heartbeat and the next, the Ventus stalled and revolved into a spin.

He countered the spin with full rudder.

It didn't work. Mountain and valley flashed by. He was in a flat spin—which should have been impossible—and falling fast. He wasted a precious second being incredulous. In desperation he shoved the control stick in the spin direction. The spin stopped with the Ventus diving into a canyon between the bulk of the mountains and a thick fin of rock.

He pulled up as hard as he dared. Ahead was the dead end of the canyon. He commanded a hard climbing turn to the left. The Ventus instantly traded speed for climb.

But the canyon wall loomed too close. The canyon was full of wind pushing the Ventus toward a rock wall with a deep notch on the top edge of it. He shoved the controls to the right limit of travel. The Ventus rolled into a climbing right turn and tilted through the notch between two granite spires. Rock flashed by on the other side of the canopy. Something cracked.

Then he was out of the canyon over falling terrain with the cracking sound ringing in his ears and his neck hairs standing up in terror. He twisted his head left and right to check the wingtips. They looked fine. He craned his neck to check the tail. It looked intact. The ship flew straight. *What the hell just happened?!*

The vario had given a false reading. The thermal had been treacherous. The very air had impossibly worked against the airfoils of the sailplane. The Ventus had stalled into a nearly unrecoverable spin into the canyon under Dragon's Tooth. There it nearly slammed into the canyon wall like Flight 260.

Almost no other aircraft on Earth could have escaped the trap. Only the superb performance of the Ventus, making a knife-edge turn through that notch between granite spires, had saved him from the fate of Flight 260. By the way, today was July 13 *and that was too damn close to 7:13.* He'd broken a quarter-century-old promise to himself. He'd been unwary. And the dragon under the pinnacle almost got him.

He cursed himself and thanked the designers of the Ventus. Sweating and shaking with adrenaline aftershock, he reached out to turn the variometer back on.

The switch felt icy cold. He snatched his hand back. The air in the cockpit suddenly cooled. His sweat felt like ice water. The canopy began to frost over. His throat closed up as he watched frost spread up from the edges of the canopy. The Ventus lost altitude while unnatural frost spread over the canopy, and he didn't know what in God's world to do.

A jolt he felt through the seat pan broke his paralysis. He turned the Ventus into a strong thermal and circled. He found himself hyperventilating. *No good. Breathe through the nose. Steady.* The oxygen was so cold it hurt his nasal passages. He breathed deeply anyway. He needed to clear the anoxic fog in his brain.

What was that cracking sound between the spires?

The oxygen suffusing his brain cells made his memory work lightning fast. He remembered Tia Alma's tale about the padre freeing the train wreck's captive souls.

And then they followed the padre out.

The thermal was a column of warm air taking the Ventus up in the rays of the sun. The frost stopped spreading. He could see out except for the edges of the canopy. But he was seeing double—a second set of wings superimposed on the wings of the Ventus— hazy, blunt second wings thirty feet longer on each side, with cloudy knots that looked like engines, wings like the Martin 404 propeller plane that had been TWA Flight 260.

He swallowed with the taste of metal in his mouth. *Metal.* That day in the canyon he'd found bent aluminum with part of the airliner's serial number on it. 416. The piece of metal rattled and startled him into moving away from where the boulder came down on him. Maybe the dragon under the pinnacle had hoarded the wreckage and held the spirit of the wrecked airplane ever since the wreck. But in escaping death by vaulting through the notch on the rock wall, the Ventus—marked with the letters *WAY!*—had freed the ghost spirit.

This thermal was working overtime like some of the best from his hang-gliding days. As he circled, Dragon's Tooth shrank with the speed of his climb. A puff of rock dust signaled a rockslide. Thwarted, the dragon was mad.

It must hate all kinds of flying machines—made of metals and minerals extracted from rock, changed, given wing. Stone twists wind. Wind carves stone. It was an ancient war.

Neil wanted out of that war and wanted out now. From here he could make a final glide into the Estancia Valley to Moriarty Municipal Airport.

Ghost spirit and all?

Unfortunately, that long glide would point away from the warm sun and out of thermal-warmed air. If the canopy frosted over, he wouldn't be able to see to land and likely crash.

He was too shocked even to curse. *Now what?*

Maybe—he didn't have even a shred of any other guess to grasp—the airliner's spirit wanted *curanderismo*. If so he was on the hook this time. It made no difference that he only wanted out.

Or was that all he wanted, really?

TWA had been bought by American, and he flew for American. He'd even flown an American airliner repainted in classic TWA livery. The war of air against rock was one he'd signed up for decades ago on the side of air.

Ascending through 17,000', he watched for traffic as best he could with a partially frosted canopy. He had a transponder, so they should see him—but with the dragon under the pinnacle able to play tricks on instruments, he couldn't count on that. If he collided with an airliner or bizjet, the dragon would win. Damned if he would give it that victory. He'd freed the ghost spirit unwittingly. Now he had to make one more thing happen. Not that he knew how.

Airliners of that era sometimes had names. He didn't know this one's name and knew only part of its serial number. He cleared his throat. "416? You're free now. The Sandias are in clear air with unlimited visibility."

He heard nothing but the air slipping across the slick fuselage of the Ventus.

"There's K-Zero-E-Zero, Moriarty Municipal Airport, out in the Estancia Valley. The old Otto intersection used to be north of there."

Nothing happened except the thermal stayed strong. Going through 18,000', the Ventus turned as though on a platter.

"There's ABQ. Albuquerque." A few moments later, "That's Double Eagle. That airport's been around a long time." The nose of the sailplane traced a smooth arc on to the northeast. "And so has—" Then he knew what to say, with a certainty as exact as fitting a key into a lock. "SAF." He rolled out of the turn. "There it is, on the nose. You were en route to Santa Fe, and after that, somewhere else."

The Ventus gave an odd, harmless shiver. Then the cold phased away. The frost on the canopy started to dissolve. The hazy double wing faded.

The horizon blurred with Neil's sudden tears. Awestruck, suddenly hungry, and overwhelmingly glad to be alive, he turned to the east. It was a good thing he had a fifty-mile glide home before the challenge of landing at Moriarty. He needed to calm down and to think. Flying eastward, toward the tomorrow he'd almost not had, he wondered if it would be the same kind of tomorrow it would have been before today. Maybe. Or maybe not. Maybe—like Flight #19 more than half his life ago—every tomorrow had just changed.

I'm alive to find out, he thought, took a deep breath, and flew the Ventus home through the clear desert air.

~ * ~ * ~

Alexis Glynn Latner's science fiction novel *Hurricane Moon* was published by Pyr in 2007 and again by Avendis Press in 2014, with sequels *Downfall Tide*, *Star Crossing*, and *Helldive*. Her Starways series began with the romantic SF novel *Witherspin*. The latest book in the series, *Adversary*, was published in 2023. Her science fiction, fantasy, horror and mystery stories have appeared in *Analog* and other print magazines and in print, online, and e-book anthologies including the USA Today bestselling Pets in Space®. She also does editing and book coaching and teaches creative writing. Living in Houston, Texas, she works at the Rice University library.

Tiffin, Taxes, and Dragons

Gregg Chamberlain

Ssarrow huffed out a skeptical puff of smoke. "So this happens every spring, you say?"

With a little snort of her own, Desolay dispersed the tiny smoke cloud. "Indeed, yes," she affirmed, nodding to her skeptical guest. "Every spring, every year, for the past, oh, ten years now I do believe." She nudged a smoke-streaked leg—minus the foot—towards the other dragon with a dainty clawtip. "Another hors d'oeuvre?"

Ssarrow's lower lip curled with amused delight. "You know me so well, my dear Desolay," she crooned. "I really shouldn't." Both of her nostrils twitched at the tempting aroma even as a forepaw hovered over the proffered delicacy. "Aged three days?"

Desolay's fangs gleamed in a broad reptilian smile. "Oh, go ahead," she urged. "You know you want to."

She waited until her guest had delicately speared the leg with one talon and, with a quick flick, tossed it down her open maw. "Mmm, I do so love smoked meat," Ssarrow murmured. Her eyes widened in surprise. "Did you soak this in wine? I'm sure I taste more than a hint of Karulian Red."

Desolay's smile transformed into a great grin of satisfaction. "Do you like it? I've been experimenting with marinades."

In reply, a large, forked tongue licked appreciatively out, over and across the ridges of a broad snout. "Exquisite. My dear Desolay, you really outdo yourself sometimes. I cannot but wonder how you find a moment for such gourmet artistry but I absolutely *must* insist you share your recipe with me." Ssarrow glanced about the cave entrance as she spoke, looking for signs of more tidbits. Seeing none, she puffed out a disappointed little steamy sigh.

"About that matter we were discussing," she murmured, settling herself into a more comfortable position on the bare stone outside the cave entrance. "Please do explain it to me. Humans are peculiar creatures at the best of times—although wonderfully tasty all the time—but this sounds outrageously strange even for them."

Desolay's knobbed head dipped slightly in agreement. "Indeed. Well, you can imagine my surprise when I woke up one morning to find this little human standing outside my cave, almost right on my front step, and he demands—demands! I tell you—squeaking so like a field mouse that it almost made me laugh, that 'by order of His Imperial Majesty' I forget what the name was, that I should allow him to come inside and 'inspect, ascertain, estimate and calculate'— his very own words, mind, I swear on my scales—*my* hoard!"

Forked tongue flickering in and out in unconcealed anger, Desolay paused, to observe Ssarrow's reaction to this incredible instance of insane audacity. She viewed with satisfaction more smoke whuffing out of her astonished guest's open mouth.

"'Inspect my hoard?' I said to him," Desolay continued. "'Whatever for?' I was that surprised, I tell you truly, Ssarrow, at the strangeness of it all, I didn't even think right then about just simply eating this pompous little person like I should."

Ssarrow nodded, murmuring agreement about "such a curious situation" for her fellow dragon.

"Well, I was quite flummoxed, I can tell you," Desolay said snorting. "First to find this human, and an ordinary-looking one at that—not one of those sword-waving, lance-poking knights— showing up at my cave unannounced and uninvited, and then, with not so much as a 'by your leave' he says I should *let* him see my hoard. Well, I never! That was no proper show of respect for myself as a dragon."

Desolay huffed and snorted with undisguised annoyance as she recalled the incident. "Then this...*human*...person starts going on about 'royal obligations' and 'needs of the realm', none of which he ever really explained. Not that I cared, mind, but it would have been simple courtesy...anyway, all of this had to do with something he called 'taxes' which I gathered everyone in the Kingdom of What-ever were obliged to provide."

A single claw struck out, gouging a furrow into the stone near the foot of a cave entry wall. Desolay paused to regard it with surprise, before sheepishly tucking her forepaws underneath her. Ssarrow affected not to notice and waited for her hostess to con-tinue with her tale.

"Well," Desolay muttered, "that's when I felt my eyes go all red. What! I should just turn over part of my hoard to some human I didn't know and didn't care to know just on his say-so? Just like that? All meek and mild, no fuss or fight? I should koko!"

Ssarrow nodded in sympathy. "Such a shameful lack of respect towards one of our own, my dear Desolay," she murmured. "Whatever did you do then?"

Desolay drew herself up to her full, impressive height, head held high with fierce pride. "I did what I should have done at the first, like a proper dragon. I ate him! Three quick bites and no more listening to that human's squeaking nonsense."

Ssarrow's eyes widened slightly. "Three bites? But I was under the impression he was a rather small human."

Desolay casually brushed away the little pile of stone dust left behind from her scratching of the cave wall. "He was, my dear," she replied, while again inspecting the depth of the groove in the stone. "Well, really, my good Ssarrow, no matter how irritating any human might be, it's no reason to forgo good manners and just gulp down one's food whole like some base-born serpent. We are civilized creatures after all."

The other dragon tilted her head aside and flicked one tip of her forked tail, conceding her hostess' point. "So then?" she prompted.

Desolay glanced up towards the cloudless blue sky. "Almost noon," she observed. "Well, I thought no more of it then, but went about my own affairs. You know how it is: ravage the countryside, terrify the locals, bring back something nice to add to the hoard, that sort of thing. The rest of that year and the beginning of the next was very much the usual, you understand? Until a little before the spring equinox when I just happened to be emerging from my cave and I looked up and saw these two humans on ponies riding out of the forest. I was a bit curious, I do confess, so I settled myself down just outside of the entry and waited to see what they would do. To make a very long story just a bit shorter, my dear Ssarrow, they proved to be two more of these 'tax collectors' sent out by that king-whose-name-I-swear-I'll-never-remember. Almost the same lecture, each of them taking turns to tell me in the end how I was 'obligated' to allow them access to my hoard, only this time one of the humans—the short one, I think—noted that now I was 'in arrears' and 'subject to additional penalty charges' because I never provided my contribution to the treasury the year before."

Ssarrow blinked. "The utter cheek! What did you do?"

"Well, I was in a bit of a hurry right then for a prior engagement, don't you know," Desolay replied, shrugging. "So I just bit the heads of both of them and their ponies, pushed the lot inside the entry for later and flew off. I thought surely that was that for the entire matter...until the next year when two more of these pompous little humans showed up again, this time with a knight in tow behind them."

Ssarrow tsked. "Quite persistent, they seem, regarding this 'tax' thing."

Desolay nodded. "I must agree with you there. This king fellow impressed me as being quite obsessed about the whole matter. Almost dragon-like, one might say. A surprisingly admirable trait to find in a human, but rather annoying for me just at that time."

"Indeed," Ssarrow agreed, nodding. "So?"

Desolay shrugged. "Well, pretty much what you'd expect. The knight and I went a round or two, but he really wasn't much of a challenge. I've fought with better. He was new to the business, I suspect. But he did manage to delay me long enough for one of those pesky 'tax collectors' to slip around and into my cave, off to find my hoard, I had no doubt. Well, a quick flame blast into the entry while I had the knight pinned to the ground took care of that impertinent little skritch. The other one, the tall one as I recall, turned his pony around and took off back to the woods. I caught up with him in one leap after first sticking a claw through the knight and his armor." Half-lidded eyes gleamed with pleasure at the memory. "It was actually quite convenient for me, in the end. The three humans plus their horses, once I'd chased down the last beast still alive and galloping. No need to go off hunting dinner that day."

"Silver linings," Ssarrow observed, with a scaly smile.

"Quite so," Desolay agreed. "Well, then, that's how it has been every spring now for the past few years. One of these 'tax collectors' always shows up, though nowadays never in the company of anything less than four knights, though half a dozen has been the general rule, and sometimes more. All of them quite professional ones, too, I have noticed. Though still not very expert, in the end, in dealing with dragons. Mind you, last year, the 'tax' fellow did manage to get away. Let his pony run free while he lost himself in the woods. I caught the beast but never did find him, though I made several broad sweeps of the forest before giving it up for a loss and settling down for dinner."

She shook her head. "It's all been somewhat of a nuisance, dealing with these pests. Mind you, on the plus side of the ledger, I've been fortunate to have a full larder for at least a month or two, so I've had more time to look after my hoard, and indulge my hobbies."

"Like experimenting with marinades?" Ssarrow asked, her eyes twinkling with amusement.

Desolay smiled. "And exercising my hostess skills by entertaining my friends," she replied, "which reminds me."

She looked away towards the edge of the woods surrounding her cave. Ssarrow followed her gaze and saw a small, mounted group of armored knights, at least a score of them, pennons waving from their lances in the breeze, emerge from among the trees. Riding a small pony in their midst was a single unarmored human, scroll tucked under one arm, and looking distinctly unhappy about being there.

"Luncheon is served!" Desolay announced.

~ * ~ *~

Gregg Chamberlain, a community newspaper reporter five decades in the trade, lives in rural Eastern Ontario with his missus, and their cats, who allow the humans the run of the house. "Tiffin, Taxes and Dragons" was his first written-to-order story and allows him to indulge several of his passions: dragons, British-style humour of the P.G. Wodehouse variety, and cooking. Past fiction credits include several dozen published stories, from microfic to novelette, in the sf, fantasy and horror genres, including webzines like *Daily Science Fiction*, anthologies like *100 Great Fantasy Short-Short Stories* (Asimov, Greenberg, and Carr, editors), and magazines like *Abyss & Apex*, *Polar Borealis*, and *Weirdbook*.

The Naming of Cats

Rebecca McFarland Kyle

One hundred and four years was long for humans. In the final flickers of her luminous life, Vivian lay in her mahogany canopy bed, covered in sumptuous velvet blankets, with her head resting on cushiony silk pillows perfumed with cinnamon and blood orange. Breaths burbled out of full lips which once brought forth notes that left audiences spellbound.

Vivian was still beautiful. Her ebon skin was smooth and flawless. Her hair, whiter than her bed linens, wreathed her face in a full silken mass. Amber eyes, which alternated between doe softness and a tiger's ferocity, gleamed with intellect.

Scuttlebutt, her thirteenth black cat in eighty years, was her sole companion. He lay curled beneath her long slender fingers, purring steadily. Only the two of them knew he'd been the same animal she'd found backstage at the Cotton when she was just starting out. He'd been Ebony, Inky, Velvet, Onyx, Jet…his final name mocked the gossip columnists who still posted rumors about her occasionally.

"Guess you'll be moving on," Vivian's voice was barely audible over the whisper of the heating system. The jewels she wore round her throat reflected in his eyes as she stroked his silken black fur.

"Your grandson is not as tolerant," Scuttlebutt said.

"Phillip will find his way." Vivian said. Phillip's occasional presence wrecked their domestic harmony. While she'd been a jazz singer, her grandson rapped. She was a viper back in the day, the cocaine he did made him dependent and vicious. Vivian never approved of his music, either. She hated the waste of a beautiful baritone on music lacking all romance and disrespectful to women. Most of all, she hated the way he dressed in more jewelry than a gold-digger and pants so loose they fell down and showed his bare butt. Occasionally, when Scuttlebutt wanted to catch her ire, he'd remind Vivian her mother said similar things to her back in the day.

Scuttlebutt waited as Vivian drew her final breath. What humans called the soul departed her body in a mist. He gently closed her eyes with the most delicate of paws, knocked the phone beside her bed off the hook to dial nine-one-one so her body would not have to wait for her maid to find, and then slid the gleaming ruby from her unresisting finger.

He dropped the ring in a heavy gold mesh purse Vivian had discarded that he'd hidden behind her headboard. Within it were treasures commemorating their time together: her long-forgotten wedding rings, heavy with gold and diamonds, an emerald earring stolen from a backup singer who'd attempted to usurp Vivian's career, a diamond-encrusted cufflink from a mob boss who'd enjoyed Vivian's bed…While most would see the items for their gold and precious stones, each evoked memories, one of the most potent forms of magic.

Scuttlebutt heard a human woman's voice from the phone: "This is nine-one-one, state your emergency."

He pawed through the jewelry on Vivian's dresser to see if there was any other worthy trinket when the scrape of keys in the penthouse door startled him.

Stealthy footsteps followed. *Phillip!*

Scuttlebutt hastened toward the terrace doors with the chain purse strap caught between his teeth. Vivian always left them ajar so she could hear the sounds of the city below and smell the perfume of the small flower garden planted there. He was almost out when Phillip entered his grandmother's bedroom.

"Thieving cat!" Phillip bellowed, enraged, kicking out with his booted foot. Of course, he'd accuse him of doing precisely what he'd come to do!

Scuttlebutt dropped the purse, transformed to his true shape gaining scales, talons, and wings, and flew in the man's face. It was an awkward, unbalanced fight. A large breed dog had broken his wing years before and the delicate bone never healed correctly. Dragons did not feel pain in the Fae realm, but his right wing ached terribly with winter's damp in the human one.

"You dare call me a thief!" Scuttlebutt hissed. "You were sneaking in to steal from a kinswoman who'd give you anything she had!"

Phillip's dark eyes widened as he backed up, swearing. He grabbed Vivian's cane which she kept by her bed, an elegant piece of ebony with a white gold and lapis handle and batted at Scuttlebutt.

Scuttlebutt spat flame setting the cane ablaze. Phillip dropped it and rushed out, slamming the heavy wooden penthouse door.

Scuttlebutt sucked back his flame. Unfortunately, he couldn't stop the smoke alarm from ringing. Sirens were coming closer. The alarm company would have a fire engine dispatched, too. Damned humans and their alarms! Vivian would be amused to go out with such a bang.

Scuttlebutt swooped down and grabbed his prize as well as a strand of black pearls and flew out the terrace door. Twenty stories down, he dared not look or he would abandon the flight. He dove down to the park and raced on four trembling legs through the darkness toward the glade where the gate to Faery lay.

~ * ~

"What the—" a late-night jogger shrieked, seeing a winged creature carrying a gleaming handbag.

Scuttlebutt took cover in the bushes, cursing the timing. It wasn't a solstice or All Hallows, the Veil to Faery was near impenetrable. It required every ounce of magic he could summon to pass and find his tiny cave before Titania or worse, his larger draconian kin, were alerted to his presence. He arrived limp with exhaustion; barely strong enough to fly the short distance to his home and work the magic to penetrate the wall of solid rock.

His home in Faery was a geode cathedral: half amethyst and half citrine, like darkness come to day. It was tucked away in a tight enough cranny only a dragonet could reach. Fortunately, hatchlings had to attain age and size before their magic manifested.

He dumped the treasure upon the small gleaming mountain of riches he'd already accumulated, then fussed when it covered up a mask of gold which he'd stolen from the tomb of a favored Pharaoh who treated him like the god he was.

He'd have to find another human soon. Too many enemies resided in Faery. For now, he needed to rest and replenish his magic. Once satisfied with the arrangement of his treasures, Scuttlebutt turned around three times, curled up, and slept, cheek pillowed on his tail.

Cracking sounds belatedly alerted him to trouble. His home shattered like a wineglass thrown against a stone hearth. He tumbled forth, struggling to shake the veil of magic-deprived slumber to see Xuihcoatl in all his fiery glory smirking down at him. He was the largest of their kind, a massive drake resplendent in his glory.

"What is this?" Xuihcoatl's roar shook the ground beneath them. "A hatchling with treasure already—no, I remember the freak…"

Scuttlebutt didn't wait around to find out what Xuihcoatl would do. He snatched the handbag and raced for the veil, feeling the heat of a gout of flame chasing him. He tore through to an unknown portion of the human world, fetching up hard against a massive oak trunk.

Re-form! re-form! A frightened voice screamed in his aching head. Instead, he dragged his handbag into the bushes and dug a hole deep enough for both of them. He used his wing to scrape leaves over his body and slept.

When he awoke, his magic was revived. It was time to change and venture forth into the human world. Scuttlebutt considered his options. He'd favored the cat-shape since his encounters with the Egyptians, but he always chose a different manifestation until Vivian. Definitely not a black cat. Humans were a superstitious lot: many of Vivian's friends commented through the years that black cats were unlucky.

Vivian had always believed just the opposite.

Knowing Vivian's life was ending, he'd watched enough Animal Planet to make more informed decisions about cats. He stroked the ruby ring and slowly took on a kitten-shape. This time, he became a fuzzy-haired reddish brown tabby kitten with white paws with two extra toes on his front feet. He'd often lamented the lack of thumbs, now he possessed as close as a feline could get. He re-buried the purse and urinated on the spot, which was enough to keep even a skunk away.

Then, Scuttlebutt set out to explore his new territory and seek a human companion. From the position of the stars and the heat, he surmised he'd emerged far southwest of New York City. The Veil was again in a park-like area which was central to low-slung housing less densely constructed than the tall structures he'd grown accustomed to. Sounds and scents of home came to him in a rush. Nearby, someone cooked fresh meat on a firepit, a woman sang quietly to a child, televisions and radios blasted a mélange of words and music.

Scuttlebutt's nose twitched at the scent of strong magic. He considered stepping back across the Veil and finding another spot, but that would use much of his power. What was it? Something shadowy cold, which fed on humans.

The trail led to the gate of a home conveniently close to the Veil. This would normally be an ideal place. He could see the fading tracks of a feline leading in and out of the gate. Catnip, garlic, and other tantalizing fragrances drifted from inside a cedar fence.

Sharp pained cries indicated the dark fae neared the end of his work. Scuttlebutt crept within cedar bushes to let the predator pass. While the creatures were truly never sated, they tended to pass lesser prey if they were fed.

The dark fae passed, a fetid wind on a cool still night. Having drunk his fill of the woman's pain, he moved with a light step humming a popular High Court tune. He was not one to partake of the bodies of humans. Their touch was offensive to him. This one stole their souls and left a hole within them few could mend.

Sounds of weeping from the house stopped Scuttlebutt from continuing. Knowing it was safe, he hopped to the top of the fence and peered in as the inhabitant opened the patio door and wandered out clad in a full-length ivory chemise, very reminiscent of olden times. Her feet were bare and no doubt cold on the flagstone patio, but she paid that no heed.

Light from the interior showed her curly hair a deep titian. Unlike modern women, she had a figure Reuben would have immortalized. He couldn't see the lines of exhaustion on her face, but he knew they were there and he sensed them from the way she carried herself. Oh yes, she'd get to sleep quickly every night, then the dark fae would find her, drink his fill of the everyday annoyances and dig deep within her psyche for more. Then, he would leave her exhausted wondering what happened. And the fae would return over and over again until he'd drained her.

He'd thought the power he'd sensed was the fae, but realized the woman possessed strong but untrained magic. This was why she managed to survive the thing harming her for as long as she had. She turned her face up to the stars and wept softly, wrapping her arms about her chilled body.

So, the fae was draining and using an untrained mage to power his own forays into the human realm. Gradually, she'd be of no use in the daytime. If she was lucky, the fae would abandon her after he drained her of her magic and memories or she'd end up a victim of an accident. It was much easier in the days of horse and carriage for one plagued with night visitors. In the modern fast-paced world, they had to drive cars and operate machinery.

So like the fae to take and take without returning any kind of blessing. It's no wonder they needed a human-based public relations campaign. If the humans ever comprehended the truth, they would burn every cute ornament which sustained their belief in Faery, close the Veil with cold iron, and abandon any celebrations of the holy days which gave the fae ingress to their realm. And, they'd take their own kind, made rich from Faery gold, and hang them for leading so many astray.

Every instinct told Scuttlebutt to leave the tainted place. Indeed the woman was a victim, but some part of her nature granted the dream creature access to her sleep.

It was folly to consider helping her. Dark fae were formidable enemies. He didn't need more than he already had.

And yet, her tears stayed him.

"Kitty?" her call nearly knocked him off the fence.

Of course, he chided himself angrily. *If you look at someone too long, they will look back.* His eyes glowed gold in darkness like an ordinary cat's.

"Kitty," she called again, her voice sounding stuffy from weeping. Before Scuttlebutt could move, she turned back to the house, leaving the patio door open. She returned just a few moments later with a delicious smelling saucer full of tuna and a bowl of fresh water with ice.

"I'll just leave this here," she said. "Come and get it…" She stepped back into her home, leaving the patio door open.

His stomach growled. He had no idea how long he'd slept, but it'd been awhile since he'd eaten. His nose advised him the food was good and safe and he should partake. One never knew when the next meal would come or whether it would be near as savory. Perhaps the fae wouldn't notice the tell-tale signs of his own magic …particularly if he hurried.

Of course, his face was buried in the tuna by the time he'd arrived at that conclusion. Whenever there was a battle between sense and stomach, the belly won. He'd think his way out of the problem after he was fed. It had worked for thousands of years after all…

"Oh, you're such a handsome fellow," Scuttlebutt hadn't noticed the woman's return, he'd been so busy sating the empty pit in his belly. She stood framed in the soft light emanating from the house.

"I miss my Frodo," she said.

Frodo! Stupid human! He wanted to spit, but he was too busy finishing off the delicious salty tuna juice. Tolkien had the wrong idea about dragons. Steal the treasure, kill them—he much preferred fans of other fantasy writers. Even the ones who thought humans should ride them like ponies were better. No fantasy at all was best.

Human ignorance was his bliss.

"Would you like some more?" she asked when he'd licked the plate to gleaming cleanness. "A baby kitten like you needs more food to grow."

Oh yes, the kitten guise was a stroke of brilliance.

Scuttlebutt licked his lips and she took that as assent, going back into the house and returning a few moments later with another plateful of food. This time she set the plate right inside the patio door.

He contemplated not crossing her threshold, but his belly roared a complaint at missing something which smelled so delightful. This time, it was roast chicken breast and cheese, the good stuff from a deli.

She closed the patio door behind him so softly, he scarcely noticed. She just stood a few feet away from him watching him with cinnamon-colored eyes, shadowed with weariness.

"I'm not going to hurt you," she said, sounding tired but very kind. "A kitty as nice as you probably belongs to someone—if you were my kitty, I would want someone to take you in and get you home."

He watched as she went to the kitchen and got him another dish of clean, fresh water. The house smelled of drying herbs and spices. Soft music, heavy on flutes and guitar, played in the background. Scuttlebutt could smell the former resident, a tom-cat of great age and wisdom. The cat had lived a long life, the end of nine, and ascended to wherever it was cats went to after the Wheel's last turn. A capacious pillow he'd used lay empty near the hearth. A carpet-covered tree sat by the front windows where he could lounge all day and preside over the neighborhood.

While the house was no penthouse, he saw the woman had means. Probably a better position long-term than being the high-profile pet of a renowned entertainer.

No!

There was no future in a house where a dark fae visited nightly. If the fae didn't eat up his magic, it might well remember who he was and hand him over to Titania.

Panicked, he looked for an escape route. The cursed patio door was closed and locked. She'd seated herself on a capacious leather sofa near the hearth and watched him intently. He could have sprung the lock on the patio door, but not while she was looking.

He couldn't use any magic in this house—not with the visitor. He finished his meal and walked to the glass door, mewing pathetically.

"Kitten, you don't need to be out in that park," she said. "Too many big dogs and there's a coyote, too. There's a litterbox in here you can use."

Scuttlebutt remained at the door when she returned to her bed for a futile attempt at rest. He supposed he could have mewed and clawed and gotten her to dump him, but he didn't have the heart to worsen her plight. She'd open the door and he'd run. She'd feel guilty for having done so and the dark fae would have an even stronger hold on her. Still, he had to leave or he'd be the fae's next meal.

He cruised the area for some souvenir. If the redhead possessed magnificent jewels, she didn't leave them lying about. He pawed through a dish full of stones and chose a magnificent obsidian cut to reveal a rainbow heart. Perfect, a black heart was precisely what he needed. He picked up the treasure and took it with him. Lacking anything more, he curled up tail-to-nose in the former feline's bed, which was stuffed with downy feathers. The bed enveloped him like an embrace and he slept.

Knocking startled him awake. When the redhead went to the door, he knew it was his chance. He darted between her feet. A strong hand caught him around the ribs and raised him up. Before he could fight, the new woman carried him back inside. She was much taller than Red, slender, bronze-skinned, dark-haired, and silver eyed. Her grasp was firm, but kind.

"It's not even dawn yet..." Red complained.

"Text said come before I went to work," her visitor replied, in a voice sounding like a cat's purr. "First surgery's at seven…You wanted me to look at this kitten to find out where he belongs…"

Red sighed tiredly, "I'll leave you to it, Tig. I'm taking a shower…"

"You need one," Tig said worriedly when the door closed behind Red. She carried a brown leather satchel, which smelled of treats and medicine. "Now, let's see about you…"

Tig cleaned off the marble kitchen counter and set down her bag. She paused, her gaze sharpening, and he felt the healer's magic swim over him. Too late, he realized she'd surmised his true shape with those healing hands.

Release me! Scuttlebutt tried to work his magic and encountered an agile mind, amused and unsusceptible to his wiles. *Release me. Now!*

What to do? Silvery eyes snared him as firmly as her grasp. Tig's exhalation was warm and smelled of strong black coffee.

"Trust Micki to find something like this," Tig said, finally. "You're from nowhere near here…"

"Mercy, healer," Scuttlebutt opted to reason, suspecting she could unweave his careful magics and leave him stuck in his original form.

Tig's eyes narrowed at the sound of his voice, but she didn't loosen her grasp.

"My friend's been ill," her eyes were narrow and suspicious. "Are you the cause?"

"I arrived here last night seeking only human companionship and shelter. She trapped me," he replied. "There's a dark fae visiting her nightly."

Her eyes narrowed. "So, how do we get rid of this dark fae?"

"Are you mad, Healer?" he hissed, twisting to free himself. "This is no Disneyland creature you think to set me on!"

"No," she agreed. "Entertainers lie about the true nature of Faery. And you would not be fighting alone."

Scuttlebutt started when his feet touched the cool rock surface and her hands released him. He contemplated flying, but couldn't bring himself to do so. In truth, she fascinated him more than her skills frightened him.

"You fight for a woman you don't actually care for?"

"Micki's family—whether I like it or not," Tig answered.

"But you two were rivals." He'd sensed that from the cautious way they handled themselves. They might have gotten along better had there been others around to interact with, but the two together were uneasy.

"Yeah," Tig admitted. "Back in school…"

"You both loved the same man," Scuttlebutt asked. He missed the titillation of the constant affairs of court.

"Sort of," she said. "But that was later. Initially, we both wanted to be the top student… Then the man came along, my brother…"

He tried to stifle a chuckle and failed. The healer didn't seem as much upset as bemused.

"Jamie, my twin brother, was set to marry Micki before he was killed…"

"Killed?" he said. "Perhaps that is the trauma the dark fae's latched onto."

"An old wound," Tig said thoughtfully. "But a deep one…"

A tear traced down her bronze cheek. She glanced down at her hands and he realized she'd abated a good deal of the pain by healing others. She was one of the worthiest members of her species he'd ever met and he'd known many. If it was possible for a dragon to love a woman, he would choose her.

"If I aid you and survive," Scuttlebutt said. "Would you give me a home for the remainder of your life?"

"Of course," Tig agreed, readily. "But I have four horses, three large dogs, and another cat. They are my family, too—and they must stay."

Scuttlebutt hadn't meant to twitch his injured wing at the mention of big dogs, but her clever eyes noted the motion.

"Dogs and I do not get along," he confessed.

"I can imagine," she said. "Animals are much more perceptive than humans and they know you do not belong. My dogs are large and protective. We would have to work hard to teach them not to harm you and it's still boisterous and noisy. If you are seeking a place of peace and shelter, Micki would provide a fine home. Frodo had everything he needed: good food, shelter, a comfortable bed, and he didn't have to share. I don't normally take care of cats, but I'd be your vet so you wouldn't have any trouble… With a regular family, you'd need annual shots, be neutered, and probably have a microchip inserted between your shoulder blades. Base metal is used with each procedure."

He hissed at the thought.

Vivian knew his true nature, but most of his human companions were not privy to his secret. She'd seen him initially while under the influence of mind-altering drugs which allowed her to see the truth. She'd never taken him to a vet. And, she'd never told anyone.

"Would Micki keep my identity?"

"It would be better if you died and returned to her at the end of a natural cat lifespan—I will help you by bringing you back to her when you've changed form."

"A generous offer," Scuttlebutt agreed, considering. Verity was not a human strongpoint, but the healer was a rarity. She would keep her oaths.

"I can heal that wing so your flight is true when you need it," Tig said, upping the offer. "It'll hurt…"

"Do so," he said. "And we have an accord." He didn't know how he could oust the dark fae, but with the healer's aid, he would stand a chance.

"We fight tonight," she said, sliding her hand in the pocket of her jeans to touch an item there—for strength, perhaps? "I can't stand to see Micki go further downhill."

Tig breathed deeply, closed her eyes, and laid her hands upon him. At first, he felt a comforting warmth and smelled the scents of a spring forest. Then, the jarring ache of the bone re-breaking and seating itself in its proper place. Another deep breath, the warmth covered him like a blanket. His eyes felt heavy with exhaustion. He did not object when the healer picked him up and settled him onto the old cat's bed by the hearth.

"Sleep," she whispered. "I'll be back with dinner tonight."

"Bring crabmeat," Scuttlebutt said, then closed his eyes.

~ * ~

"I hate seafood," Micki complained when the healer returned bearing bags scented with salt air and crabmeat.

"I like it," Tig said. "And I bet your kitten does, too. We need to feed him up. Poor baby needs his strength."

Scuttlebutt winked at the healer when she placed particularly delicious fresh morsels of crabmeat on a saucer. He'd slept through whatever she'd told Micki about him that morning, but apparently it stirred the redhead's heart and that was good. She'd returned from work with a bag full of canned foods, kibble, and toys. What she might term "bonding" was a mixture of natural magic and diplomacy. He'd done it many times, but this modern age offered so many different toys and trinkets a cat was supposed to respond to, it was exhausting.

"Still can't sleep well," Micki complained. "Nightmares…"

"Got the remedy," Tig said, pulling bottles of liquor from another sack along with boxes he recognized had films inside. "How about a movie night? You can't sleep…I'm off this weekend."

This wasn't a customary event, he saw the surprise and gratitude in Micki's eyes. Another's choice brought them together as sisters, but they both honored Jamie's memory. They'd not diminish that bond even if they quarreled.

He hopped on the couch between the two knowing both would pet him and perhaps share treats. Vivian had been a fan of classic films and she watched them on a screen that made the actors giants. Everything in Micki's home was smaller in scale, but more comfortable.

Micki's hand settled between his shoulder blades, she scratched him there and he rewarded her with a resonant purr, air kneading with his multi-toed paws.

"Such a smart kitty," Micki commented as Tig hit the remote control and they started a film he'd never seen. A fantasy epic, he was grateful it wasn't Tolkien. He'd found a well-read set of that man's books on the shelves and contemplated shredding the binding.

He'd done worse to the ones he'd read after he learned what they'd done to Smaug. Fiction, it may be, no point in setting a bad example.

A snore tore him away from the film. Tig nodded, and grinned at the half-empty bottle.

"Your protection," Tig pulled a handful of needles from her bag. "They're loaded with colloidal silver."

The plastic covering indeed protected his delicate paw from the cruel metal. She used an empty needle to help him practice depressing the plunger with his paw.

"You are good for your word, Healer," Scuttlebutt said. "It'll take strong emotion to lure the dark fae."

Tig reached into the bag and brought out a notebook full of photos of abused and starving horses. He looked away. What humans allowed to happen to noble animals was beyond contempt. Her eyes blazed with fury. She replaced the photos, stood up, and paced the area in front of the open patio door.

"Stop it, Healer. Be still and wallow in your anguish. You think the Dark Fae will come to someone who's spoiling for a fight?"

If looks could open veins, the healer's silvery gaze would. She took a seat at the couch, opened the bottle and took the remainder in one long pull.

"Damnit," Tig whispered, tears flowing faster than the amber liquid spilled down her throat. "For every animal I save, there's hundreds more—some poor kid wants a horse and her family hasn't the means. Some rich bastard has the money, but he's only keeping them for the éclat. A caretaker's careless knowing the owner won't come around…"

Grief, exhaustion, and futility came off her in waves like sultry summer heat, headier than any grief, a rich drink for those who loved to sup on the misery and pain of others. He stepped into the shadows, behind a metal sculpture and hoped the healer was correct that it would conceal his presence.

A shadow appeared in the patio door. Like his new mistress, Tig left it open. The dark fae entered. He'd have been a handsome creature had his features not been twisted with generations of cruelty. Aurim hair sparked in the light, his ocean blue eyes flamed as they lit on fresh prey. He was clad in blue velvet and silk with silvery boots and a circlet of sapphires and aquamarines the color of teardrops about his brow. He'd long been one of Titania's favored swains and knew the quarrel between them. His shadow engulfed the room, much larger than other creatures like him possessed.

A frightened part of him told Scuttlebutt to run. There was nothing he could do and everything he could lose if he remained and helped the madwoman fight a hopeless battle for the soul of a human stranger.

Yet, Scuttlebutt could not run. While his oath was only as binding as he chose it to be, the healer expended a good deal of her energy healing his wing—he knew it would take every bit of her strength to fight the dark fae off.

Tig sucked in a sharp breath at the sight of the dark fae. The purposeful dive she'd taken into liquor and despair to lure him left her floundering. She was a brave woman, but she hadn't quite expected something so large. He should have warned her the image of Tinkerbell was falsehood. Like dragons, fae came in all sizes from the miniscule to the mighty—and the dark one had grown from consuming the spoils of human pain.

The dark fae's nostrils widened—at her heightened fear from the sight of him. He bared a set of white even canines in a parody of a smile, his full generous seeming lips glistening blood red.

"You called me," he said in a sonorous basso.

"I did," Tig rose, somewhat unsteadily, her eyes never leaving the foe. "I'm telling you to leave my sister alone."

"You summon me—just to tell me to leave? What kind of hostessing is that?"

"The kind that does not wish for myself or my friends to be the main course for your amusement. You've got trouble if you choose to remain," she replied, stepping forward, her posture loose and ready.

"Come to me," he crooned. "Give me your pain and your sorrow…I'll make it go away…"

"You will?" Tig drawled, eyes wide and ingenuous. "I've carried this so long, I don't think I could stand it one more minute…"

The dark fae's lips spread in a malicious grin as he twitched his hand, expecting the healer to come. Tig did, her movements seductive and languorous. A deep breath exposed cleavage more generous than her loose top showed, she tossed her mane of dark hair back.

His hand opened and his fingers spread, beckoning her. He would drink of her sorrows—but there was always a catch. The offering would not strengthen her or ease her burden. Her back would still be bowed and he'd come to take more the next night.

Scuttlebutt itched to come from hiding, to scream a warning at the healer who'd so bravely offered herself. She had so much to give to this barren human world. He did not want to see it wasted on one such as the dark fae!

At the last moment, Tig pulled a blade from her sleeve, letting the light glint upon the metal. Her eyes blazed as sharp as the knife as she made the final step and laid the searing metal against the dark fae's throat.

A shriek of pain and indignation rose from the fae's throat. A blood red imprint of the knife's edge raised on his flesh.

"I revoke any guest right you were granted to this place or my friend's person," Tig hissed as the dark fae backed up, his eyes widening.

"You dare!" the dark fae bellowed, and he pulled a knife, which lengthened to a sword with a gleaming edge of fae metal.

Tig danced away, eyes widening as she dodged the first sweeping blow. She raced to the fireplace to grab a wrought iron poker with the fae on her heels. Sword and poker rang together. She twisted the poker adroitly, shifting the blade away from her and downward.

Their eyes locked.

"You will be mine," the dark fae growled.

"Not a chance," Tig pressed her advantage, pushing his blade back and downward to cut the leggings of its master. A breath lay between them and that was all it would take for an enchantment.

Scuttlebutt flew forward in his full form and stabbed the dark fae with a needle full of silver.

"Begone!" he shouted, racing back for the next needle.

Tig knocked the sword from the fae's grasp. She lunged, touching the fae with her free hand, her own eyes locking, commanding his gaze. Scuttlebutt sensed the magic surge in her, brightening the room, bringing with it scents of freshness and sunlight.

"End the suffering for others—and yourself," Tig whispered. "Forget the pain…"

The dark fae dropped like a stone, eyes wide and shocked a human healing could have worked a major enchantment on him.

Tig kicked the fae sword out of the dark one's reach, keeping the poker between them. "Go in peace and enter this realm no more."

The dark one nodded, but something flickered in his eyes. A hand reached into his doublet for a blade slender as a rose thorn, but tipped with deadly poison.

"Finish him," Scuttlebutt bellowed at the healer as he flew into the dark fae's face and stuck him in the cheek with another of the silver-filled needles. "Use his own knife!"

Tig grabbed the dark fae's wrist and chopped it with her other hand until he released the blade. She snatched the blade, closed her eyes and sunk the poisoned blade straight into the fae's heart.

The fae toppled, his face contorting with pain.

"Wha—what are we going to do with a dead Faery?" Tig stared at the body with wide horrified eyes, the pupils nearly white from fear and stress.

"Rest, Healer, I can handle this."

Scuttlebutt flew to the fae's body, claiming the circlet that'd adorned his brow, and a ring with much power stored in it. He didn't fear the taint of the possessions. Magic was gray. Users colored the power with their actions.

A gout of dragon fire the length of the corpse took care of the problem, but it raised a dreadful stench and turned on one of those stupid alarms.

"Gag a maggot!" Tig rushed to the kitchen and turned on a fan, then threw the patio door wide open to dissipate the smoke.

"What's going on?" Micki's yell from her bedroom alerted them both to trouble.

"I burned popcorn!" Tig shouted back at her. "Nothing to worry about!"

Scuttlebutt quickly dodged out of sight and shifted back into his feline form as Micki emerged from the bedroom, her wild curly red hair fluffed like an angry cat's. While she looked aggravated, the dark circles were gone from beneath her eyes. He could see an energy and zest returning to her she had not known for a good long time. She was a robust woman in the prime of her life. What some might initially mistake as fat was a stocky body and a solid layer of muscle. Hands capable of stroking a feline body to purring bliss were currently wasted on fists.

"What on Earth were you doing making popcorn for breakfast?" Micki huffed.

"It sounded good," Tig said.

"Crazy." Micki muttered under her breath and he knew the détente between the two was short-lived. "You have pancakes and eggs for breakfast…"

"You eat whatever you want," Tig's tone was mutinous, but she stepped aside as Micki went into the kitchen and started rattling pans. She'd moved past the slight cloud of smoke and ash where the dark fae fell without even paying attention. His gleaming sword still lay on the floor where it had fallen. The healer picked it up and casually laid it atop her bag along with the thorn-thin blade.

"Where'd you get the blades?"

"Won them," Tig responded. "Wanted to show them to you. Think I should dust off my knight's gear."

Silence. The two women stared at each other. Scuttlebutt could see the memory like one of their movies from both of them. The healer's brother Jamie was killed after a performance, driving home, still garbed. Tig had not gone back to a Renfaire since.

"You should," Micki said. Then grudgingly. "You were an amazing knight."

A smile briefly flickered across Tig's lips. She bent and picked him up, stroking his sides with deft hands until he drooled from the pleasure. Oh, if he could have her touch him every day, it might be worth living with a…dog.

But not three!

"What are you going to name your kitten?" Tig asked. "Look at him. It should be something epic."

"Grendel," Micki said after only a second's thought. She extended her hands and took him against her cushiony bosom protectively.

Grendel is a good name, he thought, wishing he could keep it for as long as he had Scuttlebutt.

"I like it," Tig agreed. "What was that in the poem—" there was no honed iron hard enough to pierce him through…"

Grendel's eyes widened as he met the healer's amused gaze. Oh yes, that was quite a blessing for a fae creature in hiding with mortal enemies among the Faery court. The healer might have been his first choice as a mistress for her fierceness and her talents, but Micki would do…and hopefully, his existence would continue blissfully dog-free.

~ * ~

"One last thing, Healer," Grendel said when his new mistress left them to take a shower. "I would like a token…"

A dark brow raised.

"I have no wish to harm you. I have tokens of every human who's been significant to me," Grendel said. He brought out the ruby ring from Vivian and conjured up a bit of her music.

Tig's breath whooshed out and her silver eyes were wide. "I've got nothing so valuable as this. Grandpa introduced me to her music… I still have the vinyl… You know, on the news her rapper grandson swears he saw her old black cat turn into a dragon the night she died. There were several items stolen, including a ring… they have film from various security cameras—but it's too blurry, just a winged thing and the grandson wasn't precisely a reliable witness, either."

"I hate this modern world," Grendel said.

"Yeah, so do I, sometimes…"

"All I was trying to do was to leave with the things she'd promised me—I took some treasures as well. I am what I am…I've taken trinkets from all the others," Grendel confessed. "But you are an ally and I would like you to choose…"

Tig nodded, then dipped her hand into her jeans pocket and withdrew a pointed stone. He sensed she'd handled the stone many times in difficult times when she'd needed the extra boost of energy it lent her. Her eyes softened to the color of dove's wings when she looked at the stone, it was valued item, perhaps even more so than the glittering trinkets he'd taken from Vivian.

"It's an arrowhead," she said. "First one I found on my Daddy's land. Warriors of my tribe made them centuries ago…"

"But this is a very dear possession," Grendel protested. "I would take the chain around your neck…or the rings…"

"If you want them, you may have them all," she replied, commencing to remove the ring from her university from her hand. "The chain and rings are replaceable. This arrowhead means more. It is a cherished memory of who I am and where I came from. It is a fitting gift for a warrior who fought valiantly by my side."

~ * ~ * ~

Born on Friday 13, **Rebecca McFarland Kyle** developed an early love for the unusual. She currently lives between the Smoky and Cumberland mountains with her husband and four cats. She has three young adult novels and a mystery novel currently in the works.

The Dragon's Clause

Kelly A. Harmon

He had to hurry.

Giuseppe Piccoli, San Marino's attorney, took the two hundred silver *soldi* collected from the San Marino citizens and poured them from the collection box into his rucksack. His fingers shook, and sweat broke out on his brow even as his stomach roiled. But what was he to do? His debt grew larger the longer he could not pay. And now they threatened the life of his children.

This would solve all his problems, and the city lost nothing.

For more than three hundred years the city threw away the coins collected for sacrifice offered during the Founder's Day festivities. Today, these garbage coins would help him and his family survive. The custom angered him, tossing good money down a well when it could be used for so much more.

Outside the *Consiglio Grande e Generale Municipio* he could hear the revelers in the street.

Merda. He had to hurry.

The sun barely crested the horizon of Monte Titano, and some were drunk already. Where were the *balesrieri*, the crossbowmen?

Preparing for the annual contest of course. They would be of almost no use to the republic today while they preened for the crowds and vied for the honor of best bowman. None would be standing guard this day.

Perhaps he could use their preoccupations to his advantage. So busy with their own importance and today's contest, it was possible his early visit to the municipal building would go unnoticed. He could only hope, for his daughters' sake.

From his rucksack, he pulled a bulging cloth parcel: his winter scarf, the four corners tied together to hold the contents. Two flicks of his thumbs and the knot unraveled, revealing a cache of small stones. None was bigger than his thumbnail, the size of a silver *soldi*. He lifted the edge of a red silk bag and thrust the stones in by the handful.

When enough stones filled the bag, Giuseppe tied it off with a cloth-of-gold ribbon and put the bag in the safe. The *Capitani Reggenti* would sacrifice it to San Marino's dragon later in the day.

~ * ~

The silk bag tumbled end over end down the dry well, once or twice hitting the natural stone sides of the chute until it landed with a *clink* on top of a large pile of gold and silver coins, then rolled down the heaped mound to bump into the grey-green scales of a dragon's thigh.

"At last," the dragon breathed, two tendrils of smoke rising out of his nostrils as gently as the first curls of steam from a teapot set to boil. He lifted his large head from slumber and blinked away the sleep.

Salga di Alato stretched his neck, craning it back almost far enough to touch his raised wings.

He extended one foot to hook the bag with a claw and drew it close. He held the heavy bag with his front feet, massaging it, then with a jerk of one hooked nail, undid the ribbon and upturned the sack with the other. Two hundred stones clanked against the metal and precious gems which made up his hoard.

"This can't be," he said, riffling through the pile, turning up stone after stone in his precious pile of coins. "Surely the people of San Marino are not trying to cheat me?"

He sat down on his haunches, puffing great clouds of smoke, as he surveyed the pile. "With whom do they think they are dealing?"

He thrust the silk bag away from him. With an uncontrollable bellow, he tipped his head back and sucked in a convulsive breath. He bent his head forward and roared in fury, spitting forth a stream of fire.

The cave lit up, revealing the humble abode of a dragon. The mound of gold and silver coins, priceless gemstones and objects d'art towered almost as high as the municipal building of San Marino. Even with a dragon sitting atop it, the large cave could have held two or even three times more. "How dare they!" he said, white smoke still roiling.

He decided he would give the Sanmariners an opportunity to make amends. They'd fulfilled their part of the bargain for more than three hundred years, after all. This had to be a mistake. If not …well, he could set them right.

Salga nodded his head thoughtfully, his anger cooling. Only the barest wisps of smoke tickled his nose. Taking a calming breath, he relaxed, calling on the air elements to help him formulate his shift to human shape.

He unfurled his wings for balance and stood on hind legs, the length of his long, scaled tail holding the brunt of his weight, keeping the ponderous body upright. Once balanced, he said the words of *change*.

He felt the magic first at the crown of his head, tiny pinpoints of light dancing on the ridge of his skull. It tingled, sending pleasant little shocks across his neck and along the length of his spine. Downward the magic sang through his veins, light gamboling across his scales, until it reached his clawed feet and the tip of his tail. The large dragon shimmered, refulgent in the glow of the flickering light. The light swelled and blinked out, soap-bubble like, and the dragon disappeared.

In his place, standing at the edge of a mound of gold stood a handsome man wearing a gray-green tunic and trousers. He bent to the pile and retrieved a ruby ring and a heavy, gold necklace with links as thick as fingers. The pendant, half the size of his human fist, depicted a flying dragon. Fashioned by some Greek artisan centuries ago, it meant nothing to him, but it usually impressed those he met when he masqueraded as a human. He donned the necklace and the ring, the latter on the third finger of his right hand. Salga smiled as the metal warmed to his touch, as if it became a part of him.

He climbed the pile, as tall as three men, and retrieved the stones, human fingers sorting the fraudulent from the authentic with the speed of a dragon's innate skill. He needed neither sight nor tactile sense to pluck the dross from gold but sensed the stones as his hands passed near. In moments, he filled the silk bag and tied it closed with the cloth-of-gold ribbon. With a sigh, he made his way to the front of the cave and the winding road that led up the Appenines and its highest peak, Monte Titano.

~ * ~

Salga di Alato arrived at the Grand and General Council Municipal building shortly before *terce*. Perfect, he thought, he could meet with the city representatives before they broke for their midday meal.

"I've come to speak with the *Capitani Reggenti*," he told the *segretario*. "Either one, or both. It matters not."

The lighting was dim inside the *municipio*, but Salga could make out the historical paintings on the far wall. Too bad one did not depict himself, he thought. There would be far less misunderstanding here if they included him within their history.

Two armored men stood equidistant from the secretary's desk, close enough to help if there were need but far enough away to stay out of council business.

"Have you an appointment?" the secretary asked, looking down at his calendar then back at Salga.

Un idiota could see the *segretario* thought he had no appointment, Salga thought.

"I have a standing appointment with the *Capitani Reggenti*. It concerns our contract business."

The secretary's eyes widened, then he cracked a smile. "You jest. The only standing appointment permitted on the books is with—"

"The agent of San Marino's dragon." It was Salga's turn to smile. He held up the necklace. "I am he."

A brief moment of silence passed before the secretary erupted in a full belly laugh. "I will share this with the *Consiglio*," he said, wiping his eyes. "They will have a good laugh, too." He smiled again at Salga. "Do you have a petition to drop off or need information? Perhaps there is something else I can help you with?"

"You can help me with facilitating the *terce* appointment," Salga said. "By the dragon's contract with San Marino, I have the right to request the next meeting time on the calendar. I am requesting it."

The secretary looked down at his books.

"There is a full council meeting at *terce*," the secretary said. "And then they break for lunch. I cannot—"

Salga felt himself losing patience. Perhaps he should have exercised this right more often over the years. "Were you not apprised of your duties when you were sworn in?" Salga asked.

"Three-hundred-year-old fairy tales do not a duty make," the secretary said. He turned to the guard at his right. "If you please."

The guard lifted his glaive and took a step toward the desk.

The council chamber door opened and two men stepped out,

the *Capitani Reggenti:* Pietro Della Baldi and Vincenzo Refi.

Pietro said, "What is going on here?"

"This man says he's an agent for San Marino's dragon," the secretary replied.

Silence greeted his announcement. Then in unison, the Captains Regent looked at each other and laughed, then looked back at the secretary and Salga as if expecting them to join in.

Pietro Della Baldi sobered first. He looked at the secretary, then faced Salga, who remained earnest in his expression.

A moment passed.

Pietro Della Baldi ran a hand through his graying hair and shrugged, looking at Refi. "The dragon's agent desires a meeting. So meet we must." He pulled the door of the council chamber open wide. "Come in, sir, and let us spend a few moments talking about the dragon's desires."

Salga couldn't tell if Capitani Della Baldi humored him or believed him. It mattered not. He was getting his audience.

Della Baldi turned to Refi. "Do you mind if we adjourn to my office?"

Refi shook his head. "We'll be more comfortable."

"Let the council know we're adjourned until after lunch," Refi told the secretary.

~ * ~

They walked through the council hall and through another door at the rear. Not much had changed in the two hundred or so years since he had been here last, Salga thought. The rooms were still dim, still furnished with dark woods, waxed and polished to a sheen. The white paint on the walls didn't do enough to brighten the style of the ancient building.

Della Baldi's office told another story. A large window dominated one side of the room, sending in a bright shower of light. Here, too, the room was painted white, but the light intensified it. A diary lay open on his desk, a quill and ink jar to the left of it. The day's outgoing correspondence lay stacked to the right, the red wax seal of the *Capitani Reggenti* declaring them official notices of the court. Evidently, Della Baldi didn't entrust the *segretario* with such tasks. So who did he and Refi trust to make certain the dragon's tribute was paid?

Della Baldi gestured to two chairs in front of his desk and waited for both Salga and Refi to sit before seating himself. "So you are the dragon's emissary," he said, eyebrows raised. "It's been quite some time since he's sent his agent to the people of San Marino."

Refi scooted his chair around to face Salga. *Allying himself with Della Baldi*, Salga thought. Unusual that he would do so, since they wore badges belonging to opposing political parties.

Refi thrust out his chin, accusing. "Do you have proof you come from the dragon?" he asked.

"I knew it would come to that," Salga said. "I have already shown you my seal, but you will also be interested in *this*." He reached into his tunic and brought out the red silk bag, laying it on Della Baldi's desk.

Refi stood, pushing his chair back with such force it tumbled over. "Where did you get that?" he hissed.

Salga turned his head toward Refi, "From the dragon, of course…*capasci?*"

"No, I don't understand," Della Baldi said. "Is the dragon rejecting our tribute this year?"

"*Sì*, in a way," Salga said. He pushed the bag forward on the desk. "Open it."

Della Baldi looked at Refi, who shrugged. It was slight, but Salga had had six hundred years to learn to read humans. He did not mistake the gesture. Clearly, the two had united against him. It was a shame, because he had hoped to use their opposing political viewpoints to his advantage. He knew the missing money would make things worse between him and the city…and Della Baldi and Refi *were* the city.

Della Baldi untied the ribbon and dumped the contents of the bag on his desk.

"Dio!" he said. "Where has the money gone? San Marino gave two hundred *soldi* to the dragon this year."

"No, *Reggente*, they did not. They gave him two hundred *sasso*. And someone went through a great deal of trouble to make sure each stone was similar in shape and size. This smacks of fraud, and the dragon is very unhappy." He offered the two of them a grim smile.

"You are the fraud," Refi said, pointing a finger at Salga. "San Marino has paid tribute and you have come here to steal from us again."

"Again?" Salga asked.

"Yes, again," Refi said. "You obviously took the first two hundred *soldi*, and now you expect us to give you another two hundred by telling us you are the dragon's agent. Be gone." He turned to Della Baldi, who nodded. "Leave, before we throw you in jail for the imposter you are."

"Your grandfathers' grandfathers' grandfathers and the dragon created a binding contract." Salga said. "If you fail to act on it, San Marino will fall."

"San Marino will never fall," Refi said.

"You place a great deal of faith in your *balesrieri*, *Reggente* Refi. They may be able to hold the walls against an invading army from below, but can they seal this city from the air? I guarantee you San Marino's legendary crossbowmen cannot keep a dragon from your ramparts."

Della Baldi stood. "Please leave, sir. It is better for you to go now, than for us to take you away."

Salga nodded. Della Baldi looked sad, as though he regretted asking him to leave. It was Refi who thought him insane, or worse, truly believed him to be a thief. Della Baldi put on a united front. Salga turned to him.

"There are a great many visitors still in San Marino for the festival," he said. "Are you certain you want to risk their lives?"

A long moment passed. Della Baldi nodded. "Please go now."

"I am instructed to tell you, as the dragon's agent," Salga said, "that the dragon himself will visit San Marino. You will not like the outcome." He turned and left the chamber, crossing the anteroom and nodding to the *segretario* on his way out.

Salga exited the high-walled gate of the city and walked the dirt road down Monte Titano to his lair. He hated that this had to be done, but a contract was a contract, after all.

Where diplomazia fails, strength prevails, he thought, entering the cave.

He took off the ring and the necklace. Standing on tiptoe, he called on the magic of the air and changed back. Lethargy stole over him as he climbed to the top of his hoard. Taking human form consumed so much of his energy. His eyes closed and he burrowed his belly into the coin, feeling the coolness of it against his scales.

Sighing, he lay his great head down on his front claws and settled into slumber. Tomorrow, approaching midday when the crowds were likely to be their thickest, he would exercise his rights of the contract.

~ * ~

The day dawned clear and cool. As the first rays of sun crept into Salga's dark lair, the dragon stirred awake. He swept his large tail back and forth then wrapped it around himself, sending an avalanche of coins rushing down his hoard of gold and silver. He could almost imagine a waterfall, the slithering coins shushing against each other until they stopped at the bottom, tinkling against the bare stone floor.

After a few moments, he stood, causing another barrage of coins to fall with every movement, first arching his back down like a sway-backed horse, then up like a spitting cat, shaking out his leather wings in unison. He couldn't unfurl them in the tight confines of the cave, but soon, when he made his way back to San Marino in his true form, he would have the luxury of stretching them wide.

It's a shame, he thought, but not wholly unexpected. This new generation considered the contract legend, not truth. They would learn, and perhaps the next would benefit.

He stepped down from the tremendous pile toward the cave opening, each foot sinking ankle deep into coins, just like a walk on a beach, and just as pleasurable. Sunlight caught him on the crown of his head, warming him. He sniffed the air, enjoying the tang of wood smoke, watching the sun creep higher into the sky.

The orb lit the hillside with its brilliant dawning, but at this hour, shadows still bathed San Marino. He sat down on his haunches and waited.

Down the mountainside, flocks of sheep grazed on the elevated hillocks, looking like white, puffy ants. He could smell their pungent odor rising on an updraft. To the east, winter crops had been sown, but he could still see the fertile, black soil of the fields.

Salga waited at the lip of his cave, watching the mountainside and her inhabitants wake to the new day. Finally, the sun reached a point where its rays crested the walls of even Monte Titano.

The dragon leapt from the mouth of his cave, unfurled his

wings, and dove down the shear side of the mountain, reveling in the air blowing in his face, the warmth of sunshine percolating under his scales and the buoyancy of flight. It had been so long since he'd been out in the daytime, he'd nearly forgotten the pleasure of it. Flipping his belly to the heat of the sun, Salga caught an updraft and turned, beating his heavy wings. He shot past the walls of San Marino, rising even higher on the wind. The sun still warmed the parts of him it touched, but the wind chilled him, slowed the beating of his wings, hardened his heart.

He leveled off and angled his nose downward toward the wide plateau which formed the city of San Marino, looking for the town square. He meant to invoke fear and panic as he swept over the main thoroughfare, gliding low and fast, casting a dark shadow as his immense body passed over.

As he imagined, crowds filled the main street and its smaller tributaries. Hundreds of people milled in the road, laughing, playing games, watching the crossbow tourney. A herd of drinkers spilled out from under a red-and-white awning, mugs and goblets overflowing in the noonday sun.

Salga found his anger climbing. *Puny humans,* he thought, daring to celebrate the founding of a fortress which they held only by his own generosity. They couldn't remember, even with their collective memories, the bargain they made with him. He had to swallow back the steam building in his throat or be consumed by it himself. Instead of letting loose the fire stoked in his breast, he tamped it down and unleashed a strident call as he approached the city.

The cry caught the revelers' attention, and they turned to face him. Salga opened his great wings and glided downward, skimming over their heads, savoring the horrified looks on their faces. They ran like sheep, bleating their fear, stampeding over one another to get to safety. Their screams echoed across the mountaintop, Salga thought, and he hadn't harmed a single one.

At the end of the city square, where a wall prevented Sanmariners from falling to their death down the cliff face, Salga caught another updraft and used it to propel himself higher. He pumped his wings, hearing the leathern creak with each downward thrust. Now he would teach them about forgetfulness.

He dived.

Gulping air on the way down, he stoked the fire that lived

within him.

As he got closer to the city, he saw a line of *balesrieri* pull back their bow strings and loose their arrows. Several found their mark. He cried out again, an uncontrolled bellow encompassing both his pain and his rage.

He flew over the city, swooping down over one large tower, and set fire to the roofs of the *municipio*, the barracks and a series of smaller buildings in his path toward the second of the three towers.

There, several *balesrieri* managed to reach the ballista. They cranked it high and ratcheted the bowstring back, loading a large, steel bolt into the slot. Before he could react, they fired the bolt, and reached for their crossbows. Salga roared, letting loose a stream of fire onto the ballista.

Agony ripped through the leather webbing of his right wing as the bolt drilled a ragged hole in his flesh. The hammer blow of it forced his wing back and he fell nearly to the ground before the weak pumping he managed between the debilitating injury and the pain of it saved him from crashing to the cobblestone. He rose, heavy and ponderous, until he found a buoyant wind to support him. The crossbowmen fired their weapons again.

He twisted around, protecting his softer belly from the bolts, jerking from pain where the arrows managed to sink into flesh. Most bounced from his hardened scales like rainwater.

Still, the pain tempted him to set fire to the entire city, to kill as many as he could, but he stifled the urge. Without the city, he had no tribute, and this was about money, after all.

When he was high enough to control a glide, he circled the city once more, then descended back to his lair. Late into the night, he could hear the sounds of the citizens rallying to douse the fires and help the injured. Finally, silence fell where there should have been gaiety.

Salga plucked the crossbow bolts one by one from his hide.

~ * ~

Giuseppe Piccoli filled his pockets with the few remaining *soldi* and made his way to the square. He knew he had to do this, yet it frightened him more than anything he had ever done. Indeed, it might cost him his life, which still might be for naught. What was the use of stealing in order to save the lives of his family if they might yet be killed by the dragon?

He tied the rope around the dry well and lowered himself down. The small, covered lantern he carried illuminated the shaft enough for him to see moss growing in tufts on the walls, and various lines where the water had rested at some point before retreating, and finally, the light disappeared into the darkness of the large cavern.

After a few moments, he saw the lantern light glint off something shiny below him.

His heart began to beat as fast as hummingbird wings. Heat rushed to his face and he began to sweat. He slid the remaining few feet to the pile of gold on hands too damp to keep his weight on the rope.

He landed with a jarring thump, sending a shower of coins rushing down the hill of gold.

~ * ~

"Who dares to enter my home?" Salga asked, resting only a few feet away. He ached, and he was in no mood for confrontation.

The lamplight brightened.

Salga watched a man, so afraid of speaking his entire body shook. He moved the lantern's hood back to shed more light, then sat down, shaking, on the pile.

"G-g-g-iuseppe P-p-piccoli," he said. "I've come to make amends."

"I thought for certain the *Reggenti* would send a knight to try to kill me." Salga looked him up and down. "You don't look capable of a fight."

"I'm not a knight, sir. I'm an attorney." His voice still trembled.

Salga raised his massive head and turned toward Giuseppe, who fell back on his hands, as if expecting the dragon to take a snap at him. Salga said, "If you're not here to try to kill me, why are you here?"

Giuseppe sat up, pushing a few coins and gems down the side of the pile as he righted himself. "I'm the one who took your silver. Please don't punish the city for my actions."

"You're a brave man to come here and admit that."

Giuseppe shook his head, swallowing so hard, Salga could see his Adam's apple fall and rise above his collared tunic. "I'm a pathetic man. I didn't want to come here today, but I knew I needed to. If there were only me to consider, I would have left well enough alone, but I have to think about my children and the people of San Marino."

Salga nodded. "Why did you take the silver?"

"I needed the money."

"There are other means to obtain money."

"Not so much and so easily. I had promised to pay off an agreement by Founder's Day. I didn't have the money, but I had means to obtain the city's."

Tiny curls of smoke drifted out of Salga's nostrils. He turned his head to the side and snorted, a tiny flame escaping. Giuseppe blanched white in the lantern light.

"You sacrificed the honor of San Marino by paying your own debts first?" Salga said.

His voice a whisper, Giuseppe said, "It wasn't like that."

"No?"

"No," he said, wiping the palms of his hands across the tops of his knees. "For hundreds of years the city has collected money and thrown it away—"

"It is rent, Signor Piccoli, no matter how the city has popularized it with festivities and crossbow tournaments."

"But no one alive has ever seen you. What are we to think? To us, it's just throwing money away." He made a gesture of throwing something down on the ground.

Salga heaved a deep sigh. These words confirmed what he thought all along.

Giuseppe said, "I beg you not to harm the people of San Marino. I'm the one at fault. Kill me, if you have to, but please leave the city alone." He dug in his pocket and retrieved the remaining *soldi*. With cupped hands, he held thirteen silver coins out to Salga. "Here is what remains of the tribute after I've paid my debt. I swear I've not kept a single one back."

"Yet you are still in my debt for over a hundred and eighty *soldi*."

"I owe the city," Giuseppe said.

"No, you owe me," Salga said. "After all, the money you took represented rent San Marino owes me." He huffed a stream of smoke straight up through his nostrils.

An idea formed.

"What price would you pay for stealing from the city?"

Giuseppe hung his head. "I would lose my position as city attorney. My family would be shamed and need to leave San Marino." He drew in a deep breath. "My right hand would be chopped off at the wrist and I would go to debtor's prison until my family could raise the funds to pay off the debt and the interest incurred while the city waited to be paid."

Salga nodded his giant head and then lowered it, resting it upon his front claws.

After much consideration, he realized the problem was not San Marino, but himself. His contract with the town was short-sighted. Although his kind is accustomed to living long lives and remembering the ages, he could not expect as much from these short-lived humans.

The fault lay with him.

He possessed a contract with forgetful beings. If not Giuseppe, it would have been someone else forgetting his existence and stealing his rents. And if he didn't find a solution to the problem now, it would continue over and over again.

He rose up on his front legs, looking down at Giuseppe who still shook with fear.

"Be thankful you owe your debt to me, Giuseppe Piccoli—"

"I am a dead man," he said, crossing himself.

"Nothing so harsh," Salga said, feeling the pain of a bolt hole in his wing. "I find I am in need of an attorney."

He pawed through the pile of gold, precious gems and jewelry until he found the heavy gold necklace with the dragon emblem and handed it over to Giuseppe. "You're now my agent," he said. "I demand complete honesty and fair representation."

Giuseppe stared at the heavy badge of office, clearly stunned. Salga continued to tickle the pile with his claws, sorting money. The Sanmariner coins should have been mostly on the top, but his hoard had been repeatedly disturbed over the last few days. He sorted a few smaller denominations from the side of the pile and handed those over to Giuseppe who asked, "And how am I to perform for you?"

"Take these coins and purchase supplies for writing: materials sound enough not to deteriorate for hundreds of years. We are amending my contract with the city." He lowered himself back to the pile, taking care not to jar the injured wing.

Giuseppe raised his brows. "You think the city will agree?"

"Of course. I'm offering them a better deal," the dragon said, sweeping his tail around to warm his feet.

~ * ~

"The council has approved the new contract," Pietro Della Baldi said. "It only remains for the three of us to sign it."

Vincenzo Refi took the heavy document from Della Baldi's hands and read the words himself, as if reading them could make them any more believable. "This is real?" he asked Giuseppe Piccolo.

"The dragon dictated the words himself," Giuseppe said. "You can see the contract is written in my hand. And here," he held up the large, dragon pendant on the gold chain. "You see I now carry his seal."

Della Baldi had his arms crossed on his chest, one hand raised to stroke his chin. "It seems too good to be true," he said. "For the same terms of rent he has always received, the dragon promises to defend the city from all invaders as long as he shall live. And when he chooses a mate and has children, he can promise their loyalty to the city until his daughters leave to reside with their chosen mates or his sons move away to collect their own hoards."

"Imagine," Giuseppe said, an excited smile brightening his face, "in a matter of time you will have an army of dragons defending San Marino. Our city shall never fall."

"He does require that we allow him to participate in the Founders Day Festival every twentieth year," Refi said, laying the contract on the table.

"It is nothing," Giuseppe said. "He only wants to ensure San Marino doesn't forget him again."

"Reasonable," Della Baldi said. "Reminding the city of his presence can only help us avoid…*misunderstandings* as we've had these past two weeks."

He turned to Refi. "I'm ready to sign. Do you agree?"

Refi nodded and picked up a quill.

Della Baldi signed his own name then asked Giuseppe. "I'm curious why a dragon even collects money. After all, where could he spend it?"

Giuseppe smiled. "He doesn't collect just money. You should see the cave. He has gold and silver, jewelry, even gemstones and precious-metal art."

"It seems like a waste," Refi said, signing his own name. "I agree paying rent seems reasonable enough, but Pietro is right. And what good is art to a dragon? Can he even appreciate it?"

Giuseppe rolled his copy of the contract and tucked it away. "Dragons hoard their riches until there is enough to weave into a nest and impress a prospective mate. Once our dragon has enough to woo a spouse, he'll settle down and rear that army he promised us."

"And has our dragon begun weaving his nest?" Refi asked.

"No," Giuseppe said, shaking his head. "He simply keeps it piled. Perhaps when we're all doddering he may have enough to begin weaving."

Della Baldi looked at Refi, but he asked Giuseppe, "So offering him more gold or silver will encourage him to mate sooner?"

"That seems likely," Giuseppe said.

Della Baldi turned to Refi. "Perhaps we can afford to be more generous in our rents. After all, our payment has not changed in over two centuries." Refi was nodding in agreement before Della Baldi could even finish his statement. "In fact, it appears our dragon has been very generous to us. I think we could do no less for him."

Giuseppe coughed, hiding a smile behind his hand.

"We can easily double our present payment," Della Baldi said, watching Refi continue to nod. "And we can add a clause to revisit the payment schedule at a later date."

"That's very generous of you," Giuseppe said, pulling another contract from his satchel and spreading it on the table. "I think you'll see this contract includes the very same terms you've named, and we can write in the new rental payment." He looked into two sets of surprised eyes and shrugged. "Salga anticipated you might consider offering more if you knew what it could buy you."

Giuseppe watched the *Capitani Reggenti* sign the new contract and placed his own signature below theirs. He sanded the ink to hurry it dry, then rolled up the scroll to take with him. He left the *municipio* and crossed the small square to the other side of the city.

Shadows covered San Marino as the sun fell below the horizon.

He walked to the third tower of San Marino, the one with no

doorway for entry, and stepped into the darkest shadow where the high wall of the city met the stone of the tower. Pressing his hands against two separate bricks, he pushed, releasing a spring mechanism and opening a small door inward.

He entered and closed the door to a room tinier than the tower was wide. A staircase led down below the city. On his way to see Salga, he reflected there would be no more trips down a dry well to meet his patron, and with a little luck, he'd be godfather to a dragon whelp before he confessed his sins before God himself.

Originally published in "Black Dragon, White Dragon" - Ricasso Press, 2008

~ * ~ * ~

Kelly A. Harmon was born on the Baltimore Beltway at 120 miles-per-hour in the front seat of a Ford Mustang. In the wee hours of the morning, with rising humidity ready to swamp the day, she took her first breath of H&S baked bread, the tang of salt air coming off the harbor and the scent of Old Bay wafting out of McCormick's. Baltimore was in her blood then, as it is now.

In the intervening years, she's lived all over Maryland, written for local newspapers and beyond, and come home to Baltimore to write her Charm City Darkness series.

When the voices in her head leave her alone, she can be found haunting Enoch Pratt Library, roaming around Canton, or stopping by the Westminster Burying Grounds for a one-sided chat with Edgar Allan Poe.

The H-Word

T J O'Hare

Simoom and Gharmattan were all the rage when they first came to New Helkath. Their debut appearance at the New Helkath Summer Fayre was a sensation, and although they fulfilled all their street-gigs for the entire eleven days of the fair, after that they never had to busk again, or sing for coppers outside taverns.

The art-lovers of the city took them under their wing, and even though they never sang on the streets again, their songs never died. Every minstrel or songstress worth their salt after that always had a large number of Simoom and Gharmattan songs in their repertoire. One or two minstrels got together and gave faux street performances as the pair, because the public loved them so much.

Despite the citizens of Helkath taking the singing duo to their hearts, there was one problem that some folk—with their narrow minds; or rigid prejudices; or, let's face it, with their eye on the main chance—couldn't quite get their heads around.

Simoom and Gharmattan were dragons, or, to be more precise —a dragon; yes, you heard me, —a dragon, but it was one with two heads, and therefore two sound-boxes. Their harmonies were pure and soaring and perfectly in step with each other. They closed their eyes and opened their mouths—and transported their listeners off to sublime counterpoints, divine descants, subtle phrasings (both musical and lyrical) and emotions that ranged from the mildly satirical to the deeply emotional. They ranged from fey to foot-stompin', from farrr-rrrr-out to family sing-alongs.

Their first set consisted of half their own material and half regular ballads. They took old-timey stuff they arranged in their own particular manner, remade what had been deemed hackneyed and out of fashion (and, okay, let's face it one more time, back-woodsy and hicksville).

With their new take on the approach to live music, they shook up the box a little. Not enough it offended anyone—more than that, it just made the whole thing more meaningful.

People kinda woke up to the new singing sensation.

Okay, so they were dragons, but not all dragons eat people. We got ourselves iguanas in the local lagoons and they seem to get by chompin' down on lily-pads and the local greenery. Sure, they might get an occasional shot of protein when they suck up a slug or two in their salad, but they sure ain't people-eaters.

So, after the first ripple of unease went through the local panic-mongers—oh, sure, we got 'em here, too. Even in laid-back, big easy New Helkath. Can't even rightly call it a ripple—more like a frisson. Know what I mean? It's bad, but it's also good. Gets the juices goin' a little—not enough to get a big reaction from the Imperial Culture College, but enough for people to stop and listen, and say, 'Hey, that's new. That's cool.'

And even if the Imperials have a big down on anything that smacks of magic, this pair—Simoom and Gharmattan—they were just so goldurn clean and dragon-next-door, and whatever the latest adjective is nowadays for what's hip 'n' happenin'. Shoot. They were dragons—or, at least *a* dragon—but—but—but—

What can I say? They could sing the heart right out of you, lube it down and spank it till it hollered, and put it right back in, the right way up and the best foot forward, and you felt all the better for hearing them.

Anyways.

They were dragons—okay, *a* dragon. And with the D-word comes a whole mess o' baggage. Well, their good appearance and calm demeanour and wholesomeness kinda covered the spittin' fire and eatin' people thing. They were as gentle as kittens. Didn't even frighten the horses.

A few guys turned up in armour—armour, I have to admit of the most dubious kind—but once they'd sniffed around our singin' duo, they sensed their innate decency and knew there was nothing to be had here in the dragon-slayin' business.

Sure they probably coulda killed Simoom and Gharmattan with two snicker-snacks of whatever blade happened to come to hand, but then they woulda had the audience on their backs. So it was not a heroism-type opportunity, and they all slunk off, back to the badlands, where there were dragons that really needed to have manners put upon them.

Dragons—their baggage consists of treasure. The T-word. Or, if you like, the H-word (and I'm whispering here, *hoard*; just make sure you spell it right).

It started off as taproom talk. The last lush of the night, mumbling into his forearms on the bar before his forehead hits the off-switch.

The T-word (rightly, in my opinion) shouldn't come up in polite company. It belongs to the dreams of drunkards and ne'er-do-wells, to whom a decent day's work would make them break out in a cold sweat.

I was there at the festival on the third night when the T-word was thrown from the anonymity of the crowd. Good-natured smiles told me the heckler was a sap and a maroon and a nogoodnik—but it had been said.

Simoom sang on through to the intro of his next song and said: 'Someone from the crowd asked us about our treasure. I think I can speak for Gharmattan and myself, when I say our treasure is this— right here and now, singing to you good folks.'

'Too right, bro,' Gharmattan added. 'Heck, if we had treasure, we'd be rolling and flopping in it, happy as a hog in mud of its own manufacture, if you get my drift.'

Nice brush-off, I thought, mentally applauding. Didn't throw them; didn't muss up the feel-good vibe of the set.

But, you know, dragons and treasure go together like 'stick and measure', as we say in these here parts. Simoom and Gharmattan got taken on board by the private villas of the merchants' party circuit. I heard through channels that they did very well. They got paid top shekel, without ever having to show their business-brains and start whining and gouging.

As a music agent, I have to confess, a lot of the love goes out of the business when the talent starts whining and gouging. It's like they invented whining and gouging, and they never heard the rest of the world has to get by on hard graft and a keen eye for a good business opportunity. Either that or slavery, but let's not go there. I got enough singin' slaves to fill the galleys of the Imperial navy twice over.

After a month or two, it came out that Simoom and Gharmattan's first set was named *Early Morning/Middle of the Night*. Groovy, as we say here in New Helkath.

The next season they hit the festival again with a big build-up for their new set which they named *New Helkath Festival Fayre*, and they rewrote the old, old song of that same name that was suppos-edly written here, and updated it with a little of the local politics, all sugar-coated so no-one, not even the old timers who had fought in the last Sorcery War, could take offence.

This season, they went over even bigger. They moved up into the top mercantile circles, and their performance fees rose accordingly.

The year after that, their third season came out with *Old Scrolls*. Another eleven songs of introspection, political commentary and comments on life as a skill you can only learn the hard way: by falling down and getting up again.

This was the year they cracked the local aristocracy. Nothing fancy; just a few of the court hangers-on; the ones who had made their money the old-fashioned way, through bribery and corruption, and had almost lost the ability to spend it.

That year you couldn't walk down a street in New Helkath without hearing a Simoom and Gharmattan cover. Personally, I could never get enough of them, but some curmudgeonly folk were getting tired of S & G's success and were impatient for the Next Big Thing to arrive and rock us all down to our sandals and skivvies.

Which meant the H-word had become modified from the Hoard they'd left in the mountains or whatever backwoods boon-docks they'd left behind; to become the Hoard they were sitting on. The stash of cash that was obviously flowing into their coffers and out of the local economy of hard-working, hard-grafting New Helkathites.

Some folks. You can't please 'em.

~ * ~

So, the fourth year, the year their set was named *Byways Of The Worlds*, trouble came to New Helkath and to Simoom and Gharmattan in the form of a treasure prospector.

The treasure prospector didn't come to make trouble. In fact, he came to retire. He'd done his 30 in the Imperial Prospectors Corps, seeking out lich-tombs and sorcery enclaves, and frankly, he was here in New Helkath to put all that behind him.

Everybody called him Yellah, which wasn't a reflection on his courage or character, but was due to the amount of gold he could sniff out. He set up a tavern in the middle range of quarters, a ways from the wharves, but not too full of civil servants and government workers they would insist on imported wines.

In order to get a good vibe going, Yellah approached me as the only music agent in town who could even talk to S & G.

I met him in my office, and he pitched his pitch. He wanted Simoom and Gharmattan to open his tavern, and get the word around that his place, Yellah's, was a cool place to be seen drinking in, or even to be barred from. It would be the opening night of the festival season, and everybody, but everybody, would want to be there, to tell their grandkids they had witnessed an historic gig.

I placed my fingertips together and flexed them, which is my body-language for deep thought. 'Thing is, Mr Yellah, S & G are at a point in their careers where opening a bar is—'

I didn't want to say 'beneath them', because they ain't that type of whining 'n' gouging a-hole no-talent talent.

'—a little too bijou for them.'

'Bijou?'

'Yeah,' I prompted. 'A little too boutique. They are spreading their wings over New Helkath. They have attracted the attention of the Imperial Culture College, and they are planning to open the new set right in the heart of the Empire. The High Planetarium, no less.'

Yellah got a mean and stony look in his eye, but I tried to soothe the bad news a tad.

'Now the guys would jump at a chance to do a tavern-opening gig here in New Helkath. I mean, this is where they broke through, dude; this is where the magic happened for them. But, you know who would look askance at them doing your gig and then doing the High Planetarium.'

He didn't nod or shake his head, but the meanness in his eyes just got meaner by the blink—and he weren't even blinkin' none neither.

I'd started, so I had to finish: 'Can you see the Master of Ceremonies on stage in the High Planetarium, rilin' up the audience with S & G and their whole back catalogue, and then saying somethin' like: "And here they are, respected citizens of the Empire, hot from the opening night of Yellah's Tavern in New Helkath—" Y'see what I'm getting at? It's not the guys, they are two grounded guys, or rather, one grounded guy, but with two heads.'

The stony meanness had spread from Yellah's eyes to the rest of his grizzled veteran's physog. He stood up, stiff with mean, just jam-packed and bristling with the stuff.

He kicked aside the chair he'd been squatting on. It didn't topple, but that wasn't from the lack of ill will on his part.

'Thank you for your time,' he barked. For a guy who had a mad-on with all that mean, he musta had a ton of self-control not to just explode with disappointment and put-out-ness.

I separated my fingertips. My knuckles were still white with the pressure. I knew I hadn't heard the last of Yellah.

~ * ~

I'd been to the Imperial capital before. Man of the world, that's me.

But it was always good to network; and make new friends and renew old acquaintanceships. And flaunt the fact you're still alive and braggin' to enemies old and new.

The city was mightier than ever. The new Empress liked to build. And even if the new style of architecture wasn't quite my cup o' meat, it still cast its old spell of imperial romance and threat over the rubes who flocked in from the surrounding provinces.

Even Yellah had come along. He'd had his opening night, and it had been a tolerable sensation when the Hagger Sisters rocked the joint, but it was, y'know, not the historical gig he'd hoped for.

The Imperial city was obviously his stompin' grounds, because he hung out with a whole mess of—I can only call them—grizzled and veteran-lookin' types. At a pre-gig bash, I saw them all turn in my direction with a stink-eye that shoulda cleared the place, but I was impervious to their narrow thinking. Just because they were a little worn around the edges, didn't mean they weren't diamond-geezers, as our friends across the pond would call 'em.

All the same, I doubled my bodyguard, and checked backstage security. You can't do any better than Imperial security, but I remembered their priority may well be a little different than mine. They might be prepared to throw my talent to the dire-wolves if it meant taking the heat off her Imperial High-up-herself-ness.

My only nervousness arose when I saw a shifty little guy, wearing an access-all-areas badge on his surcoat. He didn't smell right. For a start, he didn't smell clean, which is something that is social death in Imperial city with their imperial plumbing the envy of the civilized worlds.

My two main bodyguards, Sinner and Goon, were with me. I nudged Sinner, and nodded in Stinky's direction. Sinner and Goon knew what to do. Goon went up and faced the little stinker, while Sinner went round the back and began cleaning his fingernails with a whopping great pigsticker of a hunting knife.

Goon's face had had so many blunt-instrument interface impacts he could barely breathe. This meant he could only say one word, often only one syllable at a time.

But the size he hulks about, and the shadow he imposes on any potential interviewee is often enough to elicit the correct response by the time the third word has hit the bellows-breath of his massive ribcage.

'Hey,' Goon said.

Stinky looked up, guilt written all over his weevilly, unshaven chops.

Goon continued, 'Dude.'

Stinky turned to run and bumped into Sinner, who was just admiring the way the light fell on the cutting edge of his hunting knife.

'Wassup?' Goon added.

Stinky gulped and tried not to step on Sinner's sandalled feet.

Sinner took his eyes away from his hunting knife. 'Y'know, some folks think a knife should be double-edged. But if'n you ask me, I'd say double-edges are for pussies. This double-edged thing, it's just an urban legend put around by the knife-grinders, so they can make double-time on their knife-sharpenin' action.'

He let the gleam of the blade fall on his eyes.

'How can you call yourself a man and not know how to get the best use out of a blade with one edge? I say, I ask you, my man. How can you do that, and call yourself a man?'

I blushed, because I'd written this speech myself. But I hadda hand it to Sinner, he knew how to deliver it with redneck straight delivery. All cold-eyes, and inbred dangerousness.

Stinky fainted. Or else he lost the use of all body orifices at once, which is kind of humiliatin' in a public place.

He crashed out like a side of antelope venison, and something jingled out of his filthy sash that tied his ragged robe closed under his surcoat.

I bent low to inspect it, but I had to step back out of respect for my gag-reflex, and I ain't talkin' one-liners, mí amigo.

Goon, however, is made of sterner stuff. He leaned over, with all the creaking of a schooner doing its morning warm-up exercises. He picked up the little metal gee-gaw and held it up to inspect it in the lamplight.

It was a box of metal-mesh, with some shiny crystal wheels and cogs inside. There was a little handle to one side, and the lid was a mirror that popped up to reveal a little ballerina in a tinfoil tutu.

Unlike any other ballerinas I'd seen and lusted after, this one was a silver skeleton, with a silver skull and ruby eyes. Bad taste and bad mojo. This was a magic item. And in the Empire as it stood under the new Empress, just having one in your possession was an access-all-areas pass to the torture chambers of Artil Ereth.

Sinner looked at it, his head tilted in curiosity.

'Looks,' Goon said.

Sinner finished for him. 'Like a music box.'

'Nope. That ain't no music box, chums. That's an Un-Music Box.'

'What,' Goon began.

'Does it do?' Sinner finished.

'Depends on who made it. I hearda one that makes folk dance till they can't stop and die of exhaustion.'

'Thass,' Goon began.

'Bad, very bad,' Sinner finished.

I sighed. 'You guys have been workin' together for way too long.'

'Yeah,' Goon grunted.

'We keep each other alive,' Sinner supplied.

'Works for me.'

I closed Goon's fingers about the Un-Music Box and said, 'Keep this safe and outta sight, m'man. Sinner, you go with him and help him finish his sentences.'

'Where you goin', boss-man?'

'I gotta go check up on my talent.'

~ * ~

I high-tailed it to the green room, where I found things had gone a little awry. There, Moog, Noog and Pipsqueak, the other three-fourths of Goon's old hair-tailor quartet, were looking anxious. None of them were built as big as Goon, but since they'd all been under contract with me when Goon lost his voice in a bar-room brawl, I felt sentimental and kept them on as muscle. Even Pipsqueak, who is only knee-high to a party-favour, could scare the Cthulhu outta most sensible folks when he got riled.

Except, these weren't sensible folks we were dealin' with here. This was a grift-rakin' team of ICC Imperial Prospectors. They were big and brash and full of bring-it-on-down. They were just itching for a bribe or a fight, or both. This had Yellah's stink all over it.

I turned on my charm mojo all the way up to 11.

'Greetings, Imperial officers. How may we help you in the fulfilment of your Imperial duties?'

'We got word that your…your talent, here, had access to forbidden artefacts.'

'Forbidden artefacts? Officers, I'm sure I can't imagine what you mean. My party here is visiting the Imperial city at the direct and personal invitation of the Empress herself. We are delivering a command performance, here, tonight, in the High Planetarium.'

Each of them looked big enough to have thumbs for fingers, and bricks for knuckles, but none of them could come up with the word 'civility' in their collective rap sheet. I guess they went straight from dumb to insubordinate and larcenous without taking notice of the other letters in the alphabet.

The sergeant in charge looked like he would have preferred to rough me up rather than to defer to my good people skills. But he was outnumbered in the brain-cells count—and that was just counting me and my pinkie.

~ * ~

Simoom and Gharmattan never came home after that command performance. The Imperial performance contract extended to the rest of their natural lives. I thought I had an unbreakable contract until I met the Imperial shysters who call themselves contract lawyers. Still, I got away with my head still attached to my neck.

I go up every year for old times' sake, and listen to the guys. The after-show party is where I get to kick back and sink a few drinks with the sweetest-voiced dragon I ever hope to meet.

Occasionally I bump into Yellah, but he can never make eye-contact.

I still have the Un-Music Box, and there are one or two singers I could've used it on over the years to make the world a better place, but I couldn't bring myself to sink that low.

And after the Imperial gig each year, I consider myself lucky— lucky to have heard Simoom and Gharmattan in their heyday, when they were kids and the whole world lay at their sandalled feet.

But then I get back to New Helkath and reconsider the ways of the world, and the twists and turns life can throw at a guy.

Outside of my office, I can hear a human duo doing a cover of the latest Simoom and Gharmattan number.

I can smile.

Simoom was right all those years ago. They were dragons without a hoard—actually, the name of their most recent Imperial-backed set.

But that wasn't true. They'd let their hoard be dispersed and grow larger. From two voices blending in harmony, they had spread their hoard far and wide. Extending it. Enlarging it. Giving hope to the new kids of the next generation who wanted to charm a world grown weary with the everyday and the toilsome and the petty.

Yep, the H-word never sounded so pretty in my mouth.

~ * ~ * ~

T.J. O'Hare writes short stories, novels, song lyrics, poetry, plays and film scripts. His novel "Amnesiak: Blood Divinity" is available on Smashwords. He co-writes with many musical collaborators, including Edelle McMahon (check out her performances on soundcloud). Under the name of Jim Johnston, he has songs on Brigid O'Neill's e.p. "Arrivals & Departures". His plays have been staged in Northern Ireland and Belgium. His most recent published short story is entitled "The Steed of the Fey", in Out of the Green: Tales from Fairyland, from Urban Fey Press.

He is married to Jean and has two grown-up sons. He lives in Northern Ireland.

Shreddy and the Dancing Dragon

Mary E. Lowd

The cardboard box, labeled *Yay! PlayCube!* on its sides, was more than big enough to hold Cooper, the blonde, curly-furred Labradoodle. Yet, somehow, Shreddy knew better than to hope the Red-Haired Woman had brought in such a large, sinister box for any reason as comforting as to haul the annoying Labradoodle away.

All three of the Red-Haired Woman's pets—Shreddy the tabby, Cooper the Labradoodle, and Susie the Cavalier King Charles Spaniel—watched as she sliced through the tape on the edges of the box and unfolded the top flap to open it.

The Red-Haired Woman drew out a strange bundle of white plastic cords and a big cube. The two dogs wagged their tails happily, excited to see what their brilliant master had brought home to make their lives more magical. Shreddy twitched his tail too, but, in the language of his feline body, that twitch meant anxiety. Unlike the dogs, he didn't think the Red-Haired Woman was a brilliant sorceress who conjured strange sounds from her smartphone and warm food from the kitchen out of nothing.

Shreddy loved the Red-Haired Woman, but he knew about technology. It could be wonderful. It could also be dangerous. Either way, the Red-Haired Woman seemed to have different ideas from him about how to use it. He'd warred with her over technology before.

So it was with trepidation in his whiskers and schemes in his heart that Shreddy watched the Red-Haired Woman set up the white plastic cube beside the TV and hook it up with twisting, twining white cords. By the time she was done, the cords clung to the base of her TV like an octopus trying to strangle a diver.

Shreddy had seen ViewTube videos on the Red-Haired Woman's smartphone of octopi and their tentacle-happy ways. Nothing good could come from a piece of electronics that looked so much like one of those creepy monsters of the deep.

Shreddy lashed his tail angrily against the carpet as he watched the Red-Haired Woman take the knobby end of one of the weird white tentacle-cords in her hand. She pressed a button on the PlayCube, and the TV screen sprang to life with a flourish of music and flashy colors unlike any of the safe, wholesome videos that it usually played. The Red-Haired Woman withdrew across the room to her couch, where the two dumb dogs eagerly jumped up, mauling her as they settled onto the cushions on either side of her.

For the rest of the evening, Shreddy watched in horror as his Red-Haired Woman stared slack-jawed and zombiefied at the TV screen. She clutched the tentacle-cord's knob in one-hand, and she idly stroked Susie, curled against her side, with the other. All the while, techno-beats and synth-pop chords screeched from the TV speakers, assailing Shreddy's sensitive, feline ears, and an animated dragon danced on the TV screen.

Night after night, the demonic PlayCube with its animated dragon summoned Shreddy's Red-Haired Woman to it. Hour after hour, Shreddy watched her life being sucked away. After a full week of the intolerable situation, Shreddy had seen more than enough. The PlayCube was more than a video game system—it was a portal into a parallel dimension. An evil dimension. It had to go. And Shreddy felt Cooper should be the one to do it.

Until the PlayCube, Cooper was the worst thing the Red-Haired Woman had ever brought home. If Cooper had been a brighter dog, Shreddy might have considered him his arch-nemesis. As it was, Shreddy had to settle for considering Cooper a bumbling idiot and reserving arch-nemesis status for the crazy Calico who lived across the way.

Shreddy made his pitch to the curly-blonde Labradoodle to no avail. Cooper remembered the time Shreddy had convinced him to bury the Red-Haired Woman's smartphone in the garden. That had not gone well.

"You're just angry," Cooper said, "because you don't know how to turn it on." He knew Shreddy liked to play the games on the Red-Haired Woman's computer, whenever she left it running.

"The PlayCube is different," Shreddy spat through his whiskers. "It's evil."

"I like it," Susie commented, flouncing into the room with her curly ears flopping. She turned up her speckled nose at Shreddy and said, "When the master plays it, she lets me sit on the couch and snuggle with her."

Incited into immediate action by Susie's infuriating demeanor, Shreddy lowered himself to the carpet, raised his haunches and began to wiggle them in preparation for a terribly dangerous front-on pounce at the offending electronics. Before he could launch himself at the PlayCube, however, he was bowled over and thoroughly woofed at by Susie.

"I told you! I like it!" she barked.

Utterly surprised by the force of Susie's conviction, Shreddy escaped to the top shelf of the corner bookcase and began licking his paw diffidently.

Never mind. He could wait. Susie couldn't defend the PlayCube all the time.

~ * ~

The Red-Haired-Woman took the dogs to the dog park the next day.

Shreddy knew better than to attack the PlayCube directly with his teeth—he'd learned the hard way not to chew on electric cords. But he'd seen the Red-Haired-Woman drop her smartphone in a banana-honey sandwich she was making once. The smartphone had been covered in sticky, gold honey, and she freaked out over whether it was destroyed. (It wasn't, but the Red-Haired-Woman didn't make sandwiches one-handed while playing games on her smartphone anymore.)

Shreddy could only assume honey had magical powers to disable electronic devices. He could well believe it. The bees that lived in the garden were mysterious, mesmerizing creatures. Their buzzing held music and danger. A golden elixir drawn from a hive such as theirs must be powerful stuff.

If Shreddy could coat the PlayCube in honey, it would be safe to chew the dread thing to death.

The Red-Haired Woman kept the honey in a cupboard over the kitchen sink. Shreddy had learned how to open that cupboard long ago when she'd made the mistake of storing catnip there. Now she stored catnip in the refrigerator.

Shreddy perched on the edge of the sink, reached up to open the cupboard, and then jumped inside. He found the honey bear and clasped it with his jaw, teeth piercing its plastic belly. He shuddered at the shock of sweetness that oozed onto his tongue.

The honey bear was awkward and heavy for his jaw, but Shreddy held it tight in his mouth as he jumped down from the cupboard, trotted through the kitchen, and returned to the electronically haunted living room. He placed the honey bear on top of the PlayCube, and then he truly ripped into it, gnawing and clawing until it was a shredded, tattered, sticky wreck.

Honey dripped down the sides of the PlayCube.

Shreddy gave the honey a moment to work its magic. Then he set into the cords with a vengeance, gnawing down hard with his back teeth. His tail lashed. His eyes dilated with the satisfying joy of feeling his teeth sink right through the plastic coating of the cords and into the thin metal wires inside.

He didn't notice he'd set his back foot on the power button until he felt the unmistakable ZAP of electricity in his mouth.

Shreddy jumped back, his paws tangled in the cords, and clonked his head on the hard plastic of the knobby controller.

A buzzing in his ears joined the tingling that lingered in his mouth. Shreddy opened his eyes; he didn't remember shutting them.

Although it was midday, the living room and the windows that looked outside had gone dark as night. Shreddy could still see with his cat's eyes, but he knew something was very, very wrong. He looked up, and where the rectangular TV screen had been, there was a swirling vortex—black and purple, roiling like storm clouds, sparking with electricity. Nothing could have impelled Shreddy to enter that vortex, not willingly.

He wouldn't have done it to save the Red-Haired Woman's soul. He wouldn't have done it to save his own skin.

Yet, the twining white cords tightened around Shreddy. He struggled, but like an octopus dragging a diver into the deep, the white cords dragged Shreddy, spitting and hissing, into the vortex.

Wind battered Shreddy as he entered the swirling clouds. His ears popped, and his fur stood on end—not from fear but from static electricity. Then the wind died, and the air stood still.

The white cords dropped Shreddy on hard dirt, untwined from him, and withdrew back through the vortex that was now behind him.

Shreddy looked around the dark chamber he found himself in.

From this side, he could see his empty living room through the purple-swirling vortex. Other vortexes looked out on other rooms that he recognized from looking through the windows of other houses in the neighborhood—other houses with PlayCubes.

Shreddy considered jumping back through the vortex to the relative safety of his own living room, but his curiosity got the better of him. If the portal had carried him into a parallel dimension, how could he not explore it?

Cautiously, Shreddy crept away from the array of portals, keeping so low to the hard ground his stripy belly dragged in the dirt.

Auto-tuned laughter echoed through the cavern, and bursts of colorful light bounced off the rocky walls. A spotlight shone in a perfect circle on Shreddy, throwing his cowering body into sharp relief.

"You can't hide, Cat." It was the voice of the animated dragon from the Red-Haired Woman's game on the PlayCube. "You're in my realm now."

Shreddy's fur fluffed.

"What do you want, Cat?"

Shreddy pressed his body against the ground, but he couldn't will himself to melt into the dirt. He looked up at the dragon.

Emerald wings, ruby eyes, and belly scales that shimmered like mother of pearl. The dragon had been hidden in the shadows, but now dancing spotlights glittered off of her Technicolor body. She looked magnificent, but she was nothing more than a lowly leech, draining the life away from all the PlayCube players in the neighborhood.

"*Leech*," Shreddy murmured under his whiskers.

"What was that?" the dragon bellowed, her voice climbing to an unreasonable auto-tuned pitch.

"You're a leech," Shreddy said. "You've been draining my human's life away. And I want it back."

The dragon chuckled, her mother-of-pearl belly swelling with the laughter. "Brave cat," she said.

Shreddy didn't feel brave, only right.

"I can't give your human's life back. I need it for my hoard." The dragon swung her giant tail, covered in cobalt spikes, to gesture at a pile of gold coins heaped against the cavern's far wall. "Go, look at them."

Shreddy didn't move.

"Go!" the dragon roared. "Look at how beautiful my gold coins are!"

Terrified, Shreddy scurried across the cavern to the pile of coins. Shivering in terror, he stammered at the giant dragon watching his every move, "Yes, they're…very shiny." She seemed mollified.

The dragon reached one of her talons down and daintily grabbed a single coin between two of her silver claws. "This one belongs to your human."

Shreddy saw a number inscribed on the coin—23. He looked back at the pile of coins and saw they all had different numbers. "What does the number mean?"

"The more life a human gives me, the higher the number. Also, the more valuable." The dragon sneered, showing her topaz teeth, and tossed the Red-Haired Woman's coin back on the pile. "Twenty-three isn't very good. Your human is pathetic."

"If it's not valuable, then let me take it."

"Valuable or not, it's mine!" The tone of the dragon's voice jumped all over, not restraining itself to a single octave. Tendrils of smoke escaped her nostrils. She shifted her emerald wings. Then, she said, "However, I will dance you for it."

Confused, Shreddy asked, "*Dance* me for it?"

"You've watched me dance! I've seen you!" the dragon shouted. "Don't play dumb, Cat."

Shreddy hadn't paid much attention to the rules of the PlayCube game. He did remember the dragon dancing though. She looked ridiculous.

"Cats don't dance," he said.

"Do cats squish if you step on them?"

Shreddy considered his options. They mostly involved twining tentacle-cords and stomping dragon feet. "All right. I'll dance."

A distortion-heavy metal-rock bossa nova song rang through the cavern, drilling its way into Shreddy's spine.

The dragon swayed her tail, shuffled her talons, and flapped her wings—seemingly to three different beats. The air around her exploded in fireworks. She pirouetted looking more like a child's top than a ballerina. Yet flowers and a banner reading, "OUTSTAND-ING!" fell from the dark ceiling of the cavern.

Shreddy tried to sway to the beat, but all he managed was an irritable tail-twitch.

The dragon pirouetted again, and two more banners fell for her.

Shreddy turned in a few circles, pretending for his dignity he was settling down for a nap rather than dancing, but nothing fell from the ceiling for him.

The song ended in a hideous blare of brass.

A rainbow arched over the dragon, and her auto-tuned laughter filled the cavern. "I won, Cat. Play again?"

Shreddy grumbled.

"What was that?" she roared. "You want me to find out whether cats burn if I breathe fire on them?"

Shreddy danced again. And again. By the fifth contest, he'd worked himself up to shifting his weight from one paw to the other and swishing his tail. By the fifteenth, he raised himself to standing on his back paws and did a little jig, earning himself a banner that read, "NICE!"

By the twentieth contest, Shreddy realized the dragon was sucking his life away just like the Red-Haired Woman's. He would dance in this torture chamber until he died. He'd never ever sleep on the Red-Haired Woman's bed again, feel her idle caress in the early morning, or sit on her lap. He was doomed to be an animated, dancing fool, two-dimensional on her TV screen.

Shreddy couldn't take it anymore. Let the dragon burn him, squash him, or strangle him with white tentacle cords. Anything was better than this.

Shreddy ran for the portal home to his living room.

The music stopped.

Deathly silence.

In a small, high voice, the dragon said, "Don't you want to save your game?"

"God no!" Shreddy yowled, ready to leap into the swirling portal.

"Are you sure?" The dragon sounded so sad.

Shreddy twisted one ear to the side, intrigued. "I'm sure," he said. "Delete my game."

The dragon sighed, steam rising from her nostrils. Then she lumbered over to her pile of gold coins, lifted a single coin, and flipped it into the air. It twirled, arcing through the cavern and plopped into a well of lava on the far side.

Shreddy blinked in surprise. "Delete *all* games," he said.

"No!" the dragon wailed, her voice tripping up and down a dozen octaves. Yet, she picked up another coin.

~ * ~

The tentacle cords lay as lifeless as calimari on the living room floor. Shreddy napped smugly on the couch.

Cooper and Susie came tearing in with as much energy as if they hadn't spent the afternoon playing fetch and chase at the dog park. Susie jumped onto the couch, crowding into Shreddy's space. The Red-Haired Woman followed her, grabbing the knobby PlayCube controller off the floor on her way.

"Ew," she said. "Why is this sticky?"

Cooper slobbered the honey off the PlayCube, despite the Red-Haired Woman's protests. She cleaned the honey off the controller with a tissue. Then she tried to start her game.

"What the hell? Level one? I was on level twenty-three!" She pulled her smartphone out of her pocket, touched the screen, and then held it to her ear. "Hey, Tony, are you having trouble with *Dance, Dance, Dragon*?"

Shreddy heard the voice in the phone say, "I emailed customer support. They said it was an irrecoverable server crash. A complete wipe of the system. Everyone's saved games were lost."

"Damn."

"I know. Want to play *Space Blazer Online*?"

Shreddy's ears perked up. He loved watching the tiny space-ships fly around the Red-Haired Woman's computer screen when she played *Space Blazer Online*. And the best part: there was no room for Susie or Cooper on her desk chair.

But there was plenty of room in her lap for a brave, dragon-defying cat.

~ * ~ * ~

Mary E. Lowd is a prolific science-fiction and furry writer in Oregon. She's had more than 200 short stories and a dozen novels published, always with more on the way. Most of them involve spaceships, talking animals, or both. Her work has won numerous awards, and she's been nominated for the Ursa Major Awards more than any other individual. Mary is also the founder and editor of Zooscape.

Learn more at marylowd.com or read more stories at deepskyanchor.com.

Here by Choice

Gerri Leen

Tien Shen watched as Kuan Yin lounged by the waterfall, trailing her hand back and forth through the water as she stared up at the clouds overhead. A subtle odor of lotus surrounded her, reaching him where he sat. She gleamed like an emperor's pearl. A distressed pearl—she cocked her head, listening for some sound and frowning deeply.

"What do you hear?" he asked—he heard nothing, not even with his dragon-keen ears.

She didn't answer him, so he tried to assess her mood. Her eyes glinted, and for a moment, he thought he saw tears, but then she seemed to force a smile as she laid her head back onto the hard ground. But, he could tell she was still listening, that not even the waterfall could drown out whatever it was that called to her.

"What is it you hear?" he asked again.

She finally looked over. "Everyone." This was how she was. This was how she answered. As if she could not spare the breath she no longer needed. She had achieved enlightenment; Nirvana waited. Why was she wasting time lying by this river not answering him?

"You don't have to stay, dragon." She sounded as if she wished he would go.

"It is my honor to guard those who will enter Nirvana." Although in this case, it was rather a pain as well.

She lifted her head and gave him a look that could only be considered amused—at his expense. Then she lay back again and closed her eyes.

He made sure no one would threaten her before settling down some distance away, and she glanced at him, as if checking he hadn't gotten too close. He seemed to make her unhappy—had since he'd told her he was her guide to paradise's door. But he didn't know why that distressed her. So many were striving for Nirvana; she had achieved it, but no joy lit her face.

Letting his head come to rest on the softer scales of his side, Tien Shen listened to the water. The roaring sound of the river crashing over the rocks lulled him into sleep.

He woke slowly, blinking to clear his eyes. Then he blinked again, not believing what he saw—or didn't see: the woman he was supposed to protect was gone.

He closed his eyes, trying to find a trace of her with his inside-eyes. Nothing.

He listened, heard only the cry of the hawk, the grunt of the tiger, and the swish-snap of a squirrel in the underbrush.

He sniffed, breathing in the scent of evergreen; of hard, sandy soil; the blue smell of water; the hot, red odor of the pepper flowers he loved to eat. But no scent of pearls and lotus, no trace of the woman who had ridden the wheel of life until she'd earned paradise.

Taking to the air through force of will, he soared, annoyed by an eagle that flew near and peered at him, as if unsure how an un-winged thing like Tien Shen could live in its world. He roared at the bird, and the eagle soared away, but not without a defiant cry.

"Kuan Yin?" He formed the words slowly, sending them out into the world. They fell to the earth as rain, the drops merging to form the symbol for her name.

She did not appear. She did not call out. He still could not smell her. And the earth did not give her up, did not whisper to him that she had been there. So he flew on.

He called for her over and over. Frogs echoed her name, but they were just playing. A deer bolted from a thicket as Tien Shen's calls grew more frantic.

One woman, ready for paradise, and he had lost her.

"Dragon," he heard in his inside-ears, and then he saw her with his inside-eyes. She was with a group of women who were studying a writing of a kind he'd never seen before. Curious, he settled on the ground just beyond them.

One of the women let out a little squeak, but the rest went on writing, not even looking over. The first woman stared at him, as if she could not believe what she was seeing.

"Chao Ma, pay attention to the lesson," Kuan Yin said softly, and the woman bowed and went back to creating the simple letters, so long and angular compared to traditional writing.

Tien Shen inched toward Kuan Yin, until he was right next to her, and she turned to look at him. He found he could not meet her eyes. But what did he have to feel guilty for? He was only trying to do what he'd been told. To see her safely to her rightful reward.

"I worried you, dragon?" The lotus smell changed, grew spicy, and he imagined it was regret that caused it.

"You did." He sighed and wished he could tell what she was thinking.

"I am sorry. I do not wish to cause pain, even to you."

He accepted her apology—weak as it was—with a nod of his head. "It is time to go, my lady."

"Do you know why they're here?" She glanced down at the feet of one woman. They were bound, and Tien Shen knew the woman would hobble a little as she walked.

"They are bored?"

"Hardly." Kuan Yin laughed, and her laughter was cold and hard and full of pain he didn't expect. She glanced again at the feet of the woman. "I think it is less cruel to simply cut them off."

To his shock, he felt her hand on his back. "The language is called Nushu." She rubbed his neck softly, her fingers hitting spots he hadn't even realized were itching. "It is a language only for women.

He knew women were denied education. "You taught them this?"

"As I was taught."

"Who first handed you the brush?"

"I don't remember. So many lives. So many first lessons."

But he suspected she remembered every one of those lessons. His look must have told her he didn't believe her, because she laughed, and this time her laughter was like a brook as it bubbled over smooth stones or like the sound the sun made as the clouds tickled it.

The sounds of paradise—why was she waiting? She leaned against him, her fingers still working their magic on his scales.

"Why are we here?" he asked her.

"I am here because I want to be. Why are you here, dragon?"

"To serve you."

She looked displeased. "That is the wrong answer." And like that, she was gone.

He sighed, and Chao Ma left her writing and walked over to him. She reached out, then jerked her hand back.

"It's all right."

"You don't bite?"

"Well, I won't. This time." He let out a little rumble of pleasure as she traced the pattern of his scales. Her touch moved him almost as much as Kuan Yin's. He was used to spirit creatures, insubstantial and fey, with touches just as light.

"Why do you study the language?" he asked her.

She swallowed hard. "Because it gives us some measure of freedom. It allows us to have secrets. No man can read it."

"Why do you need secrets?" Secrets had never been a good thing among dragons. They usually meant something bad was going to happen.

"My husband is cruel to me. Tan Lao's husband cheats on her. Mei Ling's brother sold her to an old man she does not love."

"How is your husband cruel?" Tien Shen did not care about the others. But this woman who was scratching his back deserved better.

"He yells. Hits, sometimes. Not all the time. Just…when he's angry."

Tien Shen sensed Kuan Yin reaching for him, the sound of her voice loud in his inside-ears. He heard the creak of the door between the worlds being opened, the rustle of a beaded curtain being pulled back. "I have to go."

"All right." But Chao Ma held on to him.

He rested his snout on her arm for a moment, was surprised to see tears in her eyes. She pulled away, but one of her tears fell onto his leg, and it burned as it sank into his scales.

Kuan Yin called again, and he forced himself away from Chao Ma and appeared where he felt his charge calling from.

Kuan Yin stood in front of the brightest light imaginable. It was so beautiful—Tien Shen never tired of seeing the sight, but then it wasn't one he saw very often. Those who attained Nirvana were few.

Soft breezes blew out of the light. A subtle smell of flowers and spices wafted over to him; Kuan Yin's scent seemed to grow in reaction, sweet and strong and still distinct even among such glory.

"Dragon?" Her voice was so small.

"You must go." But then he heard it: a small sob. And another. And another. His leg where Chao Ma's tear had fallen began to burn.

Kuan Yin turned and stared out at the world, her back to Nirvana. Her eyes welled up, then she blinked, and the tears ran freely down her cheeks. He moved closer, lifted his leg and let her see the scales where the woman's tear had fallen were turning silver.

"I hear them all, Tien Shen," she whispered. "The cries of the whole world."

He nodded. "I hear them now, too." He looked past her, at the beauty that was Nirvana. At the peace it promised. It was everything this remarkable woman had worked for.

It was what Tien Shen wanted for her.

And yet...

"I can't go just now." She took a deep breath. "I'm needed here."

The beaded curtain fell back, dimming the light. The breeze died, and the smell of Nirvana's flowers became fainter and fainter, as the scent of Kuan Yin grew.

Compassion. This was what compassion smelled like.

She turned to look at the door. "I'm needed here."

It slammed shut.

But the light remained. Growing brighter and brighter, and Tien Shen realized it was coming from her.

"My Goddess," he murmured, bowing his head. As he looked down, he realized the silver patch on his leg was reflecting her glow.

"There is much to do," she said, pulling the light around her like a cloak. It finally dimmed, drawn inside her. But he knew she could call it back if she wanted to.

He studied his leg; it still shone just a little. Even with no light to reflect.

She began to walk back into the world.

He hurried to get in front of her, and her eyes flashed with annoyance. Then he knelt, and said, "You should ride. I can be of help to you."

She touched his head, hugged him hard, her face pressed against his. Then, without a word, she jumped on his back and waited.

He listened, heard the loudest cries to the east. Without asking her, he flew for the rising sun.

Her hand tightened on his neck, and she sang a song he did not know, her voice beautiful in its rawness.

"You gave up paradise," he said softly.

"How could I go there when even one person suffers?"

He had no answer to that. Only, he'd seen others do it. Perhaps Nirvana wasn't for the perfect. Maybe it was for the almost perfect. And someday they'd be back again to find perfection by helping those who still strove—and hurt.

"But it was beautiful, wasn't it?" she murmured. "And it smelled good."

He knew it was the last she'd ever say about it.

Originally published in "Life Without Crows" - Hadley Rille Books, 2010

~ * ~ * ~

Gerri Leen lives in Northern Virginia and originally hails from Seattle. In addition to being an avid reader, she's passionate about horse racing, tea, and collecting encaustic art and raku pottery. She has stories and poems in *The Magazine of Fantasy & Science Fiction*, *Nature*, *Strange Horizons*, *Dark Matter* and others, and is a member of SFWA and HWA.

See more at gerrileen.com.

Dragonomics

Lance Schonberg

A tiny echo of breath down one of the small ventilation tunnels pulled Kahruk from sleep. Keeping the cavern from becoming too stuffy in warmer months, the tunnels also had the disadvantage of being large enough to let in anything smaller than two cows walking abreast. But prey didn't come to him very often so he kept his eyes closed, holding as still as possible. Something itched in the back of his skull.

Soft footsteps joined the breathing near the tunnel's end. Only one set, but he wished his snack had waited another week.

Kahruk pried open one eye, watching through the tiniest slit he could manage. Something warm stepped into the cavern and took a few careful steps toward him, padding sounds absorbed by the gloom before reaching the dragon's ears. Then it stopped and stood still for a dozen slow heartbeats before sitting down on the stub of a stalagmite and lowering something to the cavern floor.

Kahruk fought the urge to frown. Usually the only mortals foolish enough to approach so close were brainless young knights trying to make a name for themselves, brainless young thieves looking to get rich quickly, or on rare occasions, brainless young virgins demanding to be sacrificed for the good of their people. The virgins, at least, he was happy to oblige. The knights and thieves, well, he was happy to oblige them in the same way, if not quite how they hoped.

But no one had ever come to stare before. It was almost, well, rude.

Tiny air currents tickled his nostrils with the prey's scent. Human and probably male. Lying on his side began to put a kink in Kahruk's neck, so he stretched and rolled onto his stomach. The human's jump of fright almost made the discomfort worthwhile and he stretched out one leg to try duplicating the reaction.

The third time he moved, the human didn't jump. Instead, it surprised Kahruk by speaking. "You're not really asleep, are you?"

He let first one eye and then the other open wide. The small warm body resolved into a more solid figure. "Er, no." Kahruk raised his head several feet and tilted it to the left, stretching the right side of his neck. Several loud pops rewarded the effort. "What gave it away, if I might ask?" He repeated the action on the left.

The human sighed, slouching a little then straightening again. "You were moving around too much. Restless sleep isn't unusual in humans but according to all the legends and songs that mention it, dragons sleep 'a deep and motionless sleep.' Too much uncontrolled thrashing around could bring the roof down or break a wing, I'd guess."

He'd never really thought about it before. "Ah. True, I suppose. You see surprisingly well in the dark for a human."

"I sat about halfway up the tunnel for an hour or so to let my eyes adjust. It's not quite completely dark in here."

"Ah." Kahruk arched his back and unfolded his wings. Several vertebrae ground together and the cracks echoed in the cavern. He didn't feel quite comfortable talking to his food and had exhausted as much mental energy as he cared to for the moment. All things considered, he'd rather go back to sleep. "Well mortal, I suppose I'll have to eat you now."

"I'm not." His snack shook its head.

The dragon blinked and cocked his head to one side. "What?"

"Mortal. I'm not mortal. I'm *im*mortal."

"Ah. Well, that doesn't really—"

"And I'd rather you didn't eat me. I came here to ask a favor of you." It flinched as if expecting some expression of draconic rage.

Caught with his mouth open, Kahruk closed it again without finding a response. The little human didn't strike him as a thief, or a knight, or a sacrificial virgin. He understood intellectually there must be other kinds of humans, but he'd never encountered one at close range before and found himself at a loss for a new category. Each statement the man made seemed to push past the boundaries of Kahruk's experience. "A favor? Well, um, I suppose I might hear you out as a sort of last request."

"That's good of you. Do you mind if I explain a little before I get to the favor itself?"

"Not at all." Playing for time. Finally something Kahruk understood. Perhaps it would provide some amusement while giving him time to gather his thoughts.

Sighing, the human ran a hand through his short hair and scratched his nose. Kahruk settled back into the mound of coins and a few rolled almost to the prey's boots. Surprisingly, it ignored the coins in favour of maintaining eye contact. "I don't know how extensive your knowledge of humans is, but a very tiny number of us are naturally immortal. One out of every ten million births, or something like that. Most humans have no idea and I don't know which of the myriad gods is responsible for the joke, but there are times I wish they hadn't bothered. Immortality is dreadfully dull most of the time." His own eyes now well awake and adjusted, Kahruk saw the human lift one side of his mouth, but couldn't quite read it as a smile. "If I might ask, how old are you?"

Gold coins made a satisfying rustle under his chin as he pressed his jaw into the comfortable pile and tilted his ears forward. "Nearly fifteen hundred years have passed since my birth."

The human nodded. "In your middle years then, assuming any accuracy at all in the legends. Would you believe I'm nearly twice your age?"

"I find that difficult to believe."

"Two thousand eight hundred and fifty-six, give or take. Every time someone changes the calendar I think I lose a few months. I've seen empires rise and fall and new ones crawl from the ashes." He waved an arm in a wide arc and grinned. "Sorry for the cliché. Getting back to the point, people who live forever eventually run into each other. And we congregate, at least a little. Who else do we really have anything in common with? Boredom loves company."

Something felt wrong with that statement, but the human didn't pause long enough for Kahruk to consider what or why.

"Six of us agreed to a decade-long scavenger hunt to amuse ourselves. We each have to find one hundred rare items, or as many as we can, and meet on a certain date to determine the winner. Everyone has a different list and every item on those lists was randomly chosen by lot from a larger list we all helped compile. I have one item left and thirty-two days to return to Shandrahar with it."

Eyes narrow, a low growl rumbled deep in Kahruk's throat. "I do not think I like where this is going." He snaked out five feet of forked tongue, tasting the air near his prey.

The human looked around the dim cavern, probably for something large and very, very strong to hide behind, but his eyes came back to Kahruk. "A hair from one of your ear tufts."

Anger burned through Kahruk's veins and he reared up on his hind legs, wings spread wide. A few coins rained down, bouncing from rocks and the human fell backwards off his seat, hands splayed out behind him.

"But I have an idea I might trade for it and my life!"

Rearing back to strike, Kahruk opened his jaws wide.

"You see, I think I know how to—"

Kahruk's snarl echoed through the cavern and his jaws sped down and forward, saliva pooling under his tongue.

"—vastly increase the size of your hoard with really very little effort on your part at all!" The words spilled out into the air so fast Kahruk didn't know if he heard them all, but his jaws snapped shut just short of the target and he exhaled, blowing hot air across the human. He let his wings drift down into a less aggressive position as his eyes focused on a distant, imagined point.

How long since he'd thought about adding to his hoard? Flying out to wreck a castle or a caravan for its gold was fine for a young dragon, but not long after you had enough to make a comfortable bed you came to realize it wasn't really worth the effort anymore. Getting the arrows out of your scales could take days. His mind drifted across those last few raids half a thousand years ago before coming back to the present. He had no idea how long he'd passed in memory and thought. "Explain." He spat the word but the human's flinch did nothing for his residual anger.

The human collapsed onto his back and blew a wisp of air across Kahruk's snout, a tiny, invisible parody of dragon flame. He took a long moment climb back onto the stalactite, pushing the shreds of Kahruk's patience aside.

"Speak."

Eyes wide, the human nodded. "Yes, of course." He took a deep breath and tried to smile. Kahruk only stared, moving his head back just far enough to properly focus his eyes. "Dragons are extremely magical creatures, aren't they?"

The question wasn't worth a response. He continued to stare as the human's eyes flicked to his jaws and back.

"Ah, yes, well then. Dragons *are* extremely magical creatures.

Gradually, over centuries, some of that native magic leeches into the gold and silver and other items that make up the hoard, giving each piece a store of magic potential energy." He waved an arm at the mound of precious metals underneath and around Kahruk. "That energy can be used by a wizard to fuel spells instead of using his or her own energy." His gaze flicked to Kahruk's teeth again. "Well, the point being, um, do you have any idea of the value of Dragon Gold on the open market?"

Kahruk let the last of his anger go in a sigh. Apparently, to have some chance of finding out what the bargain might be, he would have to participate in the conversation. "I do not." It had never before occurred to him to think about it. He didn't know what the market was or how it could be opened. Today seemed unfortunately filled with new ideas.

Hand to his forehead, the human rubbed his right temple with the thumb. "It's a matter of economics. Supply and Demand. There are a limited number of dragons in the world and you breed very slowly. I mean, how often does a she-dragon rise to mate?"

"Every century or so."

"And how many eggs will she lay?"

"One. Sometimes two."

"So even though you live for a long time, your numbers don't increase quickly. Humans, comparatively, breed like flies. In spite of a variety of wars, disasters, and plagues, there are twice as many today as there were five hundred years ago, which means there are twice as many wizards."

"So?"

"So there are only three ways I can think of for Dragon Gold to reach the market. First, a dragon dies and another dragon doesn't scoop up its treasure right away. Probably doesn't happen very often." He grinned, a brief flash of white.

"Second, some brave young knight gets lucky and actually kills the dragon he's after and lives to haul away some of its treasure before it gets scooped up by another dragon. I suspect that particular event is in the realm of legend. Collective wishful thinking on the part of bards and heroes.

"Last, a reasonably intelligent thief waits till a dragon is out hunting, runs in, stuffs a small sack, and runs out again without getting caught. Still pretty rare, but I'll bet it happens a lot more often than you're willing to admit, eh?" A new grin appeared on the human's face and didn't quite go away. "It certainly seems the most likely of the three."

"Perhaps." It happened to Kahruk just last month while he'd been out for a few cows.

The human waved one hand, palm open, vaguely in Kahruk's direction. "So not much Dragon Gold gets to the market for sale and since a single coin can fuel a large number of spells, your average wizard will pay a lot for it. Limited supply. High demand. Every piece of gold in this chamber is worth at least twenty-five times its own weight."

Kahruk looked at the human and said nothing for several seconds. Counting was one thing—he'd counted his entire hoard on more than one occasion to pass the time—but anything resembling mathematics had never been necessary in his experience. "That's a lot then, is it?"

Biting his lower lip, the human reached down and picked up one of the coins Kahruk had disturbed earlier. It seemed to pulse in the tiny fingers and his eyes narrowed, tracking the coin, *his* coin. Body tense, every instinct screaming at him to eat the thief, Kahruk waited for the human to continue.

"Because of the magic they've gained from you, selling about one coin out of twenty, would double the size of your hoard."

Kahruk's ears strained forward and his nostrils flared. Sliding his tongue across several teeth, he fixed his eyes on the human, not watching the coin as it dropped back to the cavern floor. "Double?" It skittered across the stone to bump against a claw-tip. Kahruk felt his body relax.

"Plus a little. Although, you'd need a broker."

A vision clinked into Kahruk's mind of the most comfortable sleeping mound he possibly imagine, gold enough to wallow in, gold enough to fill the cavern. Then the last word reached into his brain to push the vision a little to the side. He wiggled his massive body, burrowing into a pile of gold that suddenly seemed much smaller. "What is a broker?" Gold coins kept dancing in his head and he found it hard to focus.

The human shrugged, still smiling. "An agent who sells the gold for you, taking a small portion as payment for the transaction, usually three or four percent. Um, three or four coins out of a hundred."

The human held up his hands at Kahruk's narrowed gaze. "Unless, of course, you plan to go to the market and sell it yourself."

Kahruk considered for a moment. He couldn't carry more than a very small part of his hoard and would certainly lose some as he did. While gone, he would leave the greater part vulnerable to thieves. And the inevitable panic his appearance would generate could hardly be conducive to any kind of business. "I suppose a broker would be necessary. The difficulty would be in finding someone I could trust." The word nearly stuck on his lips.

"Yes, I can see how that could be an issue. Still, there are any number of reputable brokers in every major city. I'd be happy to make a few discreet inquiries for you as part of our exchange."

"Exchange?"

"Please don't tell me you've forgotten. I'd hate to have to go through it all over again, especially the bit with the teeth."

"I have not forgotten, but neither have I agreed."

"I know. Take your time thinking it over. I'm not *really* in a hurry." The human cocked his head to one side as if some strange thought had occurred to him and didn't quite make sense. "It just struck me that there's something odd about your speech."

"How so?" Kahruk thought his speech perfectly fine, cultured even, though he had only other dragons to compare to, and not many of those or very often.

"Well, maybe I've heard too many legends and sagas, but they all hold dragon speech as very formal and usually archaic, full of thees and thous and so on."

Kahruk shook his head twice. "Not that I've ever noticed. Storytellers like to dress things up a bit, I expect."

"Probably. They do it with nearly everything else, but it seems universally accepted. Maybe it's meant to imply great age and wisdom."

Or flattery, which never hurt, but Kahruk knew a distraction when he heard one. "You claim twice my age. Is that how you speak?"

"No, but I'm not a dragon and I won't admit to great wisdom, either." He spread his arms. "I'm here, after all."

"Hnh. Safer perhaps, if you'd met your immortal companions one item short of your full list?"

One side of the human's mouth crept up again. "Perhaps." A

tiny rumbling sound came from its stomach. "While you're think-ing, would you mind if I had lunch?"

"Go right ahead."

"Thank you." The human picked up his bag and pulled out several small packages. Kahruk identified most by scent: bread, cheese, salted pork and a tiny flask of some sour smelling liquid. "I suppose it's impolite of me not to offer to share, but I don't think I have enough food you'd even notice."

"Enjoy your meal. I fed several days ago so I'm not exactly hungry." The human took three quick swallows from the flask and Kahruk wondered if the human understood the thought behind the words. He could find space in his stomach if he had to.

While the human ate, Kahruk relaxed on his hoard and consid-ered the proposition. It would be nice to have a little more gold lying around. Middle aged he might be, but his body grew a little longer each decade. He probably had enough gold, but a little more was always nice. And double? Well, double would be very nice. And if he didn't have quite enough, by the time he had difficulty sleeping, he'd be too old to do anything about it. With every coin turned into two…the more he considered the idea, the more attractive it became. By the time the human finished re-packing the remains of his lunch, Kahruk had reached his decision. Biting down on a yawn, he met the eyes of his former prey. "I think we have a bargain."

A bright smile blossomed on his face as the human leapt up. "Excellent!"

"Subject, of course, to one condition."

The human dropped back down onto his stone seat, not quite losing the smile. "And that would be?"

Kahruk turned his head and leaned forward, spearing the wary human with one eye. "You will act as my broker."

Seeming to shrink a bit, the human licked his lips, perhaps looking for his voice. "Um, me?"

"Who better?" Coins clinked as Kahruk pulled his head back to a more comfortable viewing position. "I do not know the precise qualifications of a broker, but I *am* certain that trust is important. You approached me openly and honestly. I do not think that trust would be misplaced." Though it might be difficult. As eyes began to droop again, Kahruk wondered why the human couldn't have waited a few more days. Resting his chin on the stone floor, he pulled his lips up in hopes of mimicking a human smile. "Plus, with nearly three thousand years of life, you have certainly had a great deal of practice in bargaining. Valuable experience. Finally, I do not think you will run from me screaming as would the average mortal. You are the logical choice." He watched the human, trying to gauge his reaction, but this conversation needed to end and soon. The coins around him seemed to be glowing, hardly an illusion produced by an alert mind. Kahruk needed to sleep.

The human sucked on his lower lip. Did an echo of his own thoughts roll through the small head? Money was nice. A little more couldn't hurt. It stood and gave a sharp nod. "Four percent."

Kahruk's drooping eyes popped open. While he had a hard time visualizing a fraction of anything, he did know four was more than three. "You said *between* three and four percent. Since you are keeping your life, long and boring as it is, you should be willing to settle for the lower figure."

"Ah, but since you'll be receiving the benefit of three millennia of experience, you should allow the higher." The human grinned and shrugged. "Besides, that experience will get you a better deal every time. You'll make more because I'll work harder for that extra percent."

Kahruk exhaled, blowing warm air across his new business associate. His eyes slid closed and a short yawn slipped past his teeth. "Very well. You will earn it, I think." The hoard warmed his body as sleep reached out for him. "But we can discuss this later."

"Of course, there's plenty of time."

Was there? Plenty of time for what? Sluggish thoughts rolled away from him. He'd been talking to someone. Something about gold. More gold? How odd. He had plenty of gold, didn't he? More than enough to be comfortable.

"Sleep well, my friend. I'll see you next month."

Original published in Cast of Wonders podcast, Episode 76, April 2013

~ * ~ * ~

In the middle of talking to one of his children about how important it is to follow your dreams, **Lance Schonberg** began to wonder why and when he'd stopped following his. Gathering up a few salvageable shreds of unfinished stories, he began writing (nearly) every day, and on Christmas Day that year, after the rest of his family had gone to bed, he began his first novel. *Dragon Summer* took exactly five months to complete and came in at just over 108,000 words. Fortunately, no one will ever be allowed to read it, but it did put him back on the writer's path.

He's written several novels and many shorter works in the years since, and has had twenty or so of the stories see publication. Continuing to heed the keyboard's call, at any given moment, Lance is working on a novel and at least one short story—probably more—most of which fall into the broad buckets of Science Fiction or Fantasy. He's currently conspiring to commit a podcast of some of his fiction.

Lance can be found lurking on his blog at lanceschonberg.com, on his Facebook author page, and sometimes even on Twitter as WritingDad.

The Price of Everything

Shenoa Carroll-Bradd

She called herself Penelope, a name she'd once heard a knight whisper with his dying breath. She had liked the sound of it, and any word worth a man's last breath must be powerful indeed. No one else used her name, though. No one knew. The robed man standing before her now called her "beast" and "magnificent" at turns, but refused to make eye contact. She guessed, from the state of his beard and the faint smell of sulfur, he was some sort of wizard. He chattered about his power, his renown, as his minions scurried behind him, carrying armloads of treasure and gifts into her cave. The sound of their offerings clattering at the foot of her hoard sent waves of pleasure up her spine and tingles down the length of her wings. She considered, while the figure rambled, how easy it would be to simply exhale, and turn all these skittering creatures to ash. But flame took so much out of her these days.

At last, the loads of treasure stopped, and the man finally fell silent. He raised beady eyes to her, waiting. Ah yes, her part of the bargain.

Penelope heaved herself up from her bed of gold and padded to the back of the cave, where she kept the bones of past meals and the least shiny of her treasures. When she returned, rolling the prismatic egg before her, the man's greedy eyes lit up. She felt a momentary pang. Was this the right decision? Her brightest memories were of teaching her whelps to fly, and watching them scorch their first rabbits. Penelope shook her head. Her scales were growing brittle, and her teeth were losing their edge. She was in no shape to raise a hatchling.

The man clapped his hands like an overeager child. "It's more beautiful than I imagined."

Penelope looked critically at the egg, but all she saw reflected on its opal shell were the painful hours she had struggled to push it out. "Your imagination does not impress." She nudged her barter forward, and held up a claw when the man looked about to speak. "Do not tell me any more of your imagination, or your intentions.

Our business is concluded."

It took four of his minions to carry the egg away. He bowed again and again. "Most gracious of you, most gracious, and please, let me know if you ever find yourself..." he waved both hands before his belly, pantomiming pregnancy.

Penelope snorted a thin, steaming cloud. "I won't."

He nodded and bowed some more, then backed out of her cave.

Penelope clambered back to the top of her treasure heap and settled in, curling her tail around the newest additions. If the egg was meant for components, that heavy orb would supply a lifetime's worth of spells. But if the wizard intended to hatch it, he'd better know what he was doing, or her final whelp would wreak havoc and death as soon as the shell cracked.

And, if she was very unlucky, it might find its way back home. Penelope shifted, loosing a clattering landslide of coins and jewels. She was too old to deal with entitled youngsters, and she'd be damned if the little brat came back expecting an inheritance.

~ * ~ * ~

Shenoa Carroll-Bradd lives in Southern California with her brother and dancing dog. She writes whatever tickles her fancy, from fantasy to horror and erotica. Say hello on twitter @ShenoaSays or drop by her digital hideout at www.sbcbfiction.net

Here be Dragons

Violet Addison and David N. Smith

He could smell trouble.

A dragon always could.

The intertwined scents of smoke and blood had reached his nostrils and interrupted the deep, comfortable sleep of his winter hibernation. Rortkazor opened his eyes, his lizard-like pupils narrowing, as they slowly became accustomed to the shafts of daylight spilling in through the shattered roof of Calling Keep. Rising up off his bed of silver coins, he unfurled his wings, stretched them out and shook off the dull ache caused by many weeks of sleep, as he breathed in the tell-tale odors through his snout.

Cattle blood.

Burning thatch.

Human fear.

He recognized them all.

One of the farmsteads on the northern edge of his territory was being raided. The small groups of humans that lived in such settlements had over recent decades started keeping increasingly large numbers of cattle, which he had become accustomed to dining on throughout the summer months, but now someone or something was destroying his precious food supply. It was an intrusion he would not tolerate.

Pulling in his wings, he leapt upwards, squeezed through the hole in the roof and launched himself out into the sky. Spreading his wings wide, he trapped the cold wind beneath them, using it to propel himself upward, rising high enough he could see the Snowtooth Mountains that marked the northern edge of his territory.

Beyond those white peaks there lay only rock, snow and The Frozen Sea. There was little worth hunting there, except sea birds and the odd snow bear, which he left to Zellith, an old Ice Dragon who had claimed the land many centuries before Rortkazor had even hatched.

The dales before the mountains were his concern; and one of the farmsteads was burning.

The Dragon's Hoard

Several columns of black smoke were drifting upward, congealing in the sky into a single massive cloud, raining down ash and fragments of burning timber as it rolled across the countryside. Through the haze of smoke, he could see the main house, stables and barns were all ablaze. This was no human raid, they would merrily loot and steal from each other, sometimes even kill one another, but rarely would they destroy their hand-built dwellings. No, this was the work of one of his own kind. This was the work of a dragon.

This was the fifth time in less than a decade another dragon had dared to raid his territory, each time he had dealt brutally with the intruder, taking an eye from one, ripping the tail from another and giving the other three significant burns. In the past this would have sent a clear message, but evidently this was no longer enough, as now yet another intruder was raiding his food reserve.

Granted, there was perhaps enough livestock available to keep at least two or three dragons fed, but he knew all too well if he took too much from the humans, then sooner or later, they would recruit experienced Dragonslayers to eliminate the problem; which is why any intruder who started attacking their farmsteads had to be dealt with rapidly and ruthlessly.

He did not recognize the scent of the intruder, which he could now detect under the blood and burning, which meant it was not one of the Forest Dragons who had previously attacked his land. This was something new.

Rortkazor descended through the smoke, settling on the ground with one final great flap of his wings, which blasted away much of the surrounding haze of smoke.

In the center of a nearby paddock lay the carcass of a partly eaten bull, around which were the smoking remains of at least three human corpses.

The humans kept only a carefully selected number of bulls for breeding, preferring instead to keep more of the milk producing females. As such, he had learnt never to take the bulls, partly as it would reduce his own future food supply, but also because due to its greater value, the humans were sometimes just foolish enough to try to defend it.

A dragon screamed; a trilling, high pitched squeal, filled with pain and fury.

Rortkazor instinctively leapt toward the sound, with two great flaps of his wings, he rose over the burning barn, swept over the flames and through the clouds of smoke, emerging directly above a furious battle. Half a dozen humans, armed with pitchforks and scythes, were ringed around the sleek black form of a snarling Sand Dragon.

He had only ever seen a few of her kind before.

Sand Dragons rarely survived long in the north. They were physically much smaller than normal dragons, being not much larger than a bear, making them potential prey for the packs of wolves or for glory seeking villagers. She was many thousands of miles from home, well beyond her normal desert habitat, hurt and bleeding, surrounded by hostile humans. Her right wing had been slashed, torn through, most likely by a scythe, meaning each time she tried to fly away, she inevitably sank back into the circle of her enemies.

The humans glanced up at him, as he hovered over them, each beat of his wings buffeting them with air, whilst also enraging the spitting, burning flames of the barn behind him. Their eyes widened with fear. Hurried glances were exchanged. Fighting one dragon, which was smaller than most, would have seemed possible to them, but facing him down was another matter entirely; whilst the prospect of being caught between two fire-breathing dragons, was a position no sane human ever wanted to find themselves in.

He should have left then, leaving them to their battle, let them kill the intruding dragon for him, but he hesitated for just a fraction of a second too long.

The humans ran.

Scythes and pitchforks were dropped, as they rushed headlong across the fields, screaming as they went, abandoning their crops, livestock and burning homes in fear of dragons.

That was the last thing he wanted.

The story would spread like fire through a dry forest.

The dragonslayers would come.

He bore down in fury on the intruder, spitting fuel from his throat, which he ignited with a blast of flame from his nostrils, covering his enemy in a rain of liquid fire. She panicked, beating her wings, trying to rise out of the spewing flames, but with her tattered wing flailing uselessly, she instead toppled to one side and crashed to the ground in a writhing, burning heap.

It should have been enough to seriously wound her, but instead she rolled across the grass, crushing out the flames, shedding her burnt scales. She rose moments later, appearing unscathed, with a layer of fresh scales revealed in the smoking holes of her hide.

He had heard of this odd physiological deformity in dragons before, it was rare, but while having multiple layers of thin scale made them more susceptible to claws, swords and lances, it also made them almost completely invulnerable to flame attacks. Most dragons saw it as a source of shame, a throwback to their ancient history, before they had needed thicker scales to survive the blades of the humans, when primitive dragons would actually kill one another, but now her layers of thin scale had momentarily given her the advantage, just as they would have done in fiery fights of the past.

She spat at him, covering him in a great arc of liquid fuel, which broke across his snout, blinding him as the acidic fuel burnt his eyes. Roaring in pain, he crashed to the ground.

Seething with fury, he blinked several times, washing the stinging fluid from his eyes, until a blurry image of the burning barn swam back into view.

The black scaled dragon had slunk inside the burning building, clambered up into a hay loft, and positioned itself amongst the burning timbers, where it sat glowering at him with thin yellow eyes.

"Come and finish me, if you can," she snarled. "Coward!"

In fury, he almost charged at her, but over the years of living alongside the humans he had learnt to be increasingly cautious, and he paused just long enough to realize she was intentionally trying to lure him into a trap.

One beat of her wings would have fanned the flames, turning the inside of the barn into an inferno, while he was still covered in her thick, sticky fuel, which by now would have seeped far beneath his scales. He would have been roasted alive.

He considered launching another stream of his own fire into the building, forcing her outside, but even a minor back wind would ignite the fuel still stuck to his snout. He took a step backwards, suddenly conscious of the burning embers drifting on the wind.

"Get out of my territory!" he roared, pawing angrily at the ground with his claws, venting his frustration by gouging huge rifts in the earth.

The Sand Dragon stared at him.

"I cannot fly," she hissed, raising her wing, revealing the bloody slit that had been scythed into her flesh. "It will take days to heal. So, if you will not permit me to stay, it would seem this duel will have to be to the death."

He growled.

It had been more than seventy years since he had taken the life of another dragon, an act for which he still felt deeply ashamed, despite the fact he had been battling to protect his life and land. He could never again bring himself to purposefully end the life of another dragon, not if there was any compromise he could offer instead.

"You have a week," he snapped. "If you cannot fly by then, you can crawl."

"And where should I go?"

Rortkazor blinked. He had not expected an argument, when he had generously decided to spare her life.

"Home! Back to which ever desert you skulked out of!"

"Impossible. The humans have staked out every stream and watering hole there is." She glanced nervously upward at the creaking, burning rafters above her; she may be impervious to the fire, but half a ton of collapsing roof was still a considerable concern. "I can never go home."

"Then go anywhere else. Not here. I don't care where. This land is mine."

"Really?" She frowned. "Because there's an awful lot of humans on it."

A rafter at the far end of the burning building suddenly snapped in the heat, bringing the far side of the roof crashing down. The Sand Dragon leapt forward, bounding down out of the hay loft, diving outside, sweeping past him, as the entire structure collapsed in on itself.

Rortkazor stamped a clawed paw down on the fleeing dragon's tail, pulling her to a sudden halt. He was half tempted to tighten his grip. Her thin scales would shatter easily under his claws; in a moment her tail would be just a bloody stump. She glanced backward, her yellow eyes widening in fear, as she evidently guessed the malicious thoughts rippling through his mind.

"Leave me no tail, and I'll be here for months, while it regrows."

He let go of the appendage, letting her pull it from his grip, as she turned to face him. Spreading his wings wide, he launched himself up into the air, in case she was tempted to make one last effort to fight him; it would only take her one blast of fire to ignite the fuel that had seeped beneath his scales. She circled beneath him, bemused by his caution.

"You're not still scared, are you?" she called. "I'm half your size, can't fly and have already been saved and defeated by you in one day. I, Elzoreth, do most gratefully accept your magnanimous offer to stay and recover. I promise you will get no further trouble from me."

"If you're still here in a week," he snarled. "I'll remove your wings, your tail and your head. In that order. Understood?"

"Yes." She lowered her eyes, with an obviously feigned humbleness. "It would be rude to out stay my welcome. Got it."

"There's a cave at the base of the nearest mountain, which will serve you well as a shelter. Stay out of my way and, most importantly, leave the humans alone."

"No humans?!" She scowled. "What am I supposed to eat?"

"Anything else!"

"Not even a little human?"

"Especially not the little humans!"

"But there is nothing else! They've domesticated every animal in a thousand miles of here, they pretend they own everything!" She glanced around at the burning ruins of the farm and shrugged. "So what should I do next time I'm hungry?"

"There are wolves in the forest."

"Too dangerous to hunt."

"They're not as dangerous as humans," he snapped. "If you're not up to hunting wolf, then stay hungry. Then leave."

He swung away from her, swooping back through the smoke, passing the burning farmhouse and flying back south across the dale.

"What did these humans do to you?!" she called after him.

"Nothing," he replied. "And I'd like to keep it that way."

She would be trouble.

She wasn't afraid of humans, which is why she had been foolish enough to attack the farmstead, and probably accounted for why she had needed to flee so far from home. Like rats, humans got everywhere. It had taken him many years to realize he had no choice but to tolerate them, now she would have to learn the same lesson, or she would inevitably end up dead on the end of a dragonslayer's spear.

He descended back to the ground, just beside the ruins of Calling Castle, took a dip in the moat to remove the Sand Dragon's fuel, then crawled back through the hole in the roof of the Keep and settled back down onto his bed of silver coins.

He curled himself into a loop, positioned his chin on the end of his tail and closed his eyes, hoping to return to the safe, comfortable sleep of hibernation. Next time he opened them , with luck, the interloper would be gone.

~ * ~

Humans.

Their smell was unmistakable.

Rortkazor's eyes flicked open, to find himself in darkness, broken only by the luminescence of the moonlight that shone through the hole in the roof.

He could hear the trample of horse's hooves outside, accompanied by the murmur of hushed voices. The local villagers would never come to Calling Castle, even during daylight hours; they all knew he would not tolerate such an intrusion.

He heard the metallic whisper of swords being pulled from scabbards.

Dragonslayers.

He quietly rose to his feet, trying to tread lightly on the silver coins beneath him, and then jumped up toward the patch of moonlight amongst the rafters. He perched himself atop the wall, waiting for his eyes to adjust to the night, so he could take measure of his would-be assassins.

There were eight horses tethered just outside the castle gatehouse, watched over by a girl of no more than thirteen or fourteen summers, which left at least seven other individuals unaccounted for, somewhere amongst the collapsed walls and turrets of the castle.

One, an old man in rusted armor, was trying to lead a pony and cart through the main gates; but the animal was proving reluctant, having detected the scent of dragon, meaning the man had now resorted to whipping it with a length of leather, forcing it forward.

He glimpsed a second intruder, a dark-haired man in a mud-stained green cloak, as he emerged onto the roof of the nearest turret. His silhouette vanished into the shadow of the battlements, as he silently pulled an arrow from his quiver and notched it into the string of his bow. If Rortkazor took to the air now, then the archer would easily be able to make three or four shots before he reached a safe distance.

"He's not 'ere,"

The voice came from beneath him.

A short woman dressed in a grubby, grey tunic had squeezed herself through a narrow crack in the wall and was now crouched beside his bed of silver coins, which had been his since he had claimed the castle more than two hundred years ago. "But his hoard is!"

She set down and lit a small oil lamp, whose flickering light reached up into the rafters where he was crouched, but fortunately her attention was focused on the glittering pile of coins at her feet.

"There's 'nough silver 'ere to keep us sitting pretty 'til next summer."

She was speaking in a language used in the great cities to the west, with an accent from the slums, where he knew the poorest humans were forced to survive on the rubbish and waste of others; so unsurprisingly her hands were moving gleefully amongst the many coins of his hoard, picking out one or two of the more valuable gem stones, the last remnants of crushed pieces of jewelry, which she secreted away within one of her boots.

He was half tempted to blast the opportunistic thief with fire, end her life in flames, for even daring to take his possessions. However, if he did, the archer on the turret would undoubtedly see him.

Leaving the silver behind, the thief scuttled across the room and removed the cross bar that had kept the great hall sealed for the last two centuries, pushing open the large double doors, allowing her comrades access to his Keep. The first dragonslayer through the door had the distinctive broad frame, beard and battle-axe of a warrior from the mountains to the east. He immediately set upon the thief, rightly suspicious she may have pocketed a handful of choice items from the hoard, but her outraged protests were just enough the next human through the doors, a tattooed tribeswoman from the islands of the far west, intervened on her behalf.

From city slums, to distant mountains and exotic islands, all had come many miles in pursuit of wealth. So, unsurprisingly, they were all now squabbling over the coins of his hoard.

He could hear the voices of two others, approaching excitedly, their previous caution abandoned in the belief they had struck on an easy reward.

They were all distracted enough he would have been able to make an escape, if it were not for the archer who was sitting in the turret, who had shown the good sense and patience not to be moved by the excitement below. Had the archer's eyes adjusted to the darkness yet? If so, there was just enough moonlight for him to be spotted, particularly with the light of the oil lamp flickering beneath him. If he moved, he would be seen, but he couldn't stay still. The dragonslayers were lighting more and more oil lamps in the great hall, and sooner or later one of them would think to look up. There were five of them in the hall now, having been joined by two more of their number; a shaven headed priest, from an order than was supposed to abhor material wealth, who was delightedly counting up their stolen riches, plus a young spearman from the desert to the south, who was packing the silver coins into chests and then carrying them outside and loading them onto the small cart, which the old man was holding just outside the doors. There were too many of them to fight, and even if he could kill them all, he still would not win.

For the dragonslayers to have come hunting for him, it meant the local lord had increased the bounty on dragons, which was undoubtedly the consequence of the incident at the farmstead. If he killed these humans, the price on his head would rise further, bringing even more would-be killers to his lair. His best bet was to sacrifice his hoard, let them take everything he owned, in the hope it would at least temporarily satisfy their taste for wealth. He would have to retire to the cave in the mountain, keep a low profile for a decade or two, then reclaim the castle once the destruction of the farm was a distant memory to the short-lived humans.

He turned away from them, spread his wings, and launched himself off the rooftop.

The archer on the turret saw him move, and immediately loosened an arrow, which shot out of the darkness and ripped into his underbelly. Ignoring the pain, he blasted the turret with fire, making sure his aim was just low and short enough it would not engulf the archer. Instead, the burning fire broke across the stone battlements, driving the man backward, making him flee back down the steps. Even as Rortkazor thundered over the burning turret, the archer swung back around and paused long enough to shoot one more arrow, which sliced past him, narrowly missing the taut and fragile skin of his wings. Had the shot been successful, he would have crashed to the ground, as unable to fly as the Sand Dragon, and would soon have been cut apart within a circle of their swords, spears and axes.

He beat his wings, putting distance and height between him and the archer, noticing at least two more arrows shoot past him, just wide of their mark.

He dove toward the mountains.

He did not look back.

He swept across the burnt-out ruin of a farmstead, thinking nothing of it at first, until he came across a second set of blackened buildings in the next valley. Realizing neither was the site of the Sand Dragon's original attack, he immediately swung back around, zigzagging across his territory, finding another three farms burnt to the ground, littered with human corpses and half-eaten cattle.

He found at least a dozen more farms abandoned by the occupants, with heavy track marks indicating the humans had fled the area days ago, taking their livestock with them.

Elzoreth had terrorized the area, while he lay sleeping.

Why would she do it?

How could she do it?

She had broken her word to him. She had killed many times more than was required to feed her. Did she despise humanity that much? Was this just slaughter for the sake of it?

How could he have been unaware of such carnage?

In simple terms, the last answer was easy enough, presuming she had determined where he was sleeping, she would just have needed to time her attacks to when the wind was blowing away from Calling Keep; so there would be no scent to rouse him from his slumber.

The dragonslayers would not back away from provocation like this, regardless of how much silver they recovered from his hoard, the bounty for dragons would now be so high they would be unable to stop themselves from pursuing him.

He glanced back down across the dale, noting that two of the horses, carrying the old man and young girl, plus the pony dragging the cart full of silver, had turned south and were headed away from him. The other six horses were moving northward, toward him, the light of their lamps and torches proudly declaring they were not the ones who were afraid to fight.

Did they know about the cave?

He did not care. It did not matter.

If Elzoreth was still there, then he would give them a dragon corpse to cart away. She would pay for her broken promise and murderous actions with her life. Then perhaps, he could return to the peaceful co-existence with the humans he had become so accustomed to.

He landed, as quietly as he could, half a mile downwind of the cave, pausing only to pluck the arrow from his side. He did not want Elzoreth to realize he was approaching; if possible he would take her by surprise, killing her before she had the chance to gather her devious wits.

Is that how it was in the ancient past? Dragon against dragon? Killing each other by any means possible? Squabbling over land, like the humans squabbled over coins?

He sniffed the air. He could detect her scent, but it was old, as if she had been there, but had left several days ago.

There was another scent though, something strange, yet familiar, something that stirred centuries old memories of being young; of occupying the cave with his brother and sisters, of learning to fly, of venturing out into the world on his own for the very first time.

He worked his way up to the cave, thoughts of revenge now banished from his mind, as he peered curiously into the darkness. He exhaled a little fuel, igniting it with a tiny flare of fire from his nostrils, the short burst momentarily illuminating the dark interior of the cave.

Then, suddenly, everything made sense to him.

There, in the flickering shadows cast by the fire, he could see numerous eggs. All of them were cracked and broken, many pieces of shell having been discarded on the floor around them as the occupants had smashed their way out.

Elzoreth had been carrying fertile eggs.

She had been looking for a place to raise her young, a land with enough food to feed six additional mouths, within easy reach of a safe base; somewhere exactly like this cave. Judging by the collection of bones in the cave, she had taken everything she needed, making no distinction between cattle or human, as she had struggled to keep all six of her hatchlings alive. She had let them grow strong enough to fly, while her wing healed, then they had fled as the outraged humans hired professional dragonslayers, leaving him, the oblivious idiot, to deal with the consequences.

It was so simultaneously devious and noble he could not help but admire it.

If they had headed east or west, they would be able to feed themselves in the forests that ran alongside the mountains; some of the hatchlings may become the prey of wolves and bears, but most would almost certainly survive.

From his vantage point at the mouth of the cave, as dawn broke, he glanced down the rocky slope to see the six dragonslayers coming over the rim of the last hill. They were relentless.

He could not turn east or west, for fear of running into Elzoreth and her hatchlings. So he had a simple choice, turn south and face the dragonslayers, or turn north and face his old rival, Zellith, the old and honorable Ice Dragon who ruled the frozen land to the north of the mountains.

It was no choice at all.

With several large flaps of his wings, he rose upward, higher than he had in many years, then turned north, diving between the white peaks of the Snowtooth Mountains. He was fleeing the humans, just as Elzoreth had done, a refugee from his own land; he too had now become an intruder in another dragon's territory.

In the red light of the dawn, the dragonslayers would have been able to see his ascent, but would they follow? Would they dare invade Zellith's territory? Would they dare to challenge the oldest and mightiest dragon of the north?

~ * ~

Zellith was dead.

His bones were slumped across a sprawling hoard of pebbles, with the last of his flesh being pecked away by the seabirds that were flocking around his carcass.

Rortkazor gave a blast of fire, burning dozens of them alive and sending the rest into a panicked flapping as they fled through the cave mouth, back out over The Frozen Sea.

The death of his old rival did provide him with a solution to his immediate problem, provided the dragonslayers did not cross through one of the mountain passes, he could claim the old dragon's territory for himself. The land may not offer him much, but it was at least relatively safe, and should provide him with just enough to survive.

He glanced at the bones.

Was that the fate that awaited him?

To die alone, in a remote cave, having scrounged a meager survival for centuries, as far away from humanity as he could possibly get.

He shivered.

Was that the fate that awaited all dragons?

A black shape flapped into the cave, which at first he mistook to be just another large sea bird, but as it began pecking at one of the burning corpses, the distinctive blue and black sheen of Sand Dragon scales caught his eye. It was far too small to be Elzoreth, but given the similarity of scales, it was undoubtedly one of her hatchlings.

It looked up at him, noticing his presence, staring at him with tiny, terrified yellow eyes.

"Hello?" he said.

The hatchling blinked, and then with a single flap of its wings, it fled the cave with dazzling speed.

Rortkazor bounded to the cave mouth, spread his wings, and flung himself after the little dragon. They swooped low across the fields of rock and ice, with the hatchling zigzagging through various natural updrafts, before he finally fled over the horizon.

Youth, size, agility and knowledge of the terrain had all worked in the little dragon's favor, but ultimately, by flying in a specific direction, it had given away the location it was headed. Rortkazor glided along the edge of the mountains, carried by the winds that were pushed upward by the change in terrain, until he came to a point where the mountains met the sea, to find a cliff face riddled with small caves.

He watched as two of the little dragons shot out of different caves, diving straight down toward the ice, their fire burning holes large enough for them to plunge through. Being engulfed by the frozen water should have been enough to kill them, but moments later they both erupted back out of the water with large silver fish clenched in their claws. Their multilayered scales protected them from the cold water, the same way they had protected their mother from his fire. The death of Zellith had created an opportunity, which they were perfectly adapted to take advantage of; they would not just survive here, they would thrive. If others of their kind came north, then within a decade this area could be swarming with Sand Dragons.

Were they still Sand Dragons? In snow covered mountains, with a keen appetite for fish from The Frozen Sea, the name suddenly seemed hopelessly wrong. They were something new.

He could not claim this territory for his own, it belonged to them.

He would not compete with hatchlings for food.

He turned back south, leaving them the mountains and everything to the north, to find Elzoreth hovering over the mountains. She suddenly swooped down between two of the peaks, issuing a great blast of fire as she descended, as arrows streaked through the sky around her.

Six familiar horses and riders were in the pass beneath her.

The dragonslayers had come north.

This was not his fight. This was not his territory to defend. Elzoreth was neither a friend, nor an ally. The safest thing for him to do was leave, let the dragonslayers kill her, so perhaps they might stop looking for him.

Rortkazor hesitated for a moment, aware all logic and reason demanded he leave; then he dove into the heart of the battle.

He swept directly over the dragonslayers, plucking two of them from the back of their horses with his claws. Flapping his wings hard, he powered upward, just avoiding an arrow that sliced through the air beneath his wing, until he had risen high above the snow-capped mountains.

The humans in his claws, the tattooed woman and the boy from the desert, were panicking, squirming in his grip. The tribeswoman was shouting above the wind in one of the southern human languages, which Rortkazor did not know, in a pleading and desperate tone.

"Impressive maneuver!" Elzoreth cried as she swooped past him, her scales glinting in the sunlight, as she began circling around him. "But it's uncivilized to play with your food."

"The humans aren't the prey here," Rortkazor snorted, looping around her, so they were flying in intertwined circles. "We're the prey. They're the predators."

The boy he held in his right paw suddenly plunged a short sword into his ankle. Rortkazor howled in agony, releasing his grip on the boy. He watched him fall, until he hit the snow in a puff of white and red.

"Now you're just wasting good food." Elzoreth sniffed the tattooed woman he still held in his other paw. "And I have six hungry hatchlings to feed."

"Kill these dragonslayers and they will only send more," Rortkazor snapped angrily, "Your hatchlings will never be safe."

Elzoreth broke out of her loop, beating her wings hard, enabling her to hover directly in front of him.

"They'll never be safe no matter what I do!" she growled. "The humans have slowly and insidiously invaded every territory, from the deserts of the south to here at the very edge of the world, driving us out, leaving us nowhere to even exist."

"Which is why you have to be discreet. Don't make them come looking for you!"

"You can go," she snarled, glancing towards the hatchlings. "But I cannot. We have nowhere else to go, but this isn't your fight."

"But it is," he replied. "Dragons are fading from the world, and I will not have that happen because I chose to do nothing. I cannot let them kill your hatchlings. They have a right to survive."

"Rortkazor," she said, her brow furrowing with an expression of regret. "They are only looking for two dragons. They are only looking for the two of us."

He looked at her, surprised and shocked by her implied suggestion; if they attacked the dragonslayers and lost, then they would take their skulls and go south to collect their reward, but they would never go looking for the hatchlings.

She was devious and noble to the very end.

Was that what they were reduced to? They had given up everything, would they have to sacrifice their lives too?

"No," he roared angrily. "We have conceded enough!"

He opened his left claw, causing the tattooed woman to panic, as she frantically tried to keep hold of him. Her grip was not strong enough, and she fell, screaming.

"There comes a time to fight, even against impossible odds. Let us not betray what we are. We will not roll over and die for them! Let them send more dragonslayers, and let us burn and claw and bite before we die, let us fight them to the end, because we are dragons! Let us fight for our lives!"

He pulled in his wings and fell, plunging back down into the mountain pass.

Elzoreth mirrored his maneuverer.

They spread their wings simultaneously, gliding with speed towards the dragonslayers, unleashing their fire as they passed overhead.

The shaven head priest fell from his burning horse, his billowing robes flaming around him, as he futilely tried to use his hands to shield his face from the melting tongues of flame. The bearded warrior, even as he was engulfed by the fire, made a pitiful attempt to hurl his axe at them, but it fell harmlessly back into the snow beside his burning corpse.

The archer, hidden in the rocks beside the path, let loose a single arrow, which sliced through the air and ripped through Rortkazor's wing. The taut skin, split wide open by the arrow, tore further apart as the air trapped beneath it gushed through the ragged wound. He fell from the sky. His body slammed forcefully into the rocks, bringing snow from higher up the mountain crashing down upon him. Momentarily stunned, he was only dimly aware of the archer leaving his hiding place, his green cloak flapping in the wind, as he closed the gap between them.

Another silver tipped shaft shot toward him, burying itself in his eye.

Rortkazor screamed, as he struggled to rise up out of the snow. With half of his vision lost, he turned his head in time to see the archer, now standing over him, notch another arrow, intent on delivering a final, lethal shot at point blank range. Rortkazor tried to blast his attacker with fire, but the fuel he spat was so diluted with his own blood it did not ignite.

The archer aimed an arrow directly between Rortkazor's eyes, and then let it fly.

The arrow twisted, then spun downward, harmlessly hitting the snow, driven off course by the buffeting of air from Elzoreth's wings as she snatched the archer from the ground.

He screamed as she bore him away.

His quiver hit the ground, breaking apart, spilling broken arrows in every direction.

Rortkazor allowed himself a smile, as he shook himself free of the snow, surveying the pass to make sure none of the dragonslayers had survived.

Counting the bodies, he knew they were one short.

The girl in the grey tunic, the thief who had broken into the great hall, was missing.

Then he saw her, dashing across the snow, trying to reach a horse. Unable to fly, he limped across the ground to catch her, ignoring the pain of the sword wound in his ankle, knowing if she reached the animal, she may well escape him. She would return to the cities and spread stories of the dragons in the mountains.

She reached the horse, vaulting into the saddle, only to find him sitting in her path, his head turned sideways so he could see her with his one good eye.

She pulled back on the reins, turning her mount, to find Elzoreth had landed in the pass behind her, penning her in.

It had been decades since Rortkazor had attempted to speak in a human language, but with great difficulty he made the necessary awkward shapes and primitive noises required.

"Tell them we are here," he growled. "Tell them to mark this place on their maps. Tell them this place is not for humans. That we claim this place for ourselves. Persuade them to stay away, to leave us alone, because we will defend it with our lives. We will kill all that come here. And if we fail, if we cannot survive even here at the edge of the world, then one day there will be no more dragons. And on that day, there will be no more dragonslayers either. Do you understand?"

The girl, pale with fear, nodded.

"The maps will say," she spoke softly, "Here Be Dragons."

"Make sure they always do."

Rortkazor limped to one side, allowing her to pass.

The thief kicked her heels into the flanks of the horse, sending it galloping back down the mountain pass.

"You don't think that'll actually work, do you?" Elzoreth gave a small snort of derisive fire. "Humans are far too dim and treacherous to be reasoned with."

"Never underestimate them. They are capable of anything." Rortkazor shrugged his torn and tattered wings. "Would you permit me to stay in your territory, while my wounds heal?"

"I'll give you a week," she grinned. "If you're still here after that, I'll remove your wings, your tail and your head. In that order. Understood?"

Half-blind and bleeding, he felt ridiculous hearing her repeat the unpitying threat he had made when they had first met.

"I'd like to see you try," he snorted, pushing past her.

"Ah, it wouldn't be a fair fight anyway," she shot back, "at least not until you've recovered."

"I doubt my eye will ever heal, so I guess you may be stuck with me for a while."

"Well, this is the place for it, after all." She nodded. "Here Be Dragons."

Rortkazor glanced at the horse fleeing down the mountain pass.

"But for how long, I wonder?"

~ * ~ * ~

David N. Smith and Violet Addison are a team of UK based writers, who have written numerous short stories, and one science-fiction novel. They've also written a five-hour, full-cast, audio-drama series, based on the classic *Fighting Fantasy* gamebook range, currently available via Audible and other audiobook platforms. Full details can be found on this website: www.davenevsmith.co.uk

Smelling Gold

Matthew Harrison

Carter, the first mate, looked warily at the café entrance. Their spaceship needed a new navigator, and the candidate hadn't shown yet. Carter was half hoping he wouldn't.

"This one's a dragon-slayer," Captain Mason said slowly, reading from the screen on his wrist.

Carter took a gulp of coffee and glanced at the café entrance again. A slim blond youth had entered and was looking absently up and down.

"No, not a dragon-slayer," Mason corrected himself, "a *dragon*. The guy's a dragon."

"Christ," Carter murmured. "Let's see if he can fly his way over here."

"Steady," Mason said under his breath, for the youth was closer now. "We need him—at least, we need someone like him. They're all pretty screwy, you have to accept that."

Carter nodded glumly. The youth was consulting his wrist screen, seemingly at a loss. Then messages obviously came in, as he became suddenly intent on the screen, bending over it to enter his replies.

"If he can't even find us…" Carter began.

"Relax," Mason said. "This isn't about navigating a coffee shop. It's whether he can find the real stuff, when we're out millions of kilometres from anywhere."

The youth was still absorbed in his screen.

"And just how does being a dragon help with that?" Carter asked.

It appeared the messages had been dealt with; the youth looked up. He caught sight of them immediately, and with an engaging smile strode up to their table. Shaking hands firmly with both men, he sat down and looked from one to the other expectantly.

"Now," Mason said once they had exchanged greetings, "let's talk about your—ah—*persona*…"

~ * ~

To Carter's chagrin, as their ship sped towards the asteroid belt, the youth was doing well.

His chosen name was Siegfried—which Carter already found annoying. "Surely Siegfried *killed* the dragon," he said to Mason when they were on the bridge together. "You're sure he's not a dragon-slayer after all?"

"No, he's quite clear on that," Mason replied. "Anyway, I don't give a toss what he is. He can be a parakeet if he likes, just as long as he delivers the goods."

And Siegfried, who did at least have the blond hair of his Germanic namesake, showed every sign of being able to do that. He had an impressive track record from his last flight, and came with his captain's strongest recommendation. In fact, Mason said the captain—old Hoegarten—would have kept the boy if he hadn't made enough on that single voyage to retire.

"That's exactly what we want," Mason confided in his turn. "You can't just journey up and down looking for likely spectral images, you've got to have a shortcut." He indicated the black speckled vastness through the port. "There are just too many of the bloody things, and no one pays for your searching time."

"And for a shortcut, you need a telepath," he continued.

Carter tried to accept it. But it rankled—he was an engineer, a man of science, and this was mumbo-jumbo."

"How the hell does the telepathy work?" he said at last. "He finds a metal-rich asteroid just by thinking about it?"

"That's almost what they do," Mason said. "But I just go by results. If one day they make a better spectrometer, fine. Until then…" He glanced up the corridor to where the youth's cabin was.

Carter's lack of conviction must have showed on his face, for Mason said more gently, "Look, this isn't a very profitable business, when you take into account the costs of towing the asteroid back. It's economics—without a telepath, asteroid-mining is barely viable. And if the telepaths do perform, well, like old Hoegarten said—"

Just then an alarm sounded, and the autopilot changed course so sharply they were thrown to one side.

"Bloody asteroids!" Mason exclaimed. He secured himself and called up the charts.

~ * ~

After that near-collision, luck was with them. The boy had a rare find—an asteroid more than half nickel, and at five kilometres by two a fine size. That one find would assure them a profit on the trip, but they staked their claim with a radar beacon and went on looking for more.

Carter met the youth in the corridor and grudgingly congratulated him.

"My pleasure," the youth said, smiling. He seemed rather content with himself.

"Think you're going to find another?" Carter couldn't help asking. He had a share in the profits of the trip and, unpalatable though the youth's methods were, they were delivering results.

"There's plenty about," the youth said placidly.

Carter caught his breath. *Plenty about?* Dimly, he was beginning to see the potential. No more long sweeps through the belt, hazarding their lives from collisions and ending up more often than not with a lump of silicate or carbon. This was surely the big time.

With mingled awe and irritation, he asked, "How do you know?"

"That's easy," the youth said, "I'm a dragon, remember? Dragons can smell gold."

This seemed like nonsense to Carter, but before he could ask more, the youth yawned and, propelling himself from the wall, floated off down the passage towards his room.

~ * ~

For the next few Earth-cycles, Carter was busy revamping the charts. After their narrow escape from the errant asteroid, Mason was taking no chances, and Carter had to laboriously track each object within a million kilometres and plot its position and velocity.

At last he emerged from this work and was on the way to his cabin for a proper rest when Mason caught him in the corridor.

"You'll have to tackle young Siegfried," Mason said. He seemed distraught.

Carter stared in surprise. "I thought he was doing well."

"*Was* is the operative word," Mason said grimly. "He hasn't been out of his cabin for days."

"Christ!" Carter exclaimed. "What happened to the dragon thing?"

"He's asleep. Asleep on his hoard."

"What?"

Mason took a breath. "I'm speaking figuratively. The boy's a dragon, right; he sees the good asteroids as gold, sniffs them out, and when he's got them, he brings them back to his hoard and sits on them."

Christ, Carter thought to himself, *what a fruitcake.* "Just one asteroid—that's a hoard?" he asked.

"It's a pretty big asteroid," Mason retorted. "And he'd already found several for Hoegarten."

"Anyway," the captain went on, "it's not what you think, it's what he thinks. And he thinks he's a bloody dragon, asleep on a pile of gold!"

Carter was dumbfounded. "So—so what do we do?" he finally managed to ask.

"Do?" Mason repeated grimly. "Do?" Without further words he grabbed the first mate and almost pulled him into the nearby storeroom. "Give the bugger the fright of his life, that's what!" And he gestured to what seemed a random pile of metal objects on the floor. "I had Engineering make those for you."

Carter looked. He made out a kind of winged helmet, a breast-plate, a metal shaft with a cross-guard. "What on earth?" he asked feebly.

"Get the fucking kit on, go into his cabin, and steal his fucking gold!" Mason almost screamed at him.

Shaking with confusion and fear at Mason's outburst, Carter struggled into the armor and went off up the corridor, a most unlikely knight.

~ * ~ * ~

Matthew Harrison lives in Hong Kong, and whether because of that or some other reason entirely his writing has veered from non-fiction to literary and he is currently reliving a boyhood passion for science fiction. He has published numerous SF short stories and is building up to longer pieces as he learns more about the universe. Matthew is married with two children but no pets as there is no space for these in Hong Kong.

Visit his website at: http://matthewharrison.hk/

These Things Held Most Dear

Harding McFadden

When the gremlins made their way over the Great Hill after what seemed centuries of waiting, the dragon was ready. Through her six jeweled eyes, she watched them from the bleak concealment of her home. Preparing for what must come, she could feel the smoke begin to build at the back of her throat, could see the small gray-black puffs escaping from her tear drop-shaped nostrils. Instinctively, she knew by the time the invaders had made their way over the ashy, blasted landscape, her whole body would be aglow with barely contained nuclear fire. At first slowly, she stirred, knocking dust and ash from her as she left the cave's mouth.

Her parents had named her Rainbow, seeing within the oddly hued scales that covered her a pattern more beautiful than any of her own kind had seen. Outcast and damaged, by a birth that left her birth mother a weeping, dying mess, she had been found not very far from where she now lay, under growing sediment and dust. Crying and wailing, she had been left to perish by her own kind, unable to fly or follow, still a babe. It had only been through the kindness of her parents she had even survived.

As she watched the gremlins advance, she could see the exact moment when they noticed her. Within the growing dusk, they had seen her sparkling hide from miles off, sizzling and cracking at the mouth of her lair. At first shocked, they had halted, their manner full of anxiety, until after a great long wait, they saw something: she did not advance.

Like a child of their own, her parents had raised her, seeing her not as the enemy of their people, but rather as a small creature that needed their help. For more than a dozen years they had seen to her, feeding and caring for her, until she was not merely their daughter, but was a daughter of the community. In her own way, she had loved them; and mourned them when they were taken away.

It took the gremlins mere moments to arm and shield themselves, before they were off again. Bloodlust was in their eyes. They were diminutive, at best, barely half the size of a man. Even though there were more than a dozen of them, under normal circumstances, they would never have attempted an attack on a dragon. Rainbow, however, was not a usual specimen of her kind. Even at this great distance, they must have seen this. Small from birth, she was hardly the height of a man herself. Thin framed and wiry, with the loss of substance due to her birth-torn left wing, she could not have weighed more than two men. A dragon she might have been, but one they felt well capable of taking advantage of.

Legends and half-truths would pull them toward her. The need for gold and jewels would make them risk life and limb for a chance at this dragon. Gold and jewels, a dragon's hoard, a lie told by wizards for thousands of years to make the stupid, and the greedy, and the fool-hearty throw their very existence away. The idiocy of these creatures knew no bounds. For all that she was a dragon, she had no treasure as they would see it. Her hoard was much more precious.

The first of the gremlins came at her full tilt, screaming and swinging their axes and swords, seeking her blood and gaining none of it. Her eyes ablaze, her hide sparking with retained fire, she let out a blast like the furnaces of Hades. In the blink of an eye, those first who had sought to end her were so much ash, sent to their maker so quickly they had not even had time to scream.

Shaking the rest of the dust of her home from her body, she stood her full height, not tall at all, but still more than enough to worry these raging nuisances. Their arms and armor a battered and scarred black, the gremlins themselves were thin, sickly-looking creatures, their eyes too big, their lips too small, their skin so wart and sore-covered they were unpleasant to see. In the back of her mind, she could not help but wonder what it was that had sent them into this inhospitable wasteland?

Epic, the battle was not. For no more than minutes, they fought, the gremlins jabbing and retreating, Rainbow circling them only a little, unwilling to let any of them get a free hand at the entrance to her cave, and the riches that lay within. Save for the tracks made by the approach of the gremlins, and the scuffling made by their small conflict, there was no sign of life around them. A once green and lively place, her home had been laid waste by some wizard or another decades ago, in a conflict she could not even guess at. Now here it was, a place of love for her, reduced to a joke of a war between an outcast, and the little nothings who sought to enter her den.

When the last of the gremlins made as if to escape, she moved from the mouth of her home, and chased him. Unable to fly, she was nevertheless quick on her feet, and had him through her jaws and into her belly in moments. With that, it was all done. Nothing may as well have happened, for all the world seemed to care. The gremlins were shadows now, just more ash in the air, to blow around forever.

Slowly, more tired than she had been in many a month, she stalked back to her cave. While not large, the entrance was more than wide enough to allow her entry. After the rain of smoke and disaster that had taken this place, her cave was the only home she could find. The fire that had scoured the rest of her world had not touched her. At their core, dragons were more than a bit fire themselves, after all. Alone for the first time since she had been outcast, she had found this hole in the ground, and pulled her treasure in after her. Like she always did when a melancholy overcame her, she retreated to it now.

The residual light of her enflamed body illuminated the place for a few moments before going out entirely. Because of it, she could see her treasure again, making sure it was here, and not taken by another sneaky gremlin who had escaped her notice. With a sigh that disturbed the dust and ash, she lay about it, encircling it, forever keeping safe the bones of her loving parents.

for Naomi, Eleanor, and Iris

~ * ~ * ~

Harding McFadden is an obsessive reader and an addict of all things written. He is proud to be the father of two wonderful daughters, Eleanor and Iris, and the lucky husband of Naomi, the world's greatest woman. He lives in a rotating library in Pennsylvania.

The Dragon
at the End of Time

Kathleen Townsend

The end of time was tedious, more than anything else. There was still quite a lot to do, actually, and the dragon couldn't help but feel rushed. The usual loneliness the dragon faced wasn't any greater than normal, for visitors had always been rare and often never came at all.

The earth hadn't emptied itself of living matter as quickly as he'd previously expected. There was evidence of a few small, hardy animals that had survived. Insects had waned significantly, but they too could still be found scattered about the decimated countryside. The earth was still very much populated, no matter how sparsely. In fact, at that very moment soft footfalls marched dutifully up the long, winding stair of red sandstone that led to his aerie.

Of course, the visitors had been traveling up to his aerie for an inordinately long time. The human's steps—for they were the most adventuresome folk and the only ones to ever visit—had grown slow and tired. Twice now they'd stopped for food and a few hours rest. They were tenacious, though. The dragon had to give them that. Many who discovered the stairs to his aerie decided the journey wasn't worth discovering whatever it was that lay at the top and after several hours of climbing simply turned around and went home.

The dragon strained to hear. Humans had the annoying tendency to walk like mice, and the dragon was very old indeed. Only knights in shiny metal armor made much of a sound, and none of those had turned up in several millennia.

A great, heavy sigh filled the aerie. Dust rose from where it clung to the floor and walls and was carried to the very back of the chamber where it collected in a too-deep corner already piled half a foot high with the stuff. The dragon appreciated the company, but a part of him wished they wouldn't come at all.

This time might be different, though. Maybe, just maybe…

But the dragon dismissed the idea, and went back to his endless, wearying task.

A large pedestal stood in the center of the room. Atop it sat a basin larger than any human would find useful, but a bit on the small side for a dragon. Several inches of water sat in the bottom. The dragon peered into the clear pool. A knobby, scaly face of black and silver peered back at him.

"Eek!"

The sound echoed round the chamber followed by something small scurrying away.

The dragon looked up. "Made it, did you?"

The visitors were indeed humans. Two of them, in fact. The pair stared at him. Neither seemed capable of speech. Stunned silence was a rather standard greeting he received. Even the most hardened of warriors had gone weak kneed at the sight of such a large and ancient dragon.

The one who eeked was very young, no more than six from the look of him. A mop of sandy hair and a single blue eye peered out from behind the leg of a fully grown man. Several metal baking sheets were bent and laced to the adult's chest and legs as some kind of makeshift armor. The man seemed to realize how ridiculous he looked and quickly scrambled to unlace the baking pans.

The dragon chuckled. "I haven't gotten any sudden ideas of roasting you whole. You needn't worry. Though, if you do wish to remove your outerwear and shoes, you may leave them by the doorway."

The man paused before he nodded in agreement. "Sure," he said curtly. The baking pan armor was stacked near the archway to the stairs where the pair had just entered. The shoes were left on after a moment of contemplation.

He'd have made a wonderful knight, the dragon thought, appearance-wise at least. The man had wide shoulders and dark hair that reached just above his shoulders. A smattering of stubble covered deeply tanned skin. The clothes were dirty and disheveled, but there was little hope for better. It was the end of the world, after all. The dragon wouldn't have been surprised to have found him wearing nothing but a beard with no sanity left to speak of.

The man seemed sane, though. Both of them did. And that was two more than the dragon had observed thus far.

"What's your name, little one?" the dragon asked.

The boy shifted, twisted his mouth to the side and studied the dragon for a moment. Finally, he decided the dragon didn't pose any real threat, at least not with his elder friend there, and spoke. "I'm Henry," he said. "What's your name?"

A sad look came to the dragon's eyes. "I don't have one."

The man looked questioningly over his shoulder as he removed shin guards made from older, more rusted metal sheets, though he didn't speak.

"Why not?" Henry asked.

"I had one once, I'm sure," the dragon said. "But my life began so very long ago, and I have such few visitors."

"You forgot it?" The boy contemplated it for a moment and turned to his companion. "Donald, will I forget my name too, one day?"

"'Course not. You have me to tell it to, don't you?" A hand was laid on the boy's head, and Henry smiled. "Donald Smith. We saw the stairs and thought maybe someone was alive up here."

"Donald Smith," the dragon repeated.

"You haven't heard of me, have you?" Donald asked, brow crinkling in confusion. "The only memorable thing I've ever done was survive the Cataclysm."

"Of course not. You're just one little human, after all, and you weren't the only one to survive, though I'm glad to see you still sane and free of radiation poisoning. I'm sure you've had plenty in the decade that's passed since the end of the world—if you bother to count the hours anymore. They're all chronicled here somewhere. It's just your name. Heroes always have grand, memorable names. Donald Smith is rather dull and unimaginative. How about we call you Rufus Stranger? Or maybe Amadeus Bach?"

"Donald Smith is just fine, thanks."

The dragon shrugged. "Well, then, suit yourself. But it'll be a boring start for my new collection. That is why you've come, isn't it? To restart time?"

"Time," the dragon repeated when Donald didn't speak. "It's all but stopped out there, below my aerie. Don't you want it begun again?"

Donald's eyebrows crinkled together for a moment. He glanced at Henry, who looked just as bewildered, before setting his eyes on the dragon. "Sure. But it would take a miracle to get the world back how it was."

"Or magic," Henry said.

"Neither are real," Donald said.

Henry scowled at him and shuffled a few inches away in indignation.

"What would we restart it for anyway? We've only passed a single village in three years of travel and they wouldn't let us in. Too scared to be kind to strangers, not that I can blame them, really. There's not enough food to scrounge for just the two of us. God only knows how they're getting by."

The dragon knew. He'd seen, of course. He saw everything. Nothing escaped his notice. But the story wasn't one for young ears and, if Donald was clever—and the dragon was very sure he was if he'd survived the Cataclysm—he'd have come to his own rueful conclusions long ago.

"Where's your treasure?" Henry asked. "Can I go play in it?"

"This is my treasure," the dragon said. "Every vial you see is worth more than the wealth of every kingdom combined through all of history."

"I thought dragons had gold and swords and stuff."

Myths and fairy tales must have survived the Cataclysm if the boy knew about dragons and the stories of his brothers jealously guarding their hoards. There was something reassuring in that. Now, at the end of everything, the world itself was calling out to its very beginning when dragons weren't quite so rare and heroes were populous and treasure wasn't really such an impossible thing to seek.

"All dragons hoard something. I had brothers who collected gold, or jewels, or bones of travelers. I, however, collect time."

"Time?" Donald asked.

They didn't know then. It had been foolish to think his visitors had come here with a specific purpose in mind. Still, they were the only visitors he could remember that had just stumbled in without any inkling as to what lay at the top of the tallest tower.

"Come. I'll show you."

Donald hesitated. The dark brown eyes washed over the dragon before concluding he was relatively harmless, as far as dragons came, and moved towards him. Henry had already stepped forward and clambered onto the base of the pedestal, which was slightly wider than the rest, and had his nose tipped over the edge of the basin.

"What's in the bowl?" asked Henry. "Is it water?"

"Yes and no. This is all that is left of the first rain that ever fell upon the earth. I collected it, you see. I wanted to preserve it. But I quickly realized I couldn't preserve everything in its original material form this way. There isn't the room for every object that's ever come into being to be tucked away in my halls. Much is missed, too, if you only focus on the material. So I created this. It's a mirror."

All three faces were reflected in the waters.

"All water is a mirror," Donald said.

"Ah, but not all water is a mirror to the outside world."

Donald gave the dragon a questioning look. The dragon smiled —or tried to. He'd been told by more than one human that the look seemed more ferocious than happy. Neither Henry nor Donald seemed to mind too much, though, not cringing or flinching like most of the others.

The dragon lowered his eyes back to the mirror. Donald followed suit. The dragon blew lightly out of his nose. The water rippled, violently at first but calming as each tiny wave lapped against the side of the basin. As the ripples traveled and splashed against the sides, so too did their reflections. The faces of the dragon and two humans seemed to break apart and were cast aside, crashing into thousands of droplets, each of which held the image for a brief moment before fading back into the rest.

Another image took shape. It was the earth, or what was left of it. There was nothing to see except brown dirt that hadn't seen rain in months, maybe even longer. The dragon hummed and the image seemed to change. The ground was a lighter shade of brown now. Cracks traveled through the earth, creating a vast spiders' web along the surface. Again the scene changed.

"This is the world as it appears below us at this very moment. Once upon a time, it was easy to search for something worth collecting. Now, all I find is this. The nothingness has spread. Everything looks the same, unchanging year after year. Even the ruins of human metropolises do not change any longer. There's no growth to cover them and no shifting sands to bury them Now, there's only unchanging brown rock nearly everywhere the eye can see. But, every once in a great while, there's still something special to find, some tiny fragment of the world hanging on by nothing more than hope."

The dragon hummed appreciatively as he finally found something worthy of note. In the mirror was something new. The exact location was impossible to tell without any ruins to go by. Once, it had been a great forest. It was raining, for once, not that it would do much good. Pools of a sickly green color collected at the base of long dead trees. Broken trunks reached into the sky like hundreds of fallen spears on a battlefield. The dragon wasn't sure what had happened to make the rain such an unnatural color, but it was something to be recorded.

He reached behind him where a pile of vials were stacked near the floor. A great claw hooked one and dragged it closer.

"Each moment I find that is important, different, or somehow special, I collect. Each person. Every love. Every fight. The rising and falling of every settlement and every civilization. Now, each day is much the same as the one before. Nothing changes from one moment to the next. And there's so very little life left within the world."

The vial was held aloft upside down, tilting dangerously as it threatened to slip from the dragon's claw. Carefully, the dragon dipped the vial into the pool. The image swirled and thinned as it was pulled into the container, leaving only a clear pool of water behind. The dragon put a cork stopper in the top and handed it to Donald.

"Is it real?" he asked. "How did you do that?"

"Of course, it's real. That's happening as we speak, off somewhere in your world. As for how I did it, that would be like asking a fish how he swims or you how to you breathe. I am Time's Keeper, or one of them at least. There are others I've seen. But their ways are different, writing or weaving the history of the universe and storing them where no mortal can ever find. A worthy task, to be sure. But this, my friends," the dragon tapped on the vial, "is a piece of time itself.

"I am Time's Keeper in its most literal sense. I scour the world for moments worth collecting, and I've learned that, in the end, most things are worth saving. Even the darkness I find, I still collect. Even the fall of ghastly rain is something worth remembering, even if only as a warning, or a memoriam."

Donald watched as rain fell within the vial, enraptured. "Interesting hobby," he muttered, not tearing his eyes away from the three-dimensional scene.

Henry jumped off the platform. "So they're like the movies you told me about, right Donald?"

The boy scampered to a wall and started glancing into the vials on the lower shelves. The dragon tended to keep the moments he enjoyed the most in here. There were images of the great monuments of men being built, the most beautiful ships ever made gliding across crystalline seas, moments of triumph in battle, and the first lullaby sung on earth. Henry stopped at a scene of a wounded knight fighting off a great beast and watched enraptured.

"Not really," Donald said. He bent beside Henry before moving along down the shelf, giving each vial a brief scan before continuing.

"The others are gone now, of course," the dragon continued. "The Weaving Woman who wove a tapestry of all she saw. The monk who chronicled the history of the world by quill and ink from his birth to the Cataclysm. There were others, too. They all lived within the earthly realm, though, and were subjected to the same mortalities as the rest of those who suffered the Ending of Times."

"And you don't?" Donald asked without turning to look at the dragon.

This place is outside of time. I am merely its observer. Now, though, I am the Observer of the Wasteland, Chronicler of the Vast Nothingness at the end of the universe."

"Hey," Henry said, "are you okay?"

Donald and the dragon turned. A woman wearing furs knelt before a lower shelf, eyes glued to the vial before her. She didn't respond to Henry's question, nor the hand that tapped her shoulder.

"She can't hear you," the dragon said quietly. Henry stopped tapping and turned to look at him. "None of them can."

"Why not?" the boy asked.

"They're too obsessed with what they see. All they want is that moment, whatever it is. They don't see or hear anything else. They're in their own world."

"So they're playing pretend?"

The dragon blinked at the boy. "In simplest of terms, yes. I suppose they are."

Henry turned back to the woman and peered into her face with interest. "Hey, you wanna play with me? We can play pretend together." The boy twisted his mouth to the side. "Donald, do you wanna play with me?"

"Donald?" Henry looked up and searched for his friend when there was no immediate response.

"Oh, no," the dragon said. "Henry, I'm sorry."

Donald stood facing a shelf that was about even with Henry's nose. Donald picked up the vial in front of him and cradled it in his arms, close to his chest, like the most precious of infants.

The dragon muttered a curse. He could kick himself. He really could.

Several hundred vials were crammed onto the shelf directly across from his usual place at the mirror. They'd been collected over the last several months, by a mortal's reckoning of time. The dragon hadn't bothered maneuvering through the vast, endless corridors of his aerie to shelve them all in the proper order. After all, he'd not had any visitors in decades and, at the end of the world, something as mundane as cataloging inventory seemed rather unimportant. Instead, the dragon had sat behind his mirror, searching for survivors of the cataclysm, hoping that someone, anyone, would come.

It took years for that hope to bear fruit. For so many years now, the dragon had been alone, one of the very last creatures in a world that'd passed its peak long ago. Sure, there were other humans spread throughout his aerie, but they didn't count. Each one was held self-captive, enraptured or terrified or ridden with guilt and horror at what they saw. The dragon had tried to snap them out of it. Not once had it worked.

The dragon always assumed that, one day, maybe they would come to their senses. There was that one elderly man who had arrived several ages past who, guilty of spying and treason, happened to stumble upon what became of his victims. He'd sat there, mouth open in a soundless wail with tears running down his cheeks. Then, one day, after nearly a decade, he'd stood up. The dragon had been so pleased, ready to send the man back into the world to start anew. But that was never to be. Before the dragon could prevent it, the man had slit his own throat.

The body was in a room full of shelves, meant as another space for his vials. It was a crypt now. Two or three others had joined the man.

Here, at the end of all things, the dragon was surrounded by these hapless, pitiable souls, shackled to his aerie by their own guilt, real or imagined.

"Donald?" There was fear in Henry's voice.

Even for the dragon, it felt like an eternity as Henry watched Donald. The boy's eyes grew fearful, then dejected, and finally filled with resignation. A thin line of film formed in his eyes. Just as Henry gave a long sniff, Donald did something the dragon didn't expect.

Donald turned. It was jerky at first, as if he'd forgotten how to move. Then he looked Henry dead in the eye.

"She was beautiful, wasn't she?" Donald whispered as he lifted the vial from the shelf. Henry peered over his mentor's shoulder. "Alice, her name was."

In the vial was a young woman with long brown hair and eyes that could melt a heart of ice. She smiled up as a younger, less haggard Donald lifted her by the waist and swung her in a circle.

Donald pet the side of the vial, as if petting the woman's cheek. The dragon wasn't sure who he wanted to curse more, Donald or himself. Just because he'd survived the un-survivable didn't mean Donald was particularly special, just incredibly lucky. If Donald could not tear himself away from images of his lost love, all of that would be for naught. He'd be trapped forever more, never sleeping or hungry, until even the aerie was worn away in the endless nothingness here at the end of time.

"Fledgling," the dragon whispered.

Henry turned. There was heartbreak in his young eyes. The dragon had thought he'd not understand, not without a bit of explaining, at least. That wasn't necessary, though. The boy did understand what was happening. How could he not? A small child traveling alone with a man covered in tin pans who was completely unrelated to him? Henry was no stranger to loss and death.

The small nose wrinkled and lips pursed into a small knot of a mouth. Henry took the vial from Donald's hands.

Donald blinked at the space the image he craved had just been in. Slowly, he brought his eyes to his young friend. "Henry?" he asked.

"I want to be a knight when I grow up. Like you," he said.

"You can't be a knight," Donald said defeatedly. "There are no kingdoms left to save. There are no princesses left to marry. There aren't even any monsters left to fight. Just me and you and a dragon-god who can't bring Alice back and can't save the world and can't fix time. Just let me have this, at least."

Donald reached out for the vial, but Henry backed up and clutched it to his chest like a doll.

"Henry!" he yelled angrily. "She was my wife. Give that back."

Henry looked down at the vial. Donald held his hand out. The boy clutched the vial to his chest stubbornly.

"There's a chance…" the dragon stuttered.

Cold panic gripped him, the dragon was nervous for the first time since the incident with the traitor so long ago. Slowly, both turned to him, and the dragon let out a sigh of relief.

"There's a chance," the dragon began again. "More of a theory, really. Yet, I find myself unable to validate one way or another myself, due to the nature of the thing and the possible recompense. I think there may be a way to restart time—to turn the fields green again, and the rain clear, and the oceans blue. To put birds back in the sky, beasts upon the land, and fish in the sea, and give you few, courageous little humans who still cling here at the end of the world a chance to start anew."

"Why didn't you say this to begin with?" Donald asked.

The dragon hummed deep within his throat. "Because I was afraid," he said simply.

"But you're a great big dragon," Henry said.

"Even the greatest of men are afraid sometimes. Dragon's too. And that's okay, I think. To not be afraid would mean no one looks at their own actions, or the actions of others, and sees them for what they are and what they could become. Do you understand?" the dragon asked.

Henry shook his head no.

"I was afraid Donald would find something and become trapped, a slave to his own impassioned soul, as so many others who have come here before him. I was afraid you would not understand and not know what to do and be ultimately unable to free him from a tormented future. But most of all, I was afraid you'd listen, and believe me, and my idea would not work, for then we would have nothing left at all."

"I wasn't staring that long," Donald said, eyes not quite meeting the dragon's.

"Time doesn't flow here. It's hard to keep count of the days that pass below, especially now with everything laid to waste. You've been watching that vial for more than a week by your calendar. No real fault of your own. I understand the temptation."

"What's your idea?" Henry asked, sensing something exciting and worth playing behind the words.

"Let us do an experiment, shall we? Henry, my little fledgling. I want you to find a vial you like that shows part of nature and throw it from the window at the very top of those stairs."

Henry searched high and low around the large chamber. He scurried out of sight and returned with a vial before deciding it wasn't good enough and headed out to get another. Finally, he walked towards the dragon, lips bitten between his teeth. A very old, rather worn vial was in his hands. It was bigger than most of the others, and Henry looked to be struggling beneath the weight. Donald caught the bottom as it tipped forward, Henry dragged along with it.

"This is beautiful. Where did you find this? What is it?" Donald asked.

The dragon smiled. He bent his neck low to the floor to peer at the contents one last time. "This is the very first moment I collected after I'd constructed my mirror. I'm half ashamed to admit how many days by human count I've lost to staring within its depths. This is the remnant of the first garden ever to be created in the world. It was abandoned for more than a century by the time I'd managed to finally collect it. Yes. Yes, this is quite right. If this doesn't remind the earth of its purpose, I daresay nothing will."

Henry ran into the narrow space at the top of the stairs. The dragon closed his eyes. He daren't watch. The risk of him growing cold wings was simply too great. That one, glorious image that had sparked his wild dream of collecting that single moment in time, perfectly preserved forever, had been the beginnings of his aerie and ultimate chronicling and saving of time. Watching it tip from the windowsill may have been the correct decision, but it was one the dragon simply couldn't face with open eyes.

"Sir Dragon," Donald said, "you should really come see this."

The request was easier said than done.

The time vials rattled on their shelves as the dragon circled his mirror and edged towards the door. He could fit through the archway—the dragon had made sure of that when he'd constructed the place—but the ledge at the top of the stairs was too small to fit a fully grown dragon and two humans, even if one of them was only a few feet tall. The dragon craned his neck and peered over the top of the human's heads. Hot breath from his nostrils made the pair jump in alarm.

"It's beautiful," the dragon said.

The footprints of Donald and Henry, which but a moment ago had been imprinted upon the dry, barren earth for the rest of a nonexistent eternity, had vanished. Dry ground loosened first, and then burst forth with more green life than Henry had ever seen in one place. Green grass coated the ground. Wildflowers sprouted at the base of the aerie. A long train of roses, each one a different color wound its way up the tower-like mountain as if a princess were housed within instead of the dragon. Young trees flowered. Shrubs formed themselves into little lines around beds of flowers. A large pond formed off to one side, complete with lilies, koi, and several boisterous frogs.

"It worked," Donald said. Awestruck eyes looked up at the dragon. "What would have happened if it didn't?"

"We would have lost the beginning of a world that had ended. Come along, young ones. I daresay we have a long and grueling task ahead of us. We can't very well throw every vial out the staircase window. Let us gather what we can and take to the skies."

Days passed beneath them as the dragon directed the two humans to what vials should be gathered first. Nature, the dragon decided, would be the proper thing to reinstate first. Plants had to grow and the water must be un-tainted. Of course, it was only afterwards the dragon realized they'd need to release all manner of insects and birds as well if they wanted to keep the flowers blooming and ecosystem flowing long enough to get larger creatures back into the wilds let alone humans.

"Ready," Henry said as Donald hoisted him atop the dragon's back. A heavy sack was clasped tightly in his fists.

"You may grow old upon my back before all of this is done, I fear," the dragon said as he lifted into the sky. "Though I daresay many a tale will be spun about the dragon at the end of all things and the two humans who got time to flow once again. Are you certain you don't want to change your name, Donald? It is a very boring name, after all, not the stuff of legends."

"I think the name will hold some weight after I'm through with it."

The dragon glanced at the man atop his back. "So it would seem, young human. So it would seem."

~ * ~ * ~

Kathleen Townsend is an editor of translated fiction and a Sr. Contributing Writer at Crunchyroll News. She lives in New Jersey with her husband.

More Books from
WolfSinger Publications

The Dark See – M.R. Williamson

As Helen Durkin's journey to find out about herself continues, she finally realizes she needs the help of someone with more knowledge than dwarves, elves, or even dragons. But, just how do you approach the old Wizard Andsell Phagan?

As she tries to solve that problem, yet another dangerous situation presents itself. This mysterious person is no friend of the Phagan family. And, Helen quickly finds herself on a collision course with a halfling who most refer to as Scar—one who dabbles in the dark side of magic.

With this added pressure, the effort to approach and perhaps train under Andsell Phagan intensifies. As time progresses, an old friend comes to her aid and presents the young girl's plight to Andsell. Now, the race is on and the old Dragon Pragamore takes the lead in Helen's plight.

Will Helen finally find out why the Faes are calling her Bright Helen?

What of Pragamore? Will his years keep him from helping?

And who is Scar really after—Helen, the old wizard, or Pragamore?

The Steel Fist – Rob Jackson

The survivors of Recon 9 are needed in the Ozarks where some home-grown autocrats have taken over parts of Arkansas and Missouri. They've looted National Guard armories and hoarded weapons, ammunition, and vital supplies, just waiting for the opportunity to take over the area. While most of their transport, armor, and aircraft are obsolete, they face people with no protection against such deadly equipment. And they're trying to get the local natural resources to gain control of weapons even the military have no defense against.

Recon 9 has gained four new members and formed an alliance

with locals, many of them veterans, against a common enemy. The locals have some grasp of tactics, an excellent knowledge of the hilly, forested countryside and a burning desire to be rid of the terrorists, who call themselves: THE STEEL FIST

Crisis in Big-G City – S.D. Matley

Olympus, Inc., is locked in battle with climate change!

Athena's Secret Ops program steps in when bad boy and technological genius Hermes can't come up with a carbon-curbing solution. Undercover agents Cleo Petra and Pan are deployed in the mortal world to vanquish the notorious East brothers, chthonic fossil fuel magnates who pass as human and eat humans, too...

Two-month-old Pablo, the one-quarter chthonic infant son of two fathers formerly known as P.B., employs his extraordinary abilities of adult speech and intellect in pursuit of climate justice!

Meanwhile, David Bernstein, whose hot romance with Cleo Petra meets a rocky end, recovers the memory of his century-old love affair with a beautiful Spanish nurse. He time travels to 1918 to find her and encounters love, loss, and the City of Mount Olympus —a dark and sinister place where every inhabitant lives in fear of volatile and destructive Zeus!

David's birth father and Hera's former fling, Saul Crispin, is outed as a mortal made immortal. Will Hera's high crime of granting Saul eternal life land her before a jury of her peers for judgment?

And what of baby-crazy Queen of the Underworld, Persephone, pregnant at last but not by Hades?

Intrigue, espionage, crimes of passion, secret babies and looming existential threats—everywhere you look there's a Crisis in Big-G City!

Tree of Bones – Book Two: A Familiar's Tale
- Verna McKinnon

Two Curses

A curse of Darkness... Deep within the Thill forest, stands a tree made of human bones, crowned in black leaves and red thorns.

A curse of Light... Beneath the Wastelands of Skarros, a crystal imprisons a dark, immortal queen.

The Sorceress, Runa, is tormented by horrific images of this tree of bones in a distant, lifeless forest. Even as the visions debilitate her, Mellypip, her beloved familiar, also experiences these sinister dreams, bound by the same dream seer magic as his mistress. The tree of bones summons Runa, and she must risk madness and death as obsession drives her on. What she finds reveals a devastating truth.

Koll the Sorcerer awaits trial for his crimes. His familiar, Xabral, searches for allies to free him. Driven by his own dreams of dark prophecy, Koll seeks to free Obsydia, the Bloodstone Queen, from her prison. Determined to let nothing stop him, Koll will commit any evil to achieve his goal.

Runa and Mellypip's newest journey reveals truths behind ancient secrets, as Koll's obsessive hunt for a fallen queen threatens to doom the world forever. Runa and Koll, bound by opposing magical destinies of Light and Dark, will ultimately face frightening revelations and unimagined consequences.

Gate of Souls – Book One: A Familiar's Tale
– Verna McKinnon

> Familiars.
> Magical animal companions of sorcerers.
> Keepers of spells and secrets.
> Most important, devoted friends for life.

When one such familiar, Mellypip, bonds with the young sorceress Runa, he shares in the wonders of magic. Together, Mellypip and Runa train under the tutelage of Runa's grandfather, Cathal, and his cantankerous mountain owl familiar, Belwyn. But secrets and spells do not make for good sorcery. Old friends begin to vanish even as enemies from Cathal's past return, threatening to reveal the truth of Runa's parents; a truth from which Cathal must protect his granddaughter at any cost. When Cathal is kidnapped, Runa and Mellypip rush against time to save their family and friends from dark sorcery that will not only destroy them, but shatter the Gate of Souls and release demonic creatures of The Otherworld into the mortal realms.

The Seven Exalted Orders – Deby Fredericks

Arkanost has Seven Exalted Orders. No more, no less. When a magus goes renegade in a far-off province, the Mage Lords demand something be done.

Ryamon is bitter and frustrated. He longs to be a Fire magus; as a Stone magus, he's miserable. If he can bring the rogue back, he has a chance—his last chance—to fulfill his dream.

It's a great plan—until he actually meets Valdira.

Tails from the Front Lines 2: The Thin Blue Line
– edited by Carol Hightshoe

Come meet some of the four-legged members of Law Enforcement who also serve and protect.

Here our authors will introduce you to the brave K9 officers who serve alongside their human partners. They are their eyes, ears, noses and sometimes when necessary they are their shield, protecting others.

Proceeds from this anthology will be donated to the El Paso County (Colorado) Sheriff's Office K9 program in memory of K9 Jinx who was killed in the line of duty on April 11, 2022.

Ring of Fire – edited by Dana Bell

Enter the Ring of Fire, as unpredictable as the land masses shaking a city and volcanoes erupting covering the landscape. Could there be other reasons for these events? Or could these rings be more than a geological location.

They may be dragons playing tricks
or magic portals opened to mysterious realms
or sacrificing the best work of a lifetime.
Perhaps a rescue during a forest fire
or an attempt to raise the dead
or even while attending a high school reunion.

Journeys are taken to far off lands, another world, and through caves, each with their own unique twist.

Each tale presents a new idea on what the Ring of Fire could be. It is more than what many have been led to believe. Pull up a chair and warm yourself by our fires—just don't let yourself get burned.

Coyote – Charles Combee

While camping in a remote canyon in Utah Jim accidently sees an ancient rite taking place with a coyote like creature presiding over it. Now this creature wants Jim dead.

Audrey and her family go hiking in Utah and are attacked by this creature. Audrey is the only survivor, but she is pulled into a strange world of darkness and glass. She is 'rescued' by Jim, but is still linked to the creature, whose hold on her will end in her death unless Jim can find a way to break that link.

In his dreams, or are they ancient memories, Jim begins to learn more about Coyote as well as the magics that previously bound him. But those dreams end without teaching him the full magics. Can he find a way to free Audrey and stop Coyote from once again terrorizing humankind?

Believing is Seeing – Joanna Michal Hoyt

What we believe shapes what we see. Sometimes the stories we tell free us. Sometimes they trap us.

Some people see things their neighbors can't or won't see. Are they inspired? Delusional? Who decides?

As the faithful people of her village cry out for their god's help in disaster, a young peasant woman faces the terrifying possibility that she may be that god.

A time-traveling Jewish refugee visits 21st-century churches and confronts almost unrecognizable versions of himself.

Three troubled people make the dangerous visit to The Library where the maddening stories lodged inside them can be removed—on certain demanding conditions.

Having been warned away from the vacant lot which is said to house a portal to Hell, the new girl in town naturally goes to investigate.

Early in the grid collapse—or apocalypse?—a Christian lesbian farm couple paint "WELCOME" on their barn and await visitors.

An old man in the Terran diaspora enlists in a crusade to save humanity and belatedly wonders if he's on the wrong side.

Step inside these stories and see what you believe—but don't believe everything you see.

Out of the Darkness – edited by Carol Hightshoe

Mental Health issues have long been stigmatized, with those facing them pushed into the shadows, often unable to deal with the darkness they find themselves trapped in.

In this collection, stories explore many types of darkness— Suicidal Ideation, Death from Suicide, Survivor's Guilt, PTSD, Chronic Pain, Chronic Illness, Depression, Death of a Loved One, Secrets, Bullying, and other forms of darkness are explored. Some related to mental health issues and some not, but all of them offer very human perspectives. As in real life, some stories have happy endings and sadly others don't.

We offer these stories of darkness without judgement, but with hope and compassion. Some roads should never have to be traveled —but we understand that for many they are being traveled alone.

Proceeds from sales of Out of the Darkness will be donated to the American Foundation for Suicide Prevention—or more information on AFSP please visit their website at: afsp.org.

Never Cheat a Witch – edited by Carol Hightshoe

Magical curses. Arcane revenge. Being transformed into a frog. Things evil witches do to mere mortals who cross their path. But, what if there is more to the story...

Deals made with a witch are magically binding and can bring dire consequences to those who even think about breaking them.

Whether they are seeking revenge for wrongs done to them, helping others or simply trying to live their lives—it is NEVER wise to try and cheat a witch.

Open your spell book and join our authors as they relate tales of witches and mortals. From classic fantasy witches to modern day witches and even the legendary Baba Yaga. Good and Evil as well as every shade of gray in between.

And, yes—there is a prince who is turned into a frog.

And more – check out our books at

www.wolfsingerpubs.com